# Praise for Paul Vidich

'In the manner of Charles Cumming and recent le Carré, Vidich pits spies on the same side against one another in a kind of internal cold war' – **Booklist, on** *The Coldest Warrior*

'A richly detailed work of investigative crime writing perfect for fans of procedurals and spy fiction alike' – **LitHub, on** *The Coldest Warrior*

'Vivid and sympathetic… a worthwhile thriller and a valuable exposé' – **Kirkus Reviews, on** *The Coldest Warrior*

'Chilling... more than an entertaining and well-crafted thriller; Vidich asks questions that remain relevant today' – **Jefferson Flanders, author of** *The First Trumpet* **trilogy, on** *The Coldest Warrior*

'Vidich spins a tale of moral and psychological complexity, recalling Graham Greene… rich, rewarding' – **Booklist, on** *The Good Assassin*

'A cool, knowing, and quietly devastating thriller that vaults Paul Vidich into the ranks of such thinking-man's spy novelists as Joseph Kanon and Alan Furst' – **Stephen Schiff (writer and executive producer of acclaimed television drama** *The Americans***), on** *An Honorable Man*

'*An Honorable Man* is that rare beast: a good, old-fashioned spy novel. But like the best of its kind, it understands that the genre is about something more: betrayal, paranoia, unease, and sacrifice. For a book about the Cold War, it left me with a warm, satisfied glow' – **John Connolly, #1 internationally bestselling author of** *A Song of Shadows*

## ALSO BY PAUL VIDICH

*An Honorable Man*
*The Good Assassin*

For Alice, Eric, Lisa, and Nils

Political language... is designed to make lies
sound truthful and murder respectable.

– George Orwell,
*Politics and the English Language*

# PREFACE

Family tragedy drew me to Cold War literary fiction.

My uncle Frank Olson died sometime around 2:30 am on November 28, 1953 when he "jumped or fell" from his room on the thirteenth floor of the Statler Hotel in New York City. The New York Medical Examiner's report contained that ambiguous description of how Frank came to land on the sidewalk early that morning. Frank Olson was a highly skilled Army scientist who worked at Fort Detrick in Frederick, Maryland, a top-secret US Army facility that researched biological warfare agents. He had gone to New York to see a psychiatrist in the company of a CIA escort. This was all the family knew about Frank's death for twenty-two years.

Then, in June 1975, one bit of new information came to light. Buried inside a report by The Rockefeller Commission, which had been established by President Ford to investigate allegations of illegal CIA activity within the US, was a two-paragraph account of an army scientist who had been unwittingly given LSD and died in a fall from a hotel window in New York. To the conflicting theories that Frank Olson "jumped or fell" another possibility was added: he was thrown out. Frank Olson's death came to embody our collective fascination with the Cold War's dark secrets, and it has shined light on the dubious privileges men in the CIA gave themselves in the name of national security.

Frank Olson left behind his wife, Alice, my aunt, and three

young children, Eric, Lisa, and Nils. Their lives went on, but were never the same, and Frank's death traumatized each of them in deeply personal ways. Eric, the eldest, dedicated his life to unpacking the mystery of his father's death.

I observed this tragedy over the years from within the tenuous intimacy of our family connection. I witnessed how my cousin Eric's search was frustrated by an agency clinging to it secrets. None of the volumes of books on the CIA and biochemical warfare dug deeply into the minds of the men who inhabited Frank's world – and even today questions about his death remain unanswered. I was curious about the men who were responsible, but they remained hidden, opaque, masked, and the secrets were hidden inside an obfuscating mist. I believe that is why, some years ago, I decided to put the story inside a novel.

My account of the case is told from within the CIA – an inside-out approach – not the outside-in view of Errol Morris's documentary on the subject, *Wormwood*, which recalls the frustrating effort of my cousin Eric to penetrate the opaque barrier that hides everything inside the Agency. *The Coldest Warrior* is not an effort to recreate the past, but rather, characters and a plot are grafted onto the original incident, and it imagines an outcome. Albert Camus said it well: "Fiction is the lie through which we tell the truth."

My novel puts a human face on the Cold War by focusing on the psychological burdens of its characters rather than on Byzantine plot, or high politics. Doubt and paranoia bred in a culture of secrecy characterize the novel, as does a sophisticated amorality of men at the top of intelligence bureaucracy, and above all there is the strain put on family, friends, and faith. Men who work in covert operations inevitably bring some of that darkness into themselves, suffering the moral hazards of a line of work that sanctions lying, deceit, and murder. The interplay of state secrets and individual lives is central to the novel.

# 1

## WASHINGTON D.C., 1953

A SOLID MAN OF average height not yet thirty years old, stood in the ninth-floor hotel room and placed the telephone in its cradle, ending a difficult conversation. His tuxedo was at odds with the room's drab, charmless atmosphere, and he brushed hair from his forehead with the unconscious gesture of a man whose sense of entitlement was rattled. He walked to the window, sipping from the two fingers of scotch he'd poured into a paper cup, and gazed at the dark clouds that blanketed the resting city. A curse slipped from his lips: *Shit*.

Phillip Treacher pondered the lie that he had just told his wife to explain why he wouldn't be joining her that night at the president's Thanksgiving gala. He misled friends, misrepresented himself to neighbors, and regularly carried out assignments that required him to go dark or use an alias, but this was his first lie to his new wife.

She knew he worked for the CIA, and she had come to understand in the first months of their marriage that when he came home in a sullen mood, there had been a problem at work – and she knew not to ask. They had established boundaries for their conversations, and his grimace was a signal that he couldn't answer her questions. But when he drank heavily at dinner, she guessed that a Soviet double agent had died and his harsh interrogation had been a success.

Treacher had tried to soften the blow by starting the conversation with a few questions about inconsequential things – her gown back from the tailor for the weekend gala. *Does it fit?* And gossip about who would be at the White House and who would not. Casual chat that he kept up heroically until she interrupted. *What's wrong? Where are you?* He said something unexpected had come up and he wouldn't be able to make it. Her silence was the longest of their marriage, and without saying more, he knew she would ask the question that he couldn't answer. He felt a terrible responsibility to keep her in the dark about an urgent national security matter of acute sensitivity.

He considered letting her hold onto her shock and anger, but he felt the need to offer a plausible explanation that she could tell other guests who asked why she'd come alone. *I've been called out of town.* Regret, guilt, remorse. These were the feelings that he permitted himself in the moment of his deception. But he had not considered, even for a moment, describing what he was doing a few blocks away in the Hotel Harrington.

Treacher stared at the black telephone. He drained the scotch from his paper cup and crushed it in his big fist. Too short for college basketball, too light for football, too slow for baseball, he had tried tennis, track, even fencing, before he settled on Yale's rowing team, which was a good match for his strong hands. He still raced one-man sculls at dawn before his late-sleeping wife, Tammy, woke, and he got an hour of grueling exercise on the Potomac before going to the office. Treacher tossed the crumpled cup into the wastebasket and turned his attention to the silvered smokiness of the room's two-way mirror.

Between two queen-size beds there was a nightstand with a forest green banker's lamp, a telephone, and the afternoon's tabloid, which had been folded in thirds after having been read and discarded. A middle-aged man sat on the bed nearest the window. He wore a gray suit jacket, but he had no tie, slacks, shoes, or socks. He was morosely slumped half-undressed on the edge of the bed, cradling his head in his hands. *Quiet now,* Treacher thought.

Treacher's immediate thought was that this man, Dr Charles Wilson, couldn't possibly be a national security threat, couldn't possibly be dangerous. He moved closer to the two-way mirror and saw that the quiet man was now deeply agitated. Dr Wilson looked at his wristwatch, then stared at the telephone for a long time, visibly impatient and upset. He glanced at his watch again. His face was drawn and pale. Treacher thought the unthinkable and shuddered. The judgment winged across his consciousness: *At least he'll be at peace in his grave when this dreadful night is over.*

*

Phillip Treacher was no stranger to the Hotel Harrington. He had been in room 918 before, under different circumstances, with a different security problem – and always the sensible spirit of the place provided a gloss of normalcy to the dirty business.

It was Washington's oldest hotel and, at eleven floors, one of the tallest buildings in the city. Its location near the White House and close to the Smithsonian made it a top pick for out-of-town visitors. Its height had attracted the city's first television station, Channel 5, which maintained its antenna on the roof and operated studios in a converted ballroom on the mezzanine. There, two iconoscope video cameras pointed toward the stage where Elder Lightfoot Solomon Michaux and his choir sang hymns every Thursday for the television audience. That Thursday, Thanksgiving Day, November 26,

1953, was no different. Spectators crowded the soundproof-glass wall and watched the animated evangelist in his tuxedo lead singers through a medley of rousing spirituals.

Channel 5's popular programming drew a lively crowd of musicians, actors, and tourists to the hotel's lobby, where they mixed with loitering fans and budget-minded diners going to the self-service Kitcheteria, or their elegant opposite, who came with reservations to the Pink Elephant Cocktail Lounge. Diplomats, lobbyists, and out-of-town businessmen moved swiftly to the elevators in the company of girlfriends or prostitutes without attracting the disapproval of the concierge, a smartly dressed professional, who noticed everything and remembered nothing. Lively social commerce made the Hotel Harrington a good location for a CIA safe house.

*

Again, the telephone. Treacher turned away from the sidewalk spectacle of unruly fans surrounding Elder Lightfoot's car and looked back into the room. His first thought was that his wife had found a way to trace their call and was phoning back. He picked up the receiver on the third ring. 'Hello.'

'Phil?'

Treacher recognized the voice of the head of Technical Services. 'Who else would it be?'

'What's the news? Any update?'

Treacher heard the boozy laughter of partying guests in the background. 'Are you coming over?'

'No, I can't. It's on you. What's the update?'

Treacher had been the unlucky junior man to pull holiday duty. 'Two Office of Security men found him in the television studio. He'd thrown away his wallet in the lobby. He was barefoot and extremely agitated, and he demanded to go on camera. He pushed his way to the newscaster before he was stopped.'

'Christ! Is he spinning out of control?'

'Spun. He's spun. I think he's gone. You can look forward to the arc of what he knows falling on a widening audience.'

'What is he saying?'

'Anthrax.' Treacher waited a moment. 'You're quiet, Herb.' Phillip Treacher knew that the threads of ruinous danger were unspooling in Herb Weisenthal's fevered mind. The word would have produced a chaotic montage of top secret locations – Fort Detrick's stainless-steel incubators, dark landing strips on the Korean Peninsula, Berlin Station's basement interrogation cells, Porton Down's locked gates guarded by men with tommy guns – the vast sweep of a covert enterprise that was their sworn duty to keep secret.

'Herb, you've never been this quiet.'

'Where is he now?'

'Next door.' Treacher looked through the two-way mirror at Dr Wilson. The overhead light was off now, but the shaded bedside lamp illuminated a pale perimeter. 'He's on the bed in his boxer shorts. His head is in his hands, and he keeps looking at his watch.'

'Ainsley?'

'He's there. Next bed. He's asleep. It's been a tough couple of days.' He paused. 'You should come by and see for yourself.' He didn't expect an answer and he didn't get one.

'What does he know?'

'He's a chaperone from Chemical Branch to keep Wilson calm. He's a chemist, not a bodyguard.'

'I think we know the danger. We don't have a choice.'

'Yes, yes. We know the danger,' Treacher snapped.

'Phil, we have to contain this before we fall into a bottomless perdition. We've let it go too far. A mistake – yes, my mistake – is about to become an intolerable catastrophe.'

'An unforgivable mistake.'

There was a pause.

'Let me remind you that we are at war,' Weisenthal said. 'We don't want to wake up one morning to find this problem has come front and center overnight in big newspaper headlines. War itself is regrettable.'

'Don't lecture me.'

'It's time to move. We can't weigh our options any longer. I've got clearance. It's vetted, blessed, approved. It's now for you to act and the operations team to take care of the rest.'

'Christ!'

'Do you hear me?'

'Loud and clear.'

'Good. The decision has been made. It's done. Let's do what we need to. We are beyond sentiment and regret. Keep your doubts to yourself and do your duty. Move forward.'

Treacher felt anger rise up again, but his memory of their bitter weeklong quarrel was quelled by the inevitable. They were beyond trying to convince each other that one opinion was right and the other wrong. They agreed to disagree. A decision had been made at the top of the Agency, confirmed by Weisenthal, and now he would reluctantly proceed. Treacher felt a cold hollow in his chest where regret mixed with sorrow.

'We are officially horrified,' he said, 'but we move forward. You should have put more thought into your little experiment before we got here.'

'Water under the bridge. By any reasonable standard of judgment, we were careful – but now, unfortunately, we have an unstable man with state secrets in his head.'

'He's a colleague. I know his wife and children.' Treacher looked through the two-way mirror at Dr Wilson. A lonely condemned figure in boxer shorts slumped on the edge of the bed.

'What choice is there?' Weisenthal said quietly. 'His instability is fresh and speed must answer it. Arrangements are in place.'

'When does it happen?'

'Shortly. Leave the door to Wilson's room unlocked. Ainsley will stay in the bathroom, out of the way. Two security officers will be there in a few minutes.'

'What do I tell them?'

'Nothing. They have their instructions. Solid men. Veterans. They know it's an urgent matter approved at the highest level.' A pause. 'Phil?'

'What?'

'You okay? Your voice is tired. Have you been drinking?'

Treacher's mind revolted against the question. 'Yes,' he snapped.

'Get some food in you. Life goes forward. Order room service. Not a good way to spend Thanksgiving.'

Treacher hung up. He was calm and horrified, those two opposing emotions alive in him at the same time. His face had paled, drained even of its scotch flush, and he felt a great thirst in his parched mouth – as if he'd breathed in a desert wind. His eyes had narrowed, and behind the lenses of his wire-frame glasses he appeared to squint. He felt particularly out of place standing in the safe house in his tuxedo, but the call to duty had come suddenly.

Treacher checked the 16mm camera that stood on a tripod in front of the two-way mirror, and he did the same with the Nagra recording deck. Equipment lights were dark, both machines dormant, but out of an excess of caution he unplugged the Nagra and pointed the camera away from the mirror. There was to be no record.

*

The beginning of the end had come unexpectedly, during a Monday staff meeting at Navy Hill Headquarters. Treacher had been discussing the Agency's liability in the aftermath of its botched effort to test the dispersion properties of bacteriological agents released from a lightbulb dropped on subway tracks, when Herb Weisenthal summoned him from the conference room.

Treacher followed Weisenthal past late-arriving secretaries for whom the presence of the TSS chief on the second floor would be a lively topic of gossip. 'No reason to start any rumors,' Weisenthal had whispered, smiling at the astonished women as he led Treacher to the stairwell.

'How's the wife? Newlyweds? How long has it been?' Weisenthal felt it necessary to precede an urgent work matter with a not-quite-cordial personal question.

'Not long,' Treacher replied vaguely. 'When do we stop calling ourselves newlyweds?'

'When sex slows down.'

Treacher smiled vaguely, refusing Weisenthal the satisfaction of an insight into the state of his marriage. They were unalike – Treacher the Ivy League man with roots in an established New York banking family close to Cardinal Spellman, who mentored Treacher and gave him standing among Washington's elite. He was well-schooled, well-spoken, well-liked, ambitious, and conventionally patriotic. He had been an aide to the under secretary of state fresh out of law school, special assistant to the Agency's inspector general at twenty-eight, and his name was among the privileged few of a new generation cultivated by Washington's social circles. He and Tammy were invited to smart parties with smart people.

Weisenthal was a Brooklyn immigrant's son raised on a

tough street who'd gone to public high school and then a Midwestern state university on scholarship. He found his way into Washington's burgeoning intelligence bureaucracy with a doctorate in agronomy that was useful for a nation secretly developing its germ warfare capability. He spoke with the determined speech of a recovered childhood stutterer. He was an ordinary dresser, preferring to look like the other men who arrived early to the office and left late. Except for his club foot, which gave him a slight limp, nothing about the man stood out or drew unwanted attention.

'I haven't met him before, but I know him by reputation,' Weisenthal said, answering the question that was on Treacher's mind. His eyes invited Treacher up the stairwell. 'He's in my office. MI6. Very British. Our liaison to Porton Down. Staff intelligence officer. He said he had to speak to us in person.'

Weisenthal's sparsely furnished corner office had a gunmetal-gray desk, wooden chairs, a sofa, and a glass coffee table with that week's issues of *Time* and *Newsweek*, and against the wall, completely out of proportion to the rest of the room, was a large black combination safe, door ajar. There were no family photographs, no memorabilia, no hint of a life beyond the office except for his brown fedora hanging from a coat stand.

The Englishman rose abruptly from the sofa to greet the two Americans. 'Thank you for seeing me on short notice,' he said. His overnight bag was on the floor, and his tan mackintosh draped a chair. 'Mark Leyland.' He eagerly thrust his hand forward to Weisenthal and then to Treacher.

'I didn't call before I left London. I wasn't comfortable discussing the matter on the telephone, so I took the overnight flight through Gander.'

A brisk smile parted his lips, half explanation and half apology.

Treacher remembered much of the hour-long conversation, but as with all things that come suddenly and upend your comfortable perspective, he had been skeptical of the case Leyland was making against Dr Wilson. The Englishman's corpulent bulk was squeezed into a dark wool suit that had wrinkled on the long flight and made him seem comical. Leyland kept touching his cufflinks, an odd tic that distracted Treacher. He was obviously uncomfortable and awkward knowing that he was providing compromising information on a colleague of the two Americans he addressed. That's what Treacher thought as he listened. He resented being made aware of facts he found distasteful – facts that could not be ignored.

Apparently, Dr Wilson had been in Berlin, where he witnessed the harsh interrogation of an ex-Nazi weapons scientist who had then died. Wilson flew from there to London and drove to Porton Down, where he brought up the disturbing incident with an English scientist who worked in the same field of biochemical weapons research, a man he considered a confidant.

'He talked about highly sensitive matters, eyes-only stuff.' Leyland's tenor voice had deepened. 'Very inappropriate matters. Our man reported it up the chain. We felt it important to give you Americans a heads-up. These are, we believe, serious security violations.'

'What did he say?'

'He had doubts about his work. He was very specific.'

After Leyland left, Weisenthal had taken Treacher aside. That was when the quarrel began.

'It's not enough to sit with Wilson and get his view. It's not enough to remind him of the sensitive nature of our work. It's not enough that we accept his apology and his mea culpa.'

'Not enough?' Treacher had shouted. 'You hire good men, intelligent men. You trust them to keep their mouths shut. He

18

was talking to MI6, for Christ's sake. He wasn't unburdening himself to a stranger. We're educated men. We have thoughts about the work we do.'

'There is no learning curve on treason.'

Inside that abrupt beginning Treacher had seen the horizon of possible endings, none pleasant, all expedient. Weisenthal said everything he wanted to say with the numbing repetition of an aggressive salesman. *What if he were abducted while traveling overseas? What if he were drugged at a conference in Paris, where he travels three times a year? What if he were compromised? Would he talk? What would he say? That's what we need to test.*

*

Treacher heard the soft tap on the hotel door and then two more muffled strikes in quick succession. Through the peephole Treacher saw two Office of Security men standing in the hallway with the dubious calm of diligent officers on urgent assignment. Treacher undid the door chain and admitted them. He glanced into the hallway, where two women in raccoon scarfs and short skirts escorted a drunk old enough to be their father. The john wouldn't remember the encounter, and the prostitutes would have every reason to forget it. The girls moved down the hallway in a duet of giddy laughter.

Inside the room, Treacher faced the two men. The shorter one had a boxer's porcine nose, square jaw, and wide-set eyes that gave him the impression of a man capable of great malice. His taller, younger partner had a kinder rookie's face overspread with exaggerated confidence. Humble men, loyal men, who had earned a reputation for keeping their eyes open and their mouths shut. They saw the recording equipment and two-way mirror without surprise or question. They were familiar with the room and its purpose. The taller agent looked at Treacher.

'Mr Arndt?'

Treacher paused. The alias felt like a new suit he had tried on in a men's clothing store and forgotten to take off. 'I'm Nick Arndt.' Treacher repeated the name to own it, implant it, to score his memory for the way he would be known by the two officers. 'Yes, Nick Arndt. Which one are you?'

'Casey.'

Treacher had read the two-paragraph note on Michael V. Casey during his evening vigil. He'd glanced at it when he first arrived and again after he'd exhausted his interest in the room's copies of *Modern Screen* and *Photoplay*. Boston College. Wounded in the first days of the Battle of Osan. Son of a decorated Washington Metropolitan police officer. Father of a two-year-old girl. Solid Irish Catholic. Good patriot.

'And you?' Treacher asked the second man.

'Kelly.'

A knock on the door, startlingly loud in the quiet room. Treacher put his eye to the peephole and then quickly opened the door for Ainsley, who stood barefoot in a bathrobe that he tightened with an offhanded movement, closing it where it had opened. He had the wildly disheveled hair of a man awakened from restless sleep, and he was agitated. He looked past Treacher at the two security officers and his concern was amplified by his surprise. Treacher pulled Ainsley into the room.

'This is Dr Ainsley,' Treacher said brusquely to settle the men's nerves.

'For God's sake, what's happening, Phil?' Ainsley said.

Treacher turned abruptly to the officers. 'Forget that name. You never heard it. The name is Nick Arndt.' Treacher flipped open his leather wallet and displayed an FBI alias – proof of who he claimed to be.

Treacher then addressed Ainsley. 'You okay?'

'That's not the right question,' Ainsley said. 'What's going on? Who are these thugs?'

'The hour has arrived,' Treacher said. 'Where is he?'

'Asleep. *Christ.*'

Treacher looked through the two-way mirror, but he was too far away and the angle was wrong, so he couldn't see Dr Wilson's sleeping form. As he moved closer, the fullness of the room opened up. Dr Wilson lay on the bed under a pale blue blanket, knees drawn to his chest, occupying only a small portion of the mattress.

Treacher calmly rested his hands on Ainsley's shoulders. He repeated Weisenthal's instructions. *Go back to the room. Stay in the bathroom. Wait for the police to arrive.*

Treacher was again alone with the two security officers. He had been picked for the assignment, and the time to question orders had passed. He had not trained for this, but he knew what was required. The shot of scotch he threw back vanquished any doubt that remained.

'You are now initiated,' he said to Casey and Kelly. 'Nothing you will hear, nothing you'll see, nothing that happens tonight, goes outside this room. Understand?'

'Yes, sir.'

'Michael, this will be unpleasant. You're a professional. A patriot. A good Catholic. The man next door is dangerous. Unstable. You saw him in the television studio barefoot and upset. You were kind enough to find his wallet. It's all very unfortunate, but very necessary.'

Casey nodded. His eyes were wide and steady, but his companion had no reaction whatsoever. Treacher knew where the risk lay between the two men.

'You have a problem keeping quiet, Michael?' *No, sir.* 'You know what national security is?' *Yes, sir.* 'We are fighting a war, a Cold War, but a war all the same, against a Godless enemy, and our way of life is at risk. Understand?' *Yes, sir.*

*

Treacher listened. The lights in the adjoining room were now off, and darkness beyond the two-way mirror obscured the room's details. What was taking so long? He suck-started a cigarette, but after one unsatisfying pull he ground it into the overflowing ashtray. Again the darkened room. He was alert to sounds, but he heard nothing, and he impatiently clenched and unclenched his fist. His quarrel with Weisenthal was a bad memory that echoed in the quiet of his mind, lengthening the wait. Hellish time. A second became a minute, and one minute became two and then three. The tyranny of waiting.

Suddenly, through the two-way mirror, flashlight beams carved the darkness, bouncing floor to ceiling until they found a sleeping Dr Wilson. He'd shifted on the bed, his knees still curled up to his chest in a fetal position. Amber beams washed his face in hot light, waking him, and he sat up. He blinked, startled and confused, and then loud voices shouted urgent commands. Dr Wilson was rudely made to stand, and the shorter security officer pinned his right arm behind his back, immobilizing him, and the second man guided him across the room. Dr Wilson became violent in the face of his doom. He kicked fiercely, struggled to free his right arm, and made contorted efforts to cling to the bedpost with a grasping hand. Grunts, shouts, desperate cries, and the sharp crack of breaking furniture were muffled by the two-way mirror. Erratically swinging beams caught snapshots of violence. In one moment of illumination, Treacher saw a dark object come down on Dr Wilson's head. The room was suddenly quiet. Dr Wilson's slumped form was dragged forward.

Treacher turned away from the two-way mirror, heart pounding. His hands were cold. He closed his mind to what he knew was happening. He counted the seconds until three minutes passed. *Trust the plan. Clean up. Get out.*

Treacher entered the adjoining room when he found the door ajar. He passed the bathroom and saw Ainsley on the toilet, underwear at his ankles, head slumped, trembling.

Treacher turned on the bedside lamp, and the perimeter of light revealed torn pillows, a blanket crumpled on the floor, a broken chair, and the shattered globe of a standing lamp. Everywhere the signs of struggle. Treacher's eye was drawn to Dr Wilson's wristwatch on the bedside table, which he immediately recognized by the dual time-zone face set in a tonneau crystal. He had always admired the polished gold bezel and harmonious lines of the elegant watch. He knew how much it meant to Dr Wilson, and he knew too that a policeman might covet it. He worried that the chain of custody would be broken and it would be lost. He took it for safekeeping.

Treacher became aware that the room was drafty – and cold. That's when he saw that the casement window was smashed and the drapes were outside, flapping violently in the night. Shattered glass lay on the sill, on the radiator below, and in a debris field across the floor. The window's inside frame was a sawtooth of broken glass.

Treacher carefully put his head through the jagged opening and saw a luminous White House under the limpid night sky. Dead of night in the sleeping city. Suddenly, an ear-splitting shriek amplified by the dry November air and the early-morning quiet. It was a strange cry of surprise and distress followed by the sharp clap of shoe leather running on the sidewalk. Treacher followed the uniformed doorman as he hurried from the opposite side of the street where he'd been speaking to the driver of a lone Checker cab.

Treacher saw the doorman join three pedestrians who had collected in a tight circle, talking in a blur of excited voices and urgently calling for help from an absent authority. They stepped aside for the doorman, and a mortally wounded Dr Wilson was visible on the sidewalk. Blood leaked from his nose and mouth and stained his cotton T-shirt. His knee was twisted at a terrible angle, and a pale bone protruded from an open thigh wound just below his boxer shorts. Blood pooling on the sidewalk was black in the night. The doorman took the dying Dr Wilson in his lap and leaned forward, but then Dr Wilson's gasping effort to speak ended, and life left the body. The doorman gently laid him on the concrete.

The doorman backed away from the hotel's looming façade and looked up at drapes flapping from an open window. He counted the floors so he could know which room the dead guest had been in.

# 2

## RUSSELL SENATE OFFICE BUILDING
## TWENTY-TWO YEARS LATER

ON A GRIM, RAINY Tuesday in May 1975, a fifty-four-year-old CIA officer sat in a packed Senate hearing room and contemplated the perjury being committed by his boss, the Director of Central Intelligence, which, if known, would cost him his reputation, end his career, and possibly put him in federal prison; namely, that the Agency had no records beyond those already produced that pertained to the suicide of Dr Charles Wilson.

Jack Gabriel was with two colleagues in the rear of the room, having sat in the middle of a row to stay as inconspicuous as possible in the circus atmosphere. Tall windows accentuated the height of the hearing room, and ornate brass sconces on the wall behind the curved dais of somber senators added to the formality of the space. A giant pendant chandelier hung from a long cable over the restive crowd.

Gabriel was startled by the director's perjury, but he did not for a moment feel an obligation to bring it to anyone's attention. As a long-serving officer, he was compulsively loyal to the Agency and to the man who ran it, and he would remain silent even when it made him complicit in a crime. Their bond had been forged on the anvil of the battlefield.

James Coffin, Counterintelligence, sat on Gabriel's left, and

George Mueller, Plans, was on his right. They were men of stature in the Agency and, like Gabriel, faceless to the world. They were known to each other, but largely unknown to the men and women in the audience. Gabriel's job in the Office of Inspector General put him forward publicly more than the other two, and more than he liked, but men who knew him faced the witness stand with great interest. Gabriel recognized several journalists who sat together, but it being their job to report on the spectacle and not just the testimony, they glanced around the room, and it was then that Neil Ostroff of the *Times* spotted Gabriel. They acknowledged each other.

Gabriel had a duty to be present, but he was also there for an entirely personal reason.

Dr Wilson's family sat together in a row near the front and listened intently to the Agency's first public testimony on his death. An inadvertent mention in the Rockefeller Commission Report on CIA misdeeds had stirred up the forgotten incident. Maggie, the widow, who'd never remarried, sat on the aisle beside her eldest child, Antony, a psychology doctoral candidate at Columbia, and her daughter, Betsy, a nurse. Mother and son sat side by side, but Gabriel knew of the anger in their relationship.

Wilson's family was learning several shocking details of his death for the first time. Gabriel had been Dr Wilson's colleague and friend, so he knew Maggie, and he watched the proud widow react to the new suggestion that Dr Wilson worked for the CIA.

Gabriel was just over six feet and fit, but middle age had filled out his waist and he'd lost his lanky appearance, and gone too was his confident, youthful smile. He was the consummate intelligence officer who had risen through the ranks, dedicated to the CIA's mission to tell truth to power without shaping it to fit what the White House wanted to hear. No one was more surprised than Gabriel when he realized that, at fifty-four, he had spent his entire career in the Agency. That hadn't been the career he'd imagined when he was a twenty-two-year-old newly discharged from the OSS, looking toward the far horizon of his life. Lawyer? Investment banker? College professor? Those were the careers he had contemplated, but still the allure of espionage drew him to her bosom. The cerebral challenge of the work, the immediacy of the problems and their complexity, the adventure, and the urgent call to fight the great Cold War against Communism. These were what drew him.

The call to worldly action had been planted in him by a mother who pushed him to excel in school, who did everything in her power to have him see opportunity beyond the small Midwestern town she hated. He was to blossom into an American boy, she said, turning him against his German immigrant father, whose work selling farm equipment took him away from home for weeks at a time. She urged him to leave behind the town, its insularity, the accent, and embrace the great opportunities that college offered. When young Gabriel arrived in New Haven, he carried a bundle of hundred-dollar bills she had pressed into his hand, a fondness for Shakespeare, an affinity for his mother's Socialism, and a deep skepticism of the rituals of the Catholic Church. The world, he'd been taught to believe, was a dangerous place.

Gabriel's college friends were the privileged sons of the eastern elite. They talked carelessly of how much money they'd make, the girls they'd take to bed, their gentlemen's Cs, and the lifestyle they coveted. Gabriel too saw virtue in wealth, but he didn't aspire to own a lavish home in Southampton or on Park Avenue. He saw no purpose in belonging to an exclusive men's club in Manhattan or spending weekends with a boozy crowd of amateur sailors on Long Island Sound.

It was in college that his young intelligence matured and his self-confidence grew. He wanted to make a difference in the world. His mother's radical social views and his father's cynical disdain for politics combined to shape his own moral compass. It didn't point to religion, or convention, or any Golden Rule. A lie was permitted, sometimes required.

\*

Gabriel looked toward the chairman of the subcommittee, the senator from Massachusetts, who leaned into his microphone. He was flanked by twenty of his Senate colleagues. His eyes widened, and he looked over reading glasses poised on the tip of his bulbous nose, and he repeated in a loud hectoring voice:

'I will make myself understood. What I asked, sir: Was Dr Wilson an employee of the Central Intelligence Agency?'

'At what time?' the director said.

'At any time.'

'I believe, Mr Chairman, that I answered that.'

'And what was your answer?'

'He was not, as far as I know, employed by the CIA. We knew who worked for us and who did not.'

'And the records speak for themselves?'

'The records, such as they are, don't answer that question, but neither are they complete.'

'Your testimony is that Dr Wilson, an employee of the Army, was never an employee of the CIA?'

'It is, Mr Chairman.'

Gabriel alone knew the lie. He also knew that it wouldn't have been a lie if the director had answered the question a week earlier, before an old memo turned up explaining that Wilson had quietly joined the Agency – 'safer to have him inside,' it read. So, as with much of the morning's testimony, the question was not whether the answer was true or false but when the director had acquired the knowledge that made it true or false. Gabriel had already begun to triage the problem. How ingenious the mettle of the mind, he thought, so supple this human organ that can deceive and hope, and regret and atone, all in three pounds of organic gray matter.

'Fell or jumped,' the chairman said into the microphone, his emphasis underscoring his incredulity.

The director had folded his hands on the table like a penitent altar boy. He was impeccably dressed for his hostile Senate questioning – *my inquisition*, he'd quipped to Gabriel on the drive over. The director's thinning hair was swept back; his clear plastic eyeglasses disappeared on his face, which had the plainness of a man who could enter a restaurant without catching the waiter's eye. This man, who had managed death squads in South Vietnam, leaned into his microphone. 'Is that a question, Mr Chairman?'

'Yes, it is a question.'

'Can you repeat it?'

'Did Dr Wilson fall from the ninth floor of the Hotel Harrington, or did he jump? That's the question. The investigation, such as it was, concluded that he either fell or jumped. It had to be one or the other. Those two verbs can't both be true. Did no one question what happened?'

'It wasn't a CIA operation. As I said, he wasn't our employee. He was an employee of the Army stationed at Fort Detrick, and it was a Bureau of Narcotics safe house. I had no personal knowledge of the tragedy. At that time, November 1953, I was stationed in Berlin.'

'But he was given LSD by the CIA. By...' The chairman sifted through a stack of papers. 'By Mr Redacted, who was an employee of the CIA.'

'Mr Redacted?'

'Yes, it says "mister," and the next word is "redacted".'

Laughter filled the hearing room, and Gabriel too permitted himself to smile. He met Coffin's eye, and the two men shared the moment's levity. 'He's grandstanding,' Coffin whispered. 'He's got nothing.'

The chairman continued. 'We will call Mr Redacted to testify when we get his real name, but we do have you now. May I refresh your memory for the public record?' The senator read from a document that an aide had slipped him. His reading voice was deep and booming, and it quieted the room.

'On November 8, 1953, seven men from the CIA and Fort Detrick attended an off-site retreat at a hunter's cabin in western Maryland. Three of the men were from the CIA's Technical Services Staff.' The chairman lifted his eyes from the page, and his eyebrow arched theatrically. 'Including Mr Redacted and his two colleagues, both names also redacted – and you say the originals are lost. Four participants were from Fort Detrick's Special Operations Division, including Dr Wilson. The CIA conducted an experiment on the second night of the retreat. Unknown to them, several men were given seventy micrograms of LSD in an after-dinner drink of Cointreau. In the days that followed, Dr Wilson exhibited symptoms of depression and paranoia. He was sent to a doctor in Washington, and during this time he stayed at the Hotel Harrington. It was there, in the early morning of November 27, that he suffered some type of psychotropic flashback and fell or jumped to his death.'

The chairman looked up from the document. 'It's important to have this on the public record, sir. The incident sounds like an episode from a cheap paperback spy novel – but it wasn't. It happened to an American citizen.'

The chairman continued to read. 'Following Dr Wilson's death, the CIA expedited an effort to ensure that the family receive death benefits, but the family was never told he'd been given LSD, and they were never told the circumstances of his death. The Agency went to considerable effort to prevent his death from being connected to the Agency, and even today, I suspect, we don't have the full story.'

The chairman pushed the document aside and continued extemporaneously, his voice thick with righteous disbelief. 'We have the CIA's involvement administering the LSD, the cover-up, then the DCI's letter reprimanding Mr Redacted for authorizing the use of LSD on an unwitting basis without proximate medical safeguards. With all this, you would have us believe that Mr Wilson was an employee of the Army? Everything was planned and undertaken by the CIA, but you would have us believe he was not a CIA employee, and the CIA's hands are clean.'

'Facts are credible because they are facts.'

The chairman pondered the answer. 'Why was he given LSD? No one seems to have answered that question. I would like to know the answer to the question. His widow and children would like to know. They deserve to know. It is the right and decent thing.' The chairman leaned back in his chair, signaling the end of his questions. 'Sir, is there anything you'd like to add before we recess?'

The director cleared his throat and leaned into his microphone. He spoke in a penitent tone. 'I was shocked to learn the circumstances of Dr Wilson's suicide from the Rockefeller Commission Report. As you know, the president met with the family and offered his personal apology. I made a point of meeting the family and extended the Agency's help answering questions about the tragedy. I want you to know that was one of my most difficult assignments as head of the Agency. Thank you.'

Gabriel was surprised by the director's depth of feeling and his personal tone. Gabriel had seen hints of the man's moral footing, but he had never heard him air it publicly. Here was another side of the man he hadn't seen, even when he thought he knew him. A phrase came to Gabriel: *The past isn't dead. It's not even past.* He wrote the Faulkner quote in the margin of his newspaper, but crossed out 'dead' and wrote 'over.' The past wasn't over. The long arm of time had reached back and shaken the hearing room.

Gabriel watched his boss stand at the witness table, a courteous gentleman wrapped inside a master of politics. The past was forgotten until it unexpectedly rose from its unhallowed crypt and called attention to itself. A dead man in his grave had come to life. *Look at me. Look at me. Ask me what happened.*

Gabriel turned to Coffin, who was gathering his briefcase to make space for Mueller, who had stood to leave. Gabriel saw their hostility in a flash – Coffin resenting the need to accommodate a man he disliked, and Mueller, equally abrupt, impatient to pass. It happened in a moment. The shoulder lowered to move the attaché case, a leg moving too quickly, contact, which was hardly a blow, but the two men looked at each other with instant distrust. And then it was over. Mueller passed through to the aisle, and the moment was lost except to Gabriel, the witness, who knew of the long-standing rancor between two men equal in rank but different in worldview. Coffin, the deep-thinking, hard-drinking, longtime head of Counterintelligence, who held on to a dark vision of threat, and Mueller, the casual, teetotaler strategist who preferred transparency to obfuscation. They approached espionage from opposite ends of a telescope. Coffin looked through the telescope's viewing end into the eye of the observer, seeking to look into the mind, and Mueller was the eye looking out to the world.

'Staying?' Coffin asked Gabriel, and then nodded at Gabriel's scribbled quote. 'Don't go there.'

'I want to hear her testify. I knew the family.'

'I heard the son before you arrived. I don't need to hear the wife.'

'What did he say?'

'Well spoken, which you'd expect from an academic, but angry. He makes it very personal to him, and he's not satisfied with the answers. We'll keep an eye on him.'

Coffin pulled out his notes. 'Here are a few things. The subject was taboo in the house for a long time. Innocent questions about the father set off the mother. She'd fly into a rage and burst into tears. Screamed at the kids: "You're never going to know what happened in that hotel room!"'

Coffin arched his eyebrow. 'Let's hope she's right.'

*

The hearing reconvened after a short recess. Seats vacated by those who'd come to watch the Director of Central Intelligence were quickly filled by a curious public eager to hear from the silent widow. The chairman brought down his gavel, and when the crowd didn't settle, he struck twice more. His stentorian voice boomed, 'Ladies and gentlemen...'

Seats were taken, loud conversations ended in clipped whispers, and suddenly the room was quiet.

'Thank you. I am sure the silence has nothing to do with the power of my authority and everything to do with your interest in our next witness. Mrs Wilson, will you come forward?'

Maggie Wilson rose from her seat in the third row. Sunlight poured through the room's tall windows and illuminated the woman in a natural spotlight. A hush fell. She wore a floral-pattern dress that hung loosely on her thin frame, and a silk scarf blossomed from her open neck like a colorful bouquet. She was tall even in flats, and she held a small purse in tightly clasped hands. She didn't smile except to apologize to the two big men who had taken the aisle seats during the recess and rose to let her pass.

She folded herself into the wood chair at the witness table. Her posture was straight and correct, and she wore her dignity defiantly. She ignored the photographers seated at the base of the dais, whose cameras burst with brilliant flashes, and looked to the senators.

Gabriel saw that Maggie had aged, made frail by illness, and her hair was the unnatural brown of a wig.

'Thank you for coming, Mrs Wilson. We appreciate the effort you made to be here.'

'Thank you, Mr Chairman, for accommodating my treatments. I have a statement I would like to read.' She was nervous, but her voice was firm. 'My husband was recruited to the Army's facility at Fort Detrick by his PhD thesis advisor at the University of Wisconsin. Charlie was honored to be part of the new program, but he said he couldn't tell me anything about it, except that it was top secret. That's all I knew. He was excited but nervous, and the war in the Pacific was at a turning point.' Mrs Wilson looked up from her written statement. 'Just as we speculated about the atom bomb project at Los Alamos, we wives at Fort Detrick knew that our husbands must be working on germ warfare.'

She adjusted her reading glasses. 'I knew very little about Charlie's work at Fort Detrick. I knew he was a biochemist, that he needed to wear a mask, but he never discussed his work. As I've told my children, there were hints. I could tell when he came home with a joyless expression that it meant all the monkeys had died and the experiment had been a success. When a colleague died, Charlie said it was from pneumonia, but the gossip among the wives was that he had been exposed to anthrax.

'My husband's work changed when World War II ended and the Cold War began. He was promoted to Acting Head, Special

Operations, in 1951, and he traveled more. He was in Paris, Berlin, London, and the Caribbean.'

'Did he talk to you about his trips?' the Republican senator from Idaho interrupted.

'No. When I left him at the airport, he said he'd be home in a few days. That was all I knew. I didn't know where he went or what he did. Before he got out of the car, he gave me his wedding ring. I returned it when I picked him up on his return. He explained that when he traveled, nothing could link him to his real life.'

'How did you know where he went?' the Republican senator asked.

'After he died, I found his passport and there were disembarkation stamps and dates of travel. At the time I didn't know anything, and as you can imagine, I have had to reconstruct my marriage.'

She cleared her throat, then continued in a firm voice.

'He drove himself to the off-site retreat the week before he died. I knew nothing about what happened there, but I know he came home visibly upset. That retreat was always a painful mystery, but two days ago, while I was in his study, preparing for my testimony, this page fell out of the family Bible.' She held up a typescript page yellow with age. 'It's the invitation to the retreat. It's titled "Deep Creek Rendezvous".'

Gabriel lurched forward, as did others in the room, trying to catch a glimpse.

'It doesn't describe why they were meeting or what they were to discuss, but it says they were all to have cover stories in case locals asked why they were there. They were told to say they were editors and screenwriters. It calls the hunter's cabin a cozy place with a stone fireplace and a comfortable atmosphere. You can just picture seven men enjoying a boys' weekend away from their wives.'

'Was that document provided by the CIA?' the chairman asked.

'No. As I said, I found it in our Bible, where my husband must have placed it. I don't know why he kept it – or hid it. I can only wonder, as you must, what meaning it holds. I recognized several names of his Fort Detrick colleagues among the attendees, but there are two other names I don't recognize.'

Maggie's face was brightly lit by television cameras recording the moment, and the room buzzed.

The chairman conferred with an aide and then spoke to a Republican senator. He leaned into his microphone. 'We'd like a copy of the invitation.' The chairman dispatched an aide and resumed his questioning. 'What was his mood when he came back from Deep Creek Rendezvous?'

'His mood?' She paused. 'I remember the moment he walked in the house. He'd been gone three days. He was very quiet, very depressed, and totally unlike himself. I said it was a shame that the adults in the family didn't communicate anymore. He said only that the meetings hadn't gone well. People had laughed at him. He was concerned about a terrible mistake he'd made, but he wouldn't tell me what that mistake was. There was no way to reason with him. Of course, I had no idea his was not a normal depression. It wasn't a normal kind of concern. It was, as I think back, the most unreal weekend.'

'Unreal?' the chairman interrupted.

'Unreal. Surreal. It was gray and rainy, a bit like today, which kept us in the house, and that didn't help his mood. Sunday night Charlie and I just needed to get out of the house, so we took the children to a movie theater downtown where a new film about the life of Martin Luther had opened. It was an odd choice to end a tense weekend. In the climactic scene Luther stands up against the corrupted Church and nails his theses to the cathedral door.'

36

Mrs Wilson paused. 'It was a serious movie – not a good one to see if you're depressed, but it was his choice. The next morning, he seemed better, and he said he'd made up his mind. He was going to resign. But then he came home from work Monday night and said he'd talked it over with his supervisor, and he'd changed his mind. He'd been told he was doing a good job and everything was fine. His mood was better that night. The next morning, he went to work but returned at noon with a man I hadn't met before, Mr Ainsley. Charlie said he had consented to psychiatric care in Washington. He was escorted home because he said they were afraid he would harm me and the children. I was shocked. I had to sit down at the kitchen table. I didn't understand what was happening.

'I insisted that I drive with them to Washington. The children were at school at the time. When we got to the city we stopped at a building near the mall, one of those temporary buildings built during the war. Later, I learned it was a CIA office. I left him there with Mr Ainsley. That was the last time I saw my husband.

'He called me that afternoon. We chatted about the children, and he talked about Elder Lightfoot's choir singing spirituals on Channel 5, which he liked very much, but he said nothing about his treatment or where he was staying. We agreed to speak at a particular time each night – nine o'clock was our agreed time. He was always the one to call me. Wednesday night he called and said he would be home for Thanksgiving. Then I got a call Thursday morning and he said there had been a change of plans and he wouldn't be coming home after all.

'The last time I spoke to him was Thanksgiving night at 9.00 p.m. It was a fine conversation. Everything was *I'll see you tomorrow*. It was not goodbye. He didn't call to say goodbye.'

\*

Maggie Wilson stood when she finished her testimony. Her two adult children joined her on her way out of the hearing room. The small family was surrounded by newspaper reporters and broadcast journalists, who thrust forward microphones, hoping to capture a sound bite for the evening news. This continued to be a sensational story – the Army scientist, unknowingly given LSD, who fell to his death.

Gabriel saw Maggie Wilson's jeopardy when the mobbing press blocked her path down the aisle. Gabriel was at her side quickly. He shielded her from the reporters' shouted questions, pushing away intrusive microphones and television cameras. *Any idea why he was given LSD? Whose names are on the invitation? Will you sue? Was it suicide?* His hand rose to protect her, but in doing so, he became the face of the family, and questions were thrown at him. Gabriel ignored the CBS News correspondent whose cameraman blocked the aisle, and he led Maggie around only to find himself confronted by a balding journalist, pen in hand, who barked manically, 'Hunter Thompson. *Rolling Stone.* What's your goddamn name?'

Gabriel ignored the reporters' questions and raised his palm to hide his face from the clicking cameras. His shoulder cleaved an opening in the crowded aisle, and he politely took Maggie in tow, but when reporters pressed in, he turned brusquely.

'This way,' he said. Gabriel headed for the private exit behind the dais used by senators and congressional staff. The Capitol Hill policeman accepted Gabriel's CIA badge and then denied access to the press. Angry reporters yelled questions past the diligent policeman, but then the door closed and a quiet settled in.

They found themselves alone in a hallway. Cold fluorescent light masked Maggie Wilson's startled flush, but not her grim expression.

'It's been a while, Maggie,' Gabriel said. He knew exactly

how long – Christmas Day at the county jail in 1966. He had been good friends with the Wilsons, but in July 1953, he'd already been posted to Berlin and would remain overseas for long periods. He'd tried to stay close after Wilson's death, but his frequent absences and Maggie's need to move on and raise her family had strained their acquaintance. He knew that she carried her grief alone, raising her children under the stigma of her husband's death. She had never been someone who admitted she needed help, nor was it in her nature to seek it. On holiday visits, Gabriel had seen her take a drink or two at night to help her cope. Her slide into alcoholism came over thirteen years, but when it finally surfaced, it was horrifying. Her kids were away at college, and she was living alone in a home with ghosts. Gabriel was the one who got the call from the sheriff's office. She had been arrested on Christmas Eve for driving while intoxicated and had spent the night in jail.

'I didn't know any of this,' Gabriel said. 'I should have asked more questions.'

Maggie Wilson was unmoved. She looked at Gabriel without sympathy. She listened but showed no emotion. Unforgiving coldness came over her face. 'It's a little late for an apology, Jack.'

She turned to her daughter, who hugged her, and the two women remained in a tearful embrace. Antony Wilson stared at Gabriel.

'We'll get to the bottom of this,' Gabriel said calmly, hearing himself parrot the director's empty assurances.

# 3

## CIA HEADQUARTERS BUILDING
## LANGLEY, VIRGINIA

THE CALL TO THE director's seventh-floor office came late in the day. The DCI's long-serving secretary, who'd been with him before he became Saigon Chief of Station and rejoined him on his return to Washington, waited for Gabriel at the door to the director's private conference room. Gabriel knew her name and was familiar with her startlingly blue eyes behind black-frame glasses, but he knew nothing else about this woman who served the nation's top spy.

'He'll be right in,' she said.

Gabriel had visited the inner sanctum of the DCI's adjacent office once, but he was more familiar with the small conference room. Curtains were drawn, and there was no sense of day or night. The air conditioning was off, which added to the sense of claustrophobia.

Framed oil paintings of former Directors of Central Intelligence formed a gallery of grim, unsmiling men. Fixed expressions, sealed lips, and opaque eyes imbued the faces with the look of men carrying the heavy burden of their work. The seven portraits reminded Gabriel of Velázquez's portrait of Pope Innocent X in Rome's Doria Pamphilj Gallery, showing him as a shrewd but aging man. Gabriel had known them all, respected one.

'They want me to sit for mine,' the director said.

The DCI had come in quietly, surprising Gabriel. He was a lean man in his fifties, impeccably dressed in a well-cut pinstripe suit, and he had the focus of a man starting his day, not ending it. The two men were physically different – Gabriel taller, grayer, more tired – but they shared the conceit that they were privileged to work in the Agency. A brace of flags stood at one end of the room.

'I asked if that meant I was being fired,' the director added, smiling. '*No, no,* they said. It takes time to find a suitable artist, and the process of sitting for a portrait is unreliable because crises tear up my schedule with the poor painter.' The director loosened his tie. 'Should I have Betty turn on the air conditioning? I got to like the heat in Saigon, and I haven't gotten used to our need to live in a climate-controlled world.'

'I'm fine.'

The director pointed to his predecessor on the canvas, a drawn, unsmiling face that was a generous likeness of the pipe-smoking patrician they both knew. 'Four months on the job. A record of sorts. His portrait was finished after he left.'

Gabriel was familiar with the circumstances of James Schlesinger's departure, its shocking suddenness coming in the midst of the Watergate scandal, which contributed to the apprehension between the two men.

The director pointed to the fifth man in the gallery, a Navy admiral in uniform. 'Incompetent outsider. He didn't understand the Agency or the intelligence business. He lasted fourteen months.'

They discussed the failed tenure, and neither Gabriel nor the director knew what the admiral was doing now. The director was philosophical. 'Having lost his seat of power, he was taken by the storm tide that sweeps the fallen into obscurity. His sudden fall was dressed up and packaged to the world as a resignation, but it wasn't. If you haven't prepared yourself for the inevitable downfall, as he hadn't, it is painful and demeaning to become an ordinary citizen stripped of the things we become accustomed to – chauffeurs, security, access to power, and the private jets. Even the most resilient ego is crushed.'

Gabriel had known the director for as long as they'd both been in the Agency, their acquaintance surviving years of little contact when one of them was stationed overseas, but most recently they had served together in South Vietnam. Their families had gotten to know each other in the close quarters of the embassy compound, protected from the brutal war by Marine guards. Their children shared the embassy swimming pool in the American enclave, while the two men were helicoptered to landing zones near the front lines. They were both outraged by the war's conduct. Young American lives were lost defending remote outposts that were promptly abandoned when the battle was over. They had spent a night together on a mortar-blasted hillock in the Central Highlands, waiting for muzzle flashes to announce the Viet Cong's attack beyond the booby-trapped perimeter, and in the hours together Gabriel had come to understand the director's disdain for Washington's politicians.

Gabriel watched the director gaze at his predecessors' portraits. Usually a study in equanimity, the director was preoccupied. His eyes came off the oil paintings.

'Why was Wilson given LSD?' the director asked.

Gabriel knew they had come to the purpose of the meeting.

The director wrote two names on a slip of paper. 'We know Herb Weisenthal and Roger Ainsley. Their names were on the invitation she brought to the hearing, and we can assume they were the ones redacted on the documents given to the family. How could originals have been destroyed? It's mind-boggling.'

He pointed at the slip of paper. 'Weisenthal retired two years ago. Ainsley is gone too, and no one misses him. This episode is a disgrace, and half the disgrace is our record keeping. I looked at what we gave the family. The memos don't provide a coherent or credible account of how Wilson died. They seem pieced together to justify a conclusion. They are a jumble of conflicting statements, possibly corrupted, almost certainly incomplete. How is that possible?'

The director's voice, always patient, had acquired an angry vibrato. 'Potomac Fever rages everywhere in this town, but it breeds most virulently on the floor of the Senate. They are political cowards who take up the popular outrage regardless of the facts, regardless of their convictions. I can't find myself in another hearing confronted by a senator looking to embarrass the Agency.'

The director replaced the cover of his Montblanc fountain pen and pushed the note across the table. 'I need to know what happened. I need the facts before I'm called back to the Senate and asked things about Wilson that I can't defend or explain.'

The director put his pen in his jacket pocket. 'I was summoned to the White House today. They're nervous about Wilson. They think our secrets will be aired in Congress. They don't trust us. They're going around us, running their own show. It's a shit storm. You're the errand boy who set up the account at Riggs Bank to receive Saudi money, and now the White House tells us to wire funds to numbered accounts, putting oil money to work against Communist insurgencies in Africa – keeping us out of the loop.'

The director leaned forward. His fist clenched. 'The president is a lean-witted nincompoop, and he has surrounded himself with awful men, *terrible* men – vainglorious liars and bullies. It's not clear to me that this Agency can survive a full-term presidency.'

Gabriel thought the director looked infinitely tired.

'The Wilson incident embarrasses all of us. He *did* work for us. I knew that when I perjured myself, but the White House demanded I hide the fact.'

Gabriel felt the director's contempt. Blood ran cold in the man's veins, but Gabriel knew that a request to lie under oath deeply offended the man's patrician sense of honor and duty.

'What the hell is going on in Washington?' the director snapped in uncharacteristic frustration. He rose, opened the drawn curtain, and looked out over the Virginia countryside to Washington, D.C.'s distant glow. 'They've got an election coming up, and they want to put our scandals behind them – illegal mail openings, our clumsy efforts to assassinate heads of state, all the terrible family jewels. Horror stories.'

The director looked at Gabriel. 'The spy business used to be a most satisfying job and at the same time the most fun thing a man could do. That's what got you and me here. Important work. Gentlemen's work.'

He sighed. 'My job is to protect the Agency and to give our people a reason to believe in their work at a time when the press harangues us. We are losing good men.' He turned to Gabriel again. 'I understand we're losing you. When were you going to tell me?'

Gabriel took an envelope from his suit jacket. 'I would have done it sooner.' He held out the envelope. 'My resignation.' Gabriel couldn't read the director's reaction.

The director took the envelope and put it in his pocket. He studied Gabriel. 'Wilson was your colleague. A friend too, I understand.'

'I knew him and his wife.' Gabriel didn't feel a need to explain his history with the dead man.

'You've taken a job with a consulting company.'

Gabriel had known that once he started his job search in the tight-knit intelligence community, word would eventually get back to the director.

'Big salary. Cashing in on your experience,' the director continued. 'Well, good for you. A daughter in middle school. College is ridiculously expensive, if you aim high, and I'm sure you're encouraging her to try New Haven now that they're taking women. And how is Claire? Still practicing medicine?'

'She's fine. She's on vacation with Sara. I'm a bachelor for the week.'

'I have no illusions about the hardships of the job. Long hours. Lost vacations. Missed piano recitals. Home life neglected. It puts a strain on a marriage. You can't make up for those absences.'

'No, you can't.'

'You sound angry, Jack.'

'I need to move on.'

'Yes, yes. But I need to know what we're facing. How bad is it? He was your friend. We owe his family an answer. I need you to stay on.'

Gabriel resented the director's presumption he would agree to stay, usurping his decision.

'Two months, that's all. Then, God bless you, go off and make a million dollars.' The director's bluster was gone, replaced by a grievance. 'There is more to Wilson's death. I need to know if the men responsible are still inside. If they are, they need to go.'

\*

The two old acquaintances left Headquarters' Building together and walked under a sheltering night sky. The director had forgone the private parking spot reserved for the DCI, and in the new egalitarian spirit of his tenure, he used the large employee lot. The two men stopped at the director's six-year-old Buick Skylark. He eschewed a chauffeured limousine and drove himself to work.

Gabriel sensed urgency in the man who, for all their time together, remained remote and distant.

'I have an obligation to the oath I took – we both took – to serve the Constitution. Loyalty, probity, decency, honor. These things matter, and they are scarce in this town.' The director's eyes came off the Headquarters' Building, and he smiled at Gabriel. 'Almost as scarce as a winning baseball team. I don't want to sound alarmist, but there are people, powerful people, in this town who want to destroy the Agency, and they aren't in the Soviet embassy.'

The director pointed to the dark tree line and beyond, an imaginary compass point. 'Eight miles in that direction is President Lincoln's cottage. He sought refuge there in the dark months of the Civil War, hoping to clear his head of the noise in the White House. It was there that he wrote the first draft of the Emancipation Proclamation. It's a small stucco home with a few rooms and a porch. No one knows it's there, but I visit from time to time.'

He paused. 'Lincoln made the journey there in the summer heat. Confederate troops were massing to the west, waiting to attack Washington. It was early in the war, and the nation was split. Imagine what he must have seen on his way to the cottage – wagons loaded with wounded Union soldiers, gravediggers opening the earth for the dead, escaped slaves in tent towns. Think of the harrowing burden Lincoln bore and what was on his mind. The stakes were high then. Principles mattered to Lincoln.' The director looked at Gabriel. 'They should matter to us.'

The two men stood quietly in the empty parking lot, close together, but distant too – two men joined by fresh memories of old dangers.

46

'How long have we known each other?'

'It's been a good run.'

The director laughed. 'Four months Schlesinger lasted. The admiral fourteen. I've been in the job almost three years. I should declare victory and quit.' He paused. 'Who would believe that a twenty-two-year-old suicide could be our undoing. I need your help.'

Gabriel nodded but said nothing.

'Two months. Then make some money. Live the rest of your life. Put all this in the novel you've never had the time to write.'

Gabriel felt the director's hand on his shoulder, and he knew they were coming to the end of the conversation.

'You get to the bottom of this. I would rather the damnable truth from you than convenient lies from the White House. You will liaise with them but work for me on this.'

The director opened his car's door. 'Only me. And Coffin and Mueller. Keep them informed.'

Gabriel was puzzled by the director's request that he involve two men who distrusted each other, and for a moment he felt the conscious maneuvering of a conspiring mind. He stepped forward, as if closing the distance might provide insight into the director's thinking, but he saw only the man's deeply creased brow and dark eyes.

'The FBI is not to know, and the Office of Security is not to know. The White House will get what we tell them. Interview those involved. Collect information. Then I'll decide what to do. Everything by the books.'

*

Later, Gabriel lay on his bed in his town house in Georgetown, alone. His wife and daughter would return in a few days, so without deciding whether to accept the director's request, and thus incur his wife's anger, he could spend a few days on the Wilson case. He made a mental list of men who'd been in senior positions in the Agency in 1953, including men still in the Agency, most prominently Coffin and Mueller. They had both been there at the Agency's birth and experienced the heady successes in Guatemala, Iran, and Berlin, which had given the Agency its early braggadocio. Hope had stirred, but then faded in the aftermath of the Bay of Pigs and Hungarian disasters, and it fell victim to the illusion that America's Brahmins, who sniffed the heady dream stuff of empire, could forge a world order sitting at their desks in Washington. Cold War failures had long ago divided the House of Dulles.

Gabriel doubted Coffin and Mueller were involved, but he knew investigations failed when conclusions were corrupted by presumptions and wishful thinking.

The next day, Gabriel walked into his Headquarters' office and wrote down his list, adding names and questions. He had known some personally, others only by reputation, and a few names were new to him. Their OSS biographies were legendary, as were their efforts to shape the Agency's Cold War mission. Men of stature from the Ivy League, who'd left lucrative careers in law for government service. All were gone from the Agency, and when Gabriel checked with Human Resources, gone from life, too. Dulles, pushed out by President Johnson, a victim of influenza complicated by pneumonia, dead in 1969. Frank Wisner had died four years before that, his notorious drinking helping him to an early grave. Gone too were Sheffield Edwards, General Counsel in 1953, who'd quietly passed away the month before.

Everyone who might clearly have known something had retired or died, so Gabriel adjusted his focus to the living. There were the two names that had become known through the happenstance of the Deep Creek Lake invitation, and there was Phillip Treacher, gone from the Agency for years, but he'd been there in 1953, and the three of them – Gabriel, Treacher, and Wilson – had once enjoyed an occasional drink together. Wives were sometimes part of it. Gabriel knew where he could find Treacher.

The pleasant woman in Records Administration didn't ask Gabriel why he wanted the home addresses where pension checks were sent to Herb Weisenthal and Roger Ainsley, but he knew it was a request she wouldn't forget, so he felt compelled to offer the plausible story. He said he'd been tasked to write a confidential history of the Agency's experiments in human behavior modification. *Really?* she'd said skeptically, living up to her reputation.

Dora Plummer had a storied career in the OSS in France during the Nazi occupation, earning commendations for her liaison with an SS colonel that provided the Allies critical intelligence on Germany's Normandy defenses, and she had used her good looks after the war in Vienna to charm secrets from an NKVD officer. When she joined the CIA after its formation, she was refused overseas assignments in a male-dominated Agency that kept women in back office jobs. She endured her move from being one of the guys to being one of the girls with dignity, and Gabriel had never heard her complain about the Agency's unequal treatment of women, but neither did she conform her opinions to a particular correctness, and her great memory and superior organizational skills protected her from men intimidated by her intelligence.

He sat across from Dora Plummer, now in her fifties, but with the luminous smile that had seduced an SS colonel. She looked at Gabriel as if looking into his mind, testing what he requested against what she thought he wanted.

'Of course, Jack, I remember them. Weisenthal left in 1973. July, I think. He arranged a great purging of his files that summer.

He had no need for the files and no space left, or so he said, and I'm sure it was true enough. Ainsley was the errand boy in Plans who brought in boxes of memos, reports, and diaries dealing with human behavior modification. There were too many for me to personally go through, but I peeked in a few to organize them better. Ainsley wasn't sloppy, but he was idiosyncratic. That would be the kind way to describe his cataloguing. We processed them as directed.' Dora gazed at Gabriel. 'What are you really after, Jack? No one comes in here with a straight story, only the story that will get them the answer they want. It's about Wilson, isn't it?' She laughed, then pulled a green folio from the bookcase behind her desk and wrote down home addresses and telephone numbers. She ripped the page from her pad and handed it to Gabriel. 'This is what you want.'

Gabriel took his first soundings of Weisenthal and Ainsley by phone that night, like a telephone solicitor, planning the call for the hour he knew they would be home. He made the calls from his home study. Gabriel didn't get past Weisenthal's wife, who asked for Gabriel's name, and when she conveyed it to her husband, he was suddenly not available.

Gabriel had more luck with Ainsley, a bachelor, who answered the phone. Ainsley was on the short list of men who'd worked under Weisenthal in the Technical Services Staff. He now lived in Watergate East on the banks of the Potomac in downtown Washington. Ainsley was talkative, and Gabriel recognized the slur of drink in his speech. Old grudges came up without provocation, and Gabriel listened to a long monologue on a minor grievance about being sidelined to the Chemical Branch after his Agency mentor, Bill Donovan, was eased out for carrying a loaded pistol to meetings. 'One of a kind,' Ainsley said. 'They made him a Knight of Malta for his work with the Vatican during the war.'

'I didn't know.'

'Jesus Christ, Jack. They all were. Dulles, McCone, Coffin, Mueller. The new guy running the shop is the only one who declined.'

Gabriel had started the conversation by sharing a personal fact to encourage Ainsley to open up, and Ainsley took the bait. 'Go ahead, Jack, resign. Get out. Don't fuss with old bones. Things happened. A lot of shit went down. Korea, the Soviet blockade of Berlin. Names? You want names? I think I've said enough.'

'You haven't said anything.'

'It's enough. Let it go.'

'What happened in that hotel room?'

'He went through the window.'

'How?'

'Easy to go through a window if you're a determined suicide. All very natural.'

'Suicide isn't natural.'

'*Dei opus est scriptor*,' Ainsley said. 'God's work.'

Gabriel sensed the end of their conversation in Ainsley's curt response, but he wasn't done with the man. He got Ainsley to agree to meet in person, and after some hesitation, Ainsley suggested the Howard Johnson Motor Lodge's coffee shop across the street from the sprawling Watergate complex.

'Come alone.'

# 4

## POTOMAC BOAT CLUB

AN INDIGNANT SENSE OF self-righteousness swept over Phillip Treacher. Perhaps it was less complicated than he was making it, and the surprising resurrection of the Wilson case was simply today's headline, soon to be eclipsed by tomorrow's. Treacher was at a small balcony table at the Potomac Boat Club, watching dawn peak over the tree line and burn mist from the dark river. After his early-morning row, he relaxed with coffee and contemplated the bizarre turn of events.

The *Washington Post* was open before him to coverage of the Senate hearings from three days before. He had looked at the photo of Dr Wilson's widow with trepidation. He'd gone out socially with the Wilsons several times, but over the years he had confined those memories to his mind's chamber of the willfully forgotten. His surprise had come when he read the caption, which identified the man at her side with his hand shielding his face from the cameras as Jack Gabriel, his old college classmate.

Treacher could still not wholly justify to himself his role in Wilson's death. Perhaps, he thought, it was nothing more complicated than supreme irritation that he'd been ordered to clean up a problem not of his making, and then denied the truth. He'd carried that grudge with him when he walked away from the Agency a few years later. It was so long ago – a different world – but now it was alive again and in the headlines.

Treacher's hour sculling on the river had helped him calm the worry that came with the surprise.

Michael Casey had joined him at the café table, but Casey had waved off the waiter's offer of a menu. He wasn't there to eat or socialize. Now, these two fiftyish men – strangers but for their brief encounter in the Hotel Harrington when they were in their late twenties – stared at each other across the table and across the gulf of time. Streaking rays breaking over the trees washed them in harsh light.

Treacher had no trouble tracking down Casey. Washington was a small town for ambitious men at the peaks of their careers. Successful men knew of, or were acquainted with, other men who enjoyed status and power. Treacher and Casey had kept their distance, but through word of mouth and happenstance, Treacher knew Casey had stayed on in the Office of Security and was now its deputy head. That the CIA secretary knew Treacher's name when he asked to speak with her boss had initially surprised Treacher. It always surprised him when people he didn't know knew his name – and she'd put his call through.

'It's the White House. The deputy chief of staff, Mr Treacher,' he'd heard her say.

Treacher put down his coffee cup and watched Casey across the table. His fingers tapped the table in a nervous tic. 'You know why I called?'

Casey was rigid in his chair. He was dressed immaculately in a summer suit, garroting tie, and polished black leather shoes. His clothes, his demeanor, and his expression were those of a man of personal discipline. He was tall and a little gray, and heavier than Treacher remembered, but still with the masculine good looks of an aspiring Hollywood extra. Treacher's mind reached back a quarter century to the young man he'd only briefly met, and that distant rookie's face reshaped itself to become the aging man sitting opposite.

Casey looked across the table and met Treacher's eyes. 'I do.'

'Your secretary knew my name.'

'Very sweet. Very punctual. Very charming, when she wants to be.' Casey pointed to the newspaper. 'Didn't take you long to call.'

Both men let the subtext of the meeting linger. Laughter of rowers returning from early-morning exercise drifted up from the boat ramp below and mixed with the first sounds of traffic crossing Key Bridge.

Casey's eyes came off the river. 'Weisenthal coming? Ainsley?'

'I thought we should talk first. Their names have been publicly associated with Wilson. Ours have not. What happened to Kelly?'

'He cleans powerboats docked in the marina. Too many bar fights.' Casey pointed to Gabriel's photograph in the newspaper. 'He's asking questions.'

Treacher nodded. 'He called me. Left a message. Wants to meet.'

'That's not a good idea.'

Treacher resisted the temptation to agree. He had been sporadically in touch with his old CIA colleague, and he didn't want any awkwardness between them. He looked off to the river and was morbidly amused by how circumstance anchored him to the past. His fingers tapped again. 'Where are you on this?' he asked.

Both men waited for the waiter to remove Treacher's coffee cup, gauging each other. They were men of stature, successful men who knew the power of innuendo to bring down careers. Treacher had already gone around and around on the danger.

Opprobrium, censure, vilification. Whose career could survive that? Jail, in the unlikely event that evidence was assembled, and a case brought to trial, was the least of his concerns. A man's reputation was a fragile thing – years in the making but lost in a moment. Slanderous whispers were the death of a high-ranking public servant.

'Where am I on this?' Casey echoed. 'Where the hell are you?' Casey looked off at the calm river with contempt before his eyes slowly settled on Treacher.

'I have three children. I am married to the same woman. I have a good position in the Agency. I don't need this bullshit.' Casey raised his palms. 'I still smell the blood. You crafted a crime that fell to me, but I won't fall to protect you.'

Casey's eyes were coals. 'I am the victim here as much as that poor man. I will not suffer the howls of shame. I go to church every Sunday. I suspect it's more than you do. Blood will have blood before I let myself be brought down for this.'

# 5

## CIA OFFICES
## DOWNTOWN WASHINGTON, D.C.

THE OFFICE OF SECURITY's new satellite location was on a high floor near the National Archives' graceful Corinthian columns and within view of the FBI's headquarters. Michael Casey hated his new office, and particularly its view of the FBI building. FBI Headquarters' overbearing concrete edifice had an uneven roof line and a gravel moat on three sides that reinforced a fortress-like appearance appropriate for a national police headquarters. The best that could be said of its stark, federal drabness was that its mediocre architecture was no worse than other soulless government buildings that had gone up in the preceding decade. Casey thought its severe brutalism was alien to the capital's spirit of democracy.

He was unhappy that he'd been moved out of Langley, away from the center of power, but when the order to move came, he obeyed. He had been served well in life by his respect for authority, but he'd also learned the price of blind obedience. The Office of Security had not fared well in the Agency's new tortured soul-searching, and they'd become easy scapegoats for the sins of the past. Charges had been made that he was too cozy with the FBI and too quick to bend the law. The new director had banished him and his department from Langley. To keep his job, he knew he only had to outlast the director.

Casey flicked off his desk lamp and rose from his chair, leaving an unfinished handwritten memo. He walked to the large fifth-floor windows, lit his third cigarette of the hour, and gazed out at the congested traffic detoured from cut-and-cover subway construction a few blocks away.

'Bastards.'

The word slipped quietly from his lips, but he said it with venom, and he followed it with a string of bitter epithets that expressed his feelings toward the new CIA and Jack Gabriel, who, without ever having met him, had become his nemesis. Somehow the FBI too had become involved and had sent a man to ask questions about Wilson.

Casey was like other Agency staff: fiercely private, smart, and a good drinker with a stern expression that he could shed or assume at will. But he was different too: his job in the Office of Security was to protect classified material and investigate breaches of security, and this kept him faceless inside the Agency. He was convinced that the CIA's new willingness to open up about its past was a terrible mistake, and he was appalled that the Agency's dirty linen was being washed in public. He was a strong advocate of the view that the ends justified the means. While he had a rigid belief in the moral force America played in the world, he was quick to ignore the moral jeopardy of controversy if national security was at stake.

His distrust of politicians found its full flowering in the aftermath of the Bay of Pigs, and he never forgave President Kennedy for betraying the CIA. Casey had once admired Kennedy's intelligence, sophistication, Irish Catholic roots, and the grace that he and Jackie brought to the White House. He'd read *Profiles in Courage* and was impressed with Kennedy's insights into the moral courage of a few senators who found a way to speak out against the mob tyranny of ignorant public opinion, but then Kennedy's abrupt betrayal of the CIA had changed his mind. He came to despise the man he once admired.

Kennedy's assassination was not a grievous blow or a surprise. He had heard the rumblings inside the Agency, and while he didn't know if the CIA was responsible, he was one of the few men inside with access to the accreting details of the assassination, and nothing he'd seen led him to reject the idea that the CIA murdered the president. Kennedy posed an existential threat to the Agency. He had planned to cut the CIA's budget; he wanted to withdraw from South Vietnam; he made the CIA a laughingstock after the Bay of Pigs. But it was two other facts, one known to only a handful of men and the other known only to him, that shaped Casey's opinion. He'd heard the four trace acoustic impulse patterns on the Dallas Police Department's Dictabelt, suggesting a second gunman. And he alone knew that the CIA had ordered Wilson killed. If the Agency could kill one American citizen with impunity, why not another?

*Bastards!* Casey ground his cigarette into an overflowing ashtray. He had let himself believe that his role in the Wilson killing would remain forever between him and his conscience, but that comfort was gone. How would he deal with the problem?

The answer came to him a few minutes later as he gazed out the window. He dismissed the thought at first, but once it entered his mind, he was stubbornly drawn back to the possibility. It was so simple, so audacious, and in the climate of public antipathy toward the CIA, quite reasonable. If only he could find a way to stop Gabriel. *If only such a thing could be done. From the inside.*

Casey had always been a methodical case officer, painstakingly slow. Just sometimes he had a flash of inspiration that turned him from a good intelligence officer into a brilliant conspirator. What if Gabriel could be discredited – forced out.

Slowly, Casey assembled a plan, testing the risks, calculating the dangers, and subjecting it to the scrutiny he knew would fall on it. The plan passed each of the tests.

By late afternoon he had retrieved the Agency's personnel file on Jack Gabriel. The CIA kept detailed files on its employees, which included regular background checks to determine if an employee's lifestyle was a security risk, and the material was used to evaluate officers for promotions. Salacious hearsay and moral turpitude were tactical weapons in the Agency's ongoing search for compromised officers.

Casey read Gabriel's three-page summary dossier, scanning it once, and then turned to the performance reviews, looking for a weakness. There was much good in his record – commendations for service in Vietnam, outstanding fitness reports, merit promotions, his marriage, old stuff about his alcoholic father, and Gabriel's half-dozen speeding tickets. Nothing useful jumped out, but Casey knew that every man has his weakness – alcohol, gambling, spending beyond his means, failed polygraphs, women, jealousy, arrogance. No man was free of corrupting sin. The only question was to find that weakness – however deep it was buried – and tempt it into the light of day. Gabriel had to be taken down.

Casey convened a breakfast meeting the next day in a Reston, Virginia coffee shop. Across from him in the booth were two ex-CIA operatives, veterans of the Bay of Pigs fiasco whom Casey had kept close to the Agency. He used them for dirty work that he didn't want traced to the Office of Security. William Barber was middle-aged Boston Irish with a big chest and a thick neck contained by a loosely knotted tie. The Cuban Eugenio Martinez was Barber's physical opposite: tall, thin, and his skin had an olive sheen. His eyes were large on his narrow face, and they had a disturbing calm. Both men wore business suits.

'Gentlemen,' Casey began, pushing the dossier across the table. 'Jack Gabriel is a problem for the Agency. He is in the inspector general's office, but he has become a security risk, a man who doesn't know how to keep his mouth shut. The work you'll do is off the books.'

Martinez sipped his coffee. 'What work?'

Casey scanned the coffee shop, again confirming there was no one who would recognize him. 'I don't know yet. But I suspect he's forgotten the distinction between what we do and what the FBI does.'

Casey gave a short lecture on the law, laying out a case for the work he wanted done. The CIA, he reminded them, gathered foreign intelligence, and the FBI pursued domestic criminal investigations and made arrests. Gabriel was stepping over the line with his investigation into the death of Dr Charles Wilson, and he was likely to stumble upon other matters that remained highly classified. 'Things that need to stay unknown. We need to stop him.' He added that laws might have to be broken, but they couldn't make stupid mistakes like the Watergate burglars had made.

'Is that clear?' Casey looked at the two men. 'I want to know who he speaks with and where he goes. Keep these names in mind.'

Casey wrote ROGER AINSLEY and HERB WEISENTHAL in neat block letters. Casey tore the sheet from his notepad and handed it across the table. He handed each man an envelope of cash. 'If you need to speak with me, tell my assistant you're security consultants from Florida.'

# 6

## HEADQUARTERS

FRIDAY AFTERNOON VESPERS AT Langley Headquarters. Jack Gabriel stood among intelligence officers and the director's top men, who gathered to end the workweek with a generous scotch. Gabriel was chatting with two recent graduates of the Farm when he spotted James Coffin arrive, and he begged an excuse to engage the head of Counterintelligence.

Gabriel's march across the room abruptly ended with a booming voice. 'Jack. Jack Gabriel.'

Gabriel found himself approached by George Mueller, the less-than-warm Deputy Director of Plans whose rise through the ranks was a tribute to organization, good luck, and his mordant humor. His voice had rolled across the room like distant thunder, getting attention from other men who, seeing it was Mueller, returned to their conversations.

'Weisenthal living up to his reputation, is he?' Mueller said. 'We're all shaped by something, and for him it was his belief he could manipulate the human mind. I heard he's had a transformation; he's an organic farmer and does volunteer speech therapy with kids. He's putting his sins behind him.'

Now facing Gabriel, Mueller dropped his voice to a cordial murmur. 'Come on, Jack, how could you not know?'

Gabriel smiled. 'I didn't say I didn't know.'

'Your face said it. His name was on the invitation the widow waved at the hearing. Now he's been called to testify in the Senate. We're all interested to hear what he has to say.'

'One did follow the other.'

'Like night the day. I hear you're staying on. Rumor true?'

Gabriel was always alert to the possibility that there were men in the bureaucracy who knew more about his prospects than he did, and rumors – sometimes true, often not – took on a life of their own. As he faced Mueller, sipping his drink and waiting for an answer, Gabriel calculated the algebra of discretion.

'For the moment, I'm here,' Gabriel said. 'We're supposed to talk about Wilson. You were in the Agency then. What do you remember?'

'I left in May 1953. I knew him, but by November that year, when it all happened, I was teaching in New Haven. I don't think I can be of any help. But look, I see you were on your way to Coffin. He's a better source than me. He has all the history in his head, if you can coax it out.' Mueller leaned forward and spoke in an intimate whisper. 'We all know there is a move to shrink our ranks and remove dead wood. The retirement package offered is an attractive inducement. What's next for you? For me? What's next for any of us? We're excoriated by the press, hounded by Congress. I don't know what's next, but yes, I do think about the possibilities of life on the outside. And *you* should, too.' Mueller smiled. 'Go ahead, speak with Coffin. See if he is willing to share anything beyond the time of day.'

Gabriel joined James Coffin at the bar, where he found the head of Counterintelligence lamenting the empty bottle of Macallan. 'I prefer scotch, but Kentucky bourbon will do. Good to see you, Jack. The Boss said we should talk. So, let's talk.' He nodded at the exit.

The two men stepped into the courtyard, out of earshot of

the noisy drinkers. The sun had sunk below the horizon, and the evening air had cooled and lost its steamy humidity. Coffin and Gabriel had circled each other in their careers as wary allies and occasional adversaries. Coffin's longtime smoking habit had given his face the pallor of death. His years in charge of CI had turned him inward, his eyes settled in their sockets, and he wore a permanently skeptical expression. Gabriel had known Coffin to smile, but it was a rare event, and it happened mostly when he was pleased to have impressed a person by quoting *Hamlet* or Ezra Pound, or offering trivia on orchids or fly fishing. Gabriel thought Coffin a cipher whose face was an inscrutable Venetian mask. Legends had built up around the man, and while Gabriel was certain Coffin did nothing to feed the stories, his rigorous work discipline, idiosyncratic habits, and passionate concern about postwar threats fed the rumors. There were those who insisted that Coffin studied Burgundy wines to impress his French counterparts, but Gabriel knew that his deep knowledge was acquired in London during the war – where he'd also acquired a taste for bespoke English suits.

Coffin lit a cigarette, waving away a cloud of smoke, and contemplated Gabriel. 'The Boss is making changes,' Coffin began, barely hiding his disdain. 'He wants to bring us in step with the times. Wants to make us more egalitarian. He parks in the employee lot, promotes women, lunches with newbies once a week. Next, we'll be hiring handicapped guards and wheelchair assassins. Then we'll be asked to give up Friday vespers.' He held up his glass. 'To the old guard.' He looked at Gabriel. 'I saw you with George. He won't give you the time of day.'

'He said the same of you.'

Coffin smiled. 'We know each other too well, or not at all. You've heard? Someone smells blood.'

'Heard what?'

'We have another name in the Wilson case. It came out in the documents, I believe, or rose from its grave, entering our consciousness like a bad dream. A name someone forgot to redact: Nick Arndt. Name mean anything to you?'

*Just like Coffin to raise a point thinking that he was clarifying when he was, in fact, adding a layer of obfuscation*, Gabriel thought.

'The name doesn't exist in Human Resources. There is no record of a man employed by us with that name.' Coffin laughed smoke from his nostrils. 'We are good record keepers. Better than the Gestapo. We have a prodigious need to record our history, which is why, when you look at the records on Wilson, it's so baffling. We can't rule out that records were destroyed or doctored. Yes?' Coffin smiled. 'How is your daughter? Have you had the conversation yet?'

Gabriel knew it was Coffin's style to suddenly switch topics to unbalance a conversation and leave it to Gabriel to bring things back. 'Not yet.'

'Don't wait long. She'll surprise you one day and ask, "Daddy, do you work for the CIA?" It's the wise father who understands his own child.'

'Good advice,' Gabriel said. 'Nick Arndt. What about him?'

'We have plenty on Weisenthal. A few bits on Ainsley. But not a whit on Arndt. So, there is your answer. Nick Arndt. Sounds like a cryptonym created by the boys in Technical Services. A man who isn't is called Arndt.'

Coffin threw back his bourbon, tolerating the taste, smiling. His eyes came off the brightly lit conference room where the boisterous laughter brightened with alcohol. 'We want our family jewels out in a public purging. That's our posture now. Redeem ourselves and move forward. Who is hurt here by having the full story come out? Answer that. Then you'll know where to look.'

Gabriel understood the bleak paradoxes of Coffin's worldview. The man lived in isolation in a world of fact and counter-fact, where everything was subject to doubt, including doubt itself.

'Fill me in on Ainsley's puffery after you'd gotten to him,' Coffin said. 'A bitter man. Passed over twice.' Coffin started back to the conference room, then abruptly stopped. 'Talk to the family. Talk to the *Times* reporter, Ostroff. Our records won't help here. Someone made sure of that long ago. Approach this orthogonally.'

# 7

## WATERGATE EAST

DEATH DRAWS THE LIVING like moths to light.

Gabriel had spent the morning reviewing Ainsley's personnel files that Dora Plummer had provided, and he'd brought two files with him to his meeting with Ainsley in the Howard Johnson coffee shop across from Watergate East's serpentine façade. Gabriel had been surprised to discover that Ainsley had spent much of his time in Technical Services at the mid-level, GS-10 pay scale, a career plateau that usually drove good men to leave. Gabriel looked for something that stood out or looked odd in the bland ordering of an undistinguished career. And he kept coming back to one thing: Ainsley's annual performance reviews were uniformly poor, and his low job assessments included specific mention of heavy drinking. It begged the question – why hadn't Ainsley been sacked?

Gabriel had still not shaped a good way to pose the question when he looked out the Howard Johnson's window and saw a crowd assembling around police cars parked haphazardly in front of Watergate East's lobby entrance. Their roof lights were rotating, and their doors were thrown open. He was early to meet Ainsley, so he dodged traffic crossing Virginia Avenue to see what the commotion was all about.

Hastily placed yellow tape marked a wide perimeter on the

sidewalk and held back a dozen men and women with handbags and attaché cases. In the distance, there was the wailing siren of an approaching ambulance. Anxious tenants looked down from their balconies at the restive crowd that pushed toward a fallen railing, necks craning to get a look at the body.

Someone pointed to the seventh-floor balcony where a section of broken railing dangled. 'He came from there. I heard him hit the ground. It was an awful sound, like a sandbag.'

A Good Samaritan knelt beside the stricken Roger Ainsley and dabbed his forehead. He was on his back, and a bloody femur protruded grotesquely from a tear in his pants. His eyes were open, and he was making a great effort to speak, but only pinkish foam came from his mouth. His words were garbled and lost. The woman continued to comfort him, but then he was dead.

Gabriel looked up at the balcony, his hand raised against the bright sun, and he felt himself pushed from behind. 'Excuse me,' Gabriel said indignantly to the policeman.

'Behind the tape.'

'What happened here?' Gabriel asked.

'I'll handle this,' a big plainclothes detective said, waving off the policeman. The detective was tall with a beer-belly gut, and his loose-fitting linen suit had lost its crease. He wiped perspiration from his forehead with a handkerchief and motioned Gabriel forward. His tie and shirt collar were loosened against the midday heat, and his cheeks were flushed.

'I'm Detective Potter. You a friend of his?' the detective asked, wheezing.

Gabriel hesitated before admitting quite so much. 'No.'

'Did you know him?'

'Never met him,' Gabriel said. He explained that he was walking by and saw the police cars. He looked down at Ainsley. 'Who is he?'

'What's your interest?' the detective asked, breathing heavily. He held up a bolt, tossing it in his hand like a juggler, gauging Gabriel. 'Just walking by and you happened to run over to see what happened?'

Gabriel nodded.

Potter caught the bolt and presented it. 'It popped out of the wall. The railing collapsed, and he fell.' He nodded at the sheeted corpse but kept his eyes on Gabriel. 'At that height it's three seconds of fall. Not much pain. Not a bad way to go. Last week we had a woman crushed by a garbage truck that was backing up. She took an hour to die. Gunshots are rarely quick, unless the bullet goes in the head.' His finger made a pistol to his temple. 'I see a lot of death in this job, as you can imagine. I could give you a lecture on the many ways people leave this world.' Detective Potter pointed at the body. 'I have two theories here. He was thrown off. Or he was drunk and jumped.'

'Pushed or jumped?' Gabriel said.

'Yeah. That's right. Pushed or jumped. But why do you care? You didn't know him. Just a guy passing by who happened to see a corpse, right?'

*

Gabriel crossed the avenue, but as he approached the other side, he happened to look back. It was an instinct he acquired over the years – the feeling of knowing when he was being observed. Ainsley's body was being lifted onto a stretcher by two EMTs, who slid the sheeted form into the back of the ambulance, and it was then, as he looked away from the ambulance, that he happened to see two men sitting in a car across the street. The black Ford sedan was parked illegally, and the men inside were watching him. Gabriel didn't think anything of it, but as he walked away, he looked again, and the two men hadn't moved, nor had their attention shifted. They had middle-aged faces and looked intent, respectful, and tough. Grim faces, he thought, that kept looking at him.

*

Langley Headquarters. All afternoon Gabriel had been at his desk struggling to understand the turn of events. Gradually, a spare profile of Ainsley emerged from the documents that he had requested: a native of the Florida panhandle; military family; divorced twice; no children; master's degree in biochemistry from the University of Michigan; twenty-five-year CIA veteran; heavy drinker.

Gabriel read the details of Ainsley's life looking for signs of depression, but he found none, nor did his psychological profile fit that of a middle-aged man who would jump off his balcony. From time to time he was interrupted by his secretary or the ringing telephone, but he found himself returning to the detective's suggestion that Ainsley had been pushed to his death.

It was late when he put together his papers. He was still perplexed why Ainsley's poor record and notorious drinking hadn't led to being fired. It was then, as he was finishing up, that he came to his conclusion. Someone had kept him inside over the years rather than unmoored on the outside. It was a theory that explained why his undistinguished career hadn't led to a dismissal, and it also explained why he was now dead.

Gabriel pulled an index card with the list of names from his wallet. Dulles, Wisner, Edwards. Each was crossed out. Gabriel took his pen and drew a line through Ainsley's name. The next name on the list was Phillip Treacher. He dialed the White House switchboard from memory and was transferred through.

Treacher's secretary put him on interminable hold, and while he waited, Gabriel doodled a man falling from a hotel window.

'I'm sorry for the wait, Mr Gabriel, but Mr Treacher is with the president. Can I take a message?'

Gabriel pondered how long it had taken her to respond. 'Have him call me. Tell him I'm leaving the office. We can talk tomorrow. It's nothing important.'

Gabriel considered what was next. It was convenient that he hadn't gotten Treacher on the line because he could say, in good conscience, that he'd done what the director asked. He'd looked into the matter, examined the files, such as they were, and contacted the two living men who might know what happened in the Hotel Harrington. All he'd found was one dead man and two dead ends. He had nothing to compromise the official story. The whole story wasn't out, but he'd only agreed to take a look. *Interview those involved. Collect information. Everything by the books.*

Gabriel typed a brief report for the director on his manual Remington. He described what he'd done, amplifying the spare facts with enough detail to fill out the substance of his effort. He concluded that he had found nothing to contradict the official story, and more work, if it was to be done, was of a police nature, and he wasn't the man for that. Gabriel reread the note and then added his postscript: *'You've already got my resignation, so I don't need to submit it again.'* Gabriel folded the note into an envelope that he addressed by hand and locked it in his desk drawer.

He could do more, but that was the nature of work in the Agency – there was always more that could be done. The trick was to learn when to stop and when to put the thing to bed. He was glad he hadn't gotten Treacher on the line.

Gabriel crossed Headquarters' vaulted lobby as he did every night. The reaching height and the tall dark windows made it cold, and it was a quiet space, except for his echoing footsteps on the huge Agency shield set in the mosaic tile floor. The security guard greeted Gabriel by name, and Gabriel returned the man's smile with a brisk nod.

He had arrived later than usual that day and felt lucky to have found a coveted parking spot near the Headquarters' entrance. And now the large employee lot was almost empty. This too was a reason to leave the Agency. He would find himself at his desk at midnight every day if he didn't set his own limits. Crises followed crises, and always the unreasonable demand to produce an instant analysis for the White House. Crushing workloads burnt out the best of them, and if you didn't believe in the work, you didn't last long.

These thoughts went through his mind as he approached his Volvo, and it also struck him that this would be one of his last trips across the lot. Key in hand, he went to open the car door but saw the button was up. He was a creature of habit, and there was nothing more habitual than locking his car door. Had he forgotten to lock it? Instinctively, he glanced around the empty lot, but seeing no one, he brushed off the oversight and slipped behind the wheel.

Gabriel was suddenly aware of a presence in the back seat.

'Close the door.'

He glanced in the rearview mirror.

'This won't take long,' the man said.

A tall streetlamp behind the Volvo shadowed the man's face, but even in the darkness Gabriel saw that a knotted woman's stocking masked his face and distorted his voice.

'We'll talk for a moment, and then I'll leave.'

Gabriel closed the door and stared at the man's disguised face. 'What do you want?' He took his wallet from his jacket and held it up for the man.

'This isn't a robbery.'

'What do you want?'

'Wilson.'

Gabriel's brow knitted, and he began to turn his head.

'Better if you don't see my face. It's not important who I am.'

'Not important to you, but I want to know who I'm talking to. Get out of the car.'

'If that's what you want. But you won't hear what I have to say.'

Gabriel knew that no one got into the parking lot unless they had CIA clearance. He was talking to an Agency employee. 'Who do you work for?'

'That doesn't matter. What matters to me, and it should matter to you, is that there are men inside who don't want the facts about Wilson out. They think the director is throwing them under a bus. Good men, angry men, who feel they're being sacrificed because the climate in Washington has changed. They're pissed off.'

Gabriel listened through the distorting nylon, but he couldn't make out the man's voice. 'Why are you telling me this?'

'What do you think happened to Ainsley?' the man snapped. 'Suicide? Really? How convenient. The new regime pushed him out, and he was a liability.'

'Liability to whom?'

'Who has the most to lose?'

Gabriel found himself disliking the man. 'What was his role?'

'Fix-it man. That was his reputation. Weisenthal used him to fix things when they broke, or do dirty work if necessary.'

'Weisenthal's responsible?'

'He's got facts in his head, but he's a scientist. He's one man.'

'Someone still inside knows what happened?'

'Too soft.'

'The men responsible are still here.'

72

'That sounds right. When you put your finger on the men who handled what happened in the Hotel Harrington, you'll turn up more dirty laundry. This isn't just about Wilson. Wilson is a symptom.'

'Names?'

'Who are you looking at?'

'I can't give you that.'

'I can't help, then.'

Gabriel snapped, 'For all I know, you're the man I'm looking for.'

There was a long silence.

'Don't waste time going down that rathole.'

'Do I know you?'

'We've met.'

Gabriel glanced again in the rearview mirror.

'I can't afford to have you know who I am. You're on your way out. You can burn your bridges, but I've got a good career here. I need to work with those angry men. I won't jeopardize my job. I need their trust. No one is cooperating with you. People avoid you. You'll have to break your own glass. Whoever was responsible for Wilson didn't know anything about political scruples, but they thought they did. Weisenthal is like that, but there are others.'

'Can you confirm a name if I give it to you?'

'I can't confirm what I don't know.'

Gabriel considered the report he'd written the director, then pondered the man in the back seat. *He didn't have to do this.*

There was a long silence in the car.

'I can point you in a direction,' the man said. 'Give you questions to ask. That's how I can help.'

Gabriel stifled an impulse to turn and get a better look at the man's face. He felt the man's skittishness. 'How do I reach you?'

'There is a mailbox at the end of your street. You drop letters in it while walking your dog. One vertical chalk mark means you have a question. Two means you want to meet. I will get you instructions on where to go and what to do. Here is a number to call in an emergency. It's unlisted, so don't bother tracking it. Use it only in an emergency.'

Gabriel heard the door open and then watched a tall man with an umbrella walk to the underground parking garage. He waited, thinking he'd see the man drive out, but no car emerged.

They would meet five times in two months, following the routine agreed in the car.

# 8

## P STREET IN GEORGETOWN

ALL OF THIS WAS on Gabriel's mind when he arrived home. He parked on the street as usual and glanced down the block at the mailbox. It bothered him to know that he had been watched and his routines observed, and the thought made the muscles on his neck constrict. As he approached his town house, he looked back but saw no one.

Finding an affordable Georgetown home had felt like a victory, and it eased his family's return to stateside living after two years in South Vietnam. By the end of his tour, Saigon had begun to seem normal, but upon returning to Washington, they realized how absurdly surreal life had been – bombs, sweltering heat, constant danger, and the growing toll of American casualties. For weeks after they moved onto P Street, the slightest noise at night pulled Gabriel out of bed and he'd stand at the window, 9mm Browning Hi-Power in hand.

Gabriel climbed the cast-iron stairs that curved gracefully up from the cobblestone path. Their three-story Federal home sat between grander Victorian houses, but they were drawn to the simple colonial style and the red front door, which the former owner had brightened with flowering vines.

Gabriel knew something was wrong when he entered the front door. His daughter's open backpack spilled clothing onto the vestibule floor, and camping gear formed a debris field of haphazardly dropped equipment. He placed the backpack on the bench, closing the zipper, and then he noticed Claire's pocketbook on the floor. His daughter's dog was not there to greet him.

He stood perfectly still and listened for sounds in the darkened home. 'Claire?'

Gabriel moved through the living room and continued to the rear of the house, where he saw the kitchen light. As he walked, he was alert to everything – the glossy magazines on the coffee table, luggage dropped where it didn't belong, and the *Washington Post* and the *New York Times* scattered violently on the floor.

Overhead light illuminated the kitchen table where Claire sat, her forehead resting on folded hands, holding house keys with her doctor's photo ID, asleep. A wrought-iron pot rack hung above the table, dominating the center of the room. Glass cupboards were neatly organized with stemware, and everywhere order and cleanliness were gifts to the eye. Grace, sophistication, good taste. These were the design qualities that Gabriel and Claire had hoped to bring to the home they planned for their retirement after years of nomadic postings. Precious objets d'art filled the house – carved masks, naïve watercolors, embroidered cloth bought in Saigon's back alleys, an antique medicine chest, and colored-glass vases from Venice.

'Claire,' he whispered.

She startled at his touch. Her red eyes greeted him fiercely, but she said nothing.

'What's wrong?'

'What's wrong?' She raised her shoulder to move from the awkward position she'd been in. She took a moment to stretch her arms over her head, and as she did, she looked at him, judging him. She reached for a newspaper at the end of the table and handed him the days-old front page of the *Times*. She pointed to his photograph beside Maggie Wilson in the Senate hearing room, his hand raised against the camera's unmasking lens, identifying him as an Agency employee.

Soviet embassy KGB staff knew who he worked for and what he did for a living. Senior congressional staff knew, as did White House aides, and Claire knew. Their close circle of friends mostly knew because over the years they found themselves making friends inside the intelligence community – men and women with whom they could be socially open without having to measure their conversations against a litmus test of what could be said and what could not. Only their fourteen-year-old daughter did not know.

'Oh, God,' he said.

Claire looked at her husband. She was calm, angry, judgmental, irritated, quiet. The full scope of her emotional range was present on her face.

'Where is she?'

'Asleep.'

'What did you tell her?'

'What could I say? The caption is wrong? I wasn't going to lie.'

Gabriel expected her to criticize him for the avoidable offense, but they'd joined in a conspiracy to keep their rebellious daughter ignorant.

'We waited too long,' she said. 'She's curious about the world, and she wanted to catch up on the week's news.' Claire had a desolate expression. 'She was appalled. She asked how we could have kept her in the dark.'

Claire crossed her arms and leaned forward. 'She knew something was wrong. She thought we were living in a witness protection program.' Her eyes widened. 'She was afraid to ask!

She didn't want to know the answer to that question, so in a way, she was relieved.'

Gabriel poured himself a scotch from the bottle Claire had opened.

'She asked if you torture people.'

Gabriel grimaced.

'That's what she'll ask you in the morning. You need to find a way to reach her. You need to figure out what you're going to say.'

Gabriel closed his eyes. *Fuck.* This wasn't how it was supposed to happen. He would have to explain doubly – what he did and why he hadn't told her. He crossed the kitchen toward the staircase.

'She's asleep.'

'I need a moment.' *To think.* 'I won't wake her.'

Gabriel knew the popular myth that wives and children were ignorant of who a CIA officer worked for, but the facts were different. Claire knew without knowing the details of his work, but she also had a career with urgent demands, and she had her own life. She played along when an awkward question arose at a dinner party or an abrupt trip needed to be explained. They had talked frequently about the conversation they needed to have with their daughter, but each time they put it off, hoping that a better moment would come. They differed on the urgency of having the conversation, and they argued in coffee shops or late at night in bed. They argued bitterly. Gabriel feared that his admission would fracture his relationship with his only child and she would reject the life he'd chosen. She was an eager reader of *Jane Eyre* and Keats's poems, but she was also among the vocal few in junior high school whose backpacks carried peace signs, who volunteered in soup kitchens, and who talked compassionately about Third World poverty. She believed that the CIA, and the men who worked there, engaged in unscrupulous foul play. She had watched the director's weeklong, televised congressional testimony, and she'd been appalled by his accounts of assassinations and drug experiments. Dinner conversation stopped when she raised the topic of the hearings and gave her opinion: 'The CIA kills people.'

*

Gabriel entered his daughter's dark bedroom. He sat on the rocking chair beside her bed. She lay on her side, knees pulled to her chest, and she'd kicked the comforter to the floor, where it had become a bed for her rescue dog, Molly. Sara had a peaceful expression, but her breathing was shallow and came fitfully. Gabriel gazed at her face and felt a terrible burden. He looked at his child, now almost a young woman, and remembered her birth. He'd felt a love for that baby he never thought he could feel for another human being, and now here she was, a fourteen-year-old with a mind of her own. Where had the years gone?

Her young mind had struggled to understand the world beyond the family, first in Saigon, and then in the raging American youth counterculture. The change, when it came, was startling. Her skirts shortened, her hair lengthened, and large silver bracelets appeared on her wrists. A new rebelliousness set in. Strong opinions about events in the news erupted, and loud rock music played on her turntable. She was indignant at the adult world's prejudices. Her idealism startled him, and they argued frequently, but nothing he said helped her understand the compromises that life required. Her commitment to eradicating poverty and to social justice made Gabriel conscious of his own lost compassion. Like her, he had once believed the world could be made a better place. The force of her naiveté challenged him. He made an effort to listen to her concerns without dismissing them, but her loud, indignant judgments tested his patience.

Gabriel had planned on being gone from the Agency before he had to reveal that he worked for the CIA and not the State Department. He rose from the rocking chair and petted Molly, who rose with him. He leaned over and kissed his daughter's forehead.

*

Claire was in bed, eyes closed, when Gabriel entered their room. He slipped under the sheet beside her and lay looking up at the ceiling. What was next? His mind unspooled options. The silence was broken by a dog's violent barking far away. Closer by, a couple on the sidewalk laughed excitedly, caught in the sudden rain.

*Christ.* The profanity was a feeble echo of his torment. Claire's breathing was loud in the quiet bedroom. Was she asleep?

They were aligned in their need to protect their daughter. Sometimes he thought it was the only thing that kept them together. Their marriage had suffered terribly on their return to Washington. The house in Georgetown was supposed to be a calm refuge after years of overseas postings, but their hopes were frustrated by the crush of work, lost weekends, sudden out-of-town trips, and fraught conversations when he called from the office to say he wouldn't be home until midnight. Claire's tolerance had stretched thin, and they'd drifted apart, strangers sharing a bed. He couldn't talk about his work, which widened the gulf, and the distance filled with resentments and suspicions.

Claire rose on her elbow and looked down at her husband. 'Is there a girlfriend?'

Gabriel wanted to laugh. 'There is no girlfriend.'

'What am I to think?' she demanded. 'You're gone evenings. You live inside yourself, consumed by God knows what. I suffer my love for you. I love you against my will. Foul love.'

Gabriel sat up. There was a beat of silence. 'I won't be leaving the Agency at the end of the month.'

Claire recoiled in panic. 'No,' she said in a convulsive gasp. Her voice was low and whispery, hardly audible against the torrent of soaking rain. 'Why?'

Gabriel was close enough to feel her dismay. 'They want me to find out what happened to Charlie Wilson.'

'"They?" You mean *him*. You *can* say no.'

'It won't take long.' He paused. 'I doubt we'll find anything.'

She stared. 'We agreed you'd leave. It was settled. You have a job waiting.'

Gabriel resisted the urge to defend himself against the indefensible. He knew that whatever he said would provoke a reaction and they'd exhaust themselves with angry accusations. Her eyes were alarmed but not cold, hurt but not unforgiving.

'He was a friend. He saved my life. I owe it to him. I owe it to Maggie.'

'What do you owe me?' Claire snapped. Her voice had the keen edge of a knife. 'What do you owe your family?' She glared. 'It's always been this way. I can't live like this anymore.'

Gabriel had heard that threat once before. They had been on a floating restaurant on the Mekong River on a warm January during the weeklong New Year's festivities. Riverboats with glowing paper lanterns floated by, and the war was still far from the city. She had said it desperately, to provoke him and get his attention. There followed an hour-long outpouring of emotion with tears and desperate crying, and it settled itself, as their arguments often did, by summoning the healing memories of their first night together. It had been a blind date in Washington during the Cuban Missile Crisis. They had sparred through the main course at Harvey's, feeling awkward in the Republican stronghold, each thinking the meeting was a favor to a mutual friend and that the evening couldn't possibly turn out to be fun. They had tested each other like adversaries, thrusting and parrying clever remarks to gain advantage. From their skirmish of wits grew a skeptical romantic interest, but by the end of the evening they had managed to annoy each other.

Only the looming nuclear holocaust drew them together. An after-hours jazz bar followed dessert, and after two rounds of Cointreau, they walked into the night and kept walking and talking until they arrived at his bachelor's apartment. Neither of them wanted to be alone when the ICBMs were launched. They made quiet frenzied love in his bedroom's darkness with the urgency of lovers who had one night to live. Then they fell asleep in each other's arms.

Memories of their early romance sustained their marriage across long, difficult periods. Both saw the danger when their individual lives flourished during his extended absences from home.

*

'We are better than this,' he said. 'I'm not giving up on this marriage.' Gabriel looked deeply into Claire's skeptical eyes, and husband and wife gazed at each other for a long moment. 'Two months. Maybe three. A few conversations and I will write up a report. I owe it to him. Then we'll move on with our lives. I promise.' Gabriel saw that his words swayed Claire little by little, and he saw an old affection weaken her resolve.

Her anger cooled and she took his hand. 'You are vain, narcissistic, and hurtful. But we *are* better than this.' She gently placed his hand on her chest. She had gone to bed naked. She kissed his lips.

Gabriel was surprised by her invitation and hesitated, but she didn't relent.

'You are a terrible husband,' she whispered. She looked into his eyes. 'How did we get here?'

He returned her kiss. Their breath came short and quick, and excitement vibrated between them. His hand went to her stomach, and they touched each other in familiar ways. Desire tangled their bodies in intimate contortions. Claire lay on her back, drawing him between her legs, and her hand shot out to grab lubricating gel from the drawer of the bedside table.

Later, they lay on their backs. Slow, labored breaths followed their exertion, and sweat moistened their bodies. Each gazed up at the shadows of branches dancing on the ceiling. Rain and wind outside quelled their surprise.

'We got an anonymous caller tonight,' she said. 'He made threats against you and hung up. It scared Sara.'

Gabriel sat up suddenly, looking at Claire.

'You've been identified. He knows you work for the CIA.' She sat up beside him and looked at her hands. 'This will come out better for you, for us, for Sara, if it's something you keep away from the family.'

A long silence opened between them.

'Let's think of this as a temporary, but necessary, separation. One of your sudden, extended trips out of town. I can say that to Sara. It's safer that way. I'll delist our number. Stay here if you want, but staying in a hotel will be safer.'

Gabriel saw the distant look on Claire's face. *Is it over? Is this how a marriage ends – suddenly? Unexpectedly? An afterthought after sex?* Gabriel felt like a stranger in his own bed. Loss presented itself as a terrible, unfamiliar color. Her suggestion was a hostile declaration, but in her calm, he felt denied the opportunity to open a discussion.

'Someone saw my photo in the paper. They used my name to find our number. I'll have the house protected. I am not going to a hotel.'

*

The next morning. Bright sunlight streamed through the kitchen's bay window, which looked onto a manicured garden in the town house's small backyard. Wind had cleared out the evening storm, and a flock of birds sounded a chirping chorus.

Gabriel entered the kitchen in pajamas and, as he did each morning, filled the kettle and measured grounds into the paper filter of the coffeemaker. He was a prisoner of a sullen routine, unaware that his daughter was at the kitchen table eating a bowl of cereal. He had turned from the stove, where he'd ignited the gas, when he saw her.

Their eyes met. Molly, an adult Malamute with lush fur, was at her side. He extended his hand to pet Molly's head when she rose to greet him. Sara had wanted a record player, and he'd bought her a Marantz stereo system. She'd wanted a puppy, and he'd helped her adopt a Malamute mix. Gabriel encouraged her to pick a big dog because she was frequently home alone. A big dog, even a gentle big dog, had the power to intimidate strangers.

He felt his daughter's hostility. 'Good morning,' he said.

Sara had always been a complicated subject for him. She was lovely and earnest in one moment and then – changing in an instant for an unknown reason – cold and unforgiving in her haste to abandon a conversation that no longer interested her.

'You work for the CIA,' she said.

Nothing in life had prepared Gabriel for the challenge of fatherhood – love and anger knotted together. He sat across from her. She continued to stare at her cereal, avoiding his eyes, and silence lingered. He didn't have the patience to find the right words for a response, and he let his urge to scold her accusatory tone pass. He didn't have it in him to do what he knew he must – to apologize without being apologetic; to defend himself without being defensive; to earn her understanding without having to be understood. Nothing challenged him like his daughter's contempt.

He rose again and turned off the gas under the whistling kettle. He poured two cups of coffee. He added half-and-half to hers, sugar to his. The two sat opposite each other across a great gulf.

Each spoke at the same time, words colliding, and then stopped speaking. Whatever thoughts had been on the verge of being voiced vanished. Sara grimaced at the moment's awkwardness.

'Will you be around for a while?' she asked.

'I live here.'

'No trips coming up?'

'I'll be around. I'm working in the office for a few weeks.'

'No coup d'etats to engineer? No governments to topple?'

Gabriel frowned.

'I'm sorry,' she said. 'I'm sure you're doing good things. Protecting us from free speech.'

Gabriel contained his anger. He stared at her, and she stared back.

'I've suspected for a while,' she said.

'When?'

'Saigon. There was another American girl who didn't like me. I ignored her, and it made her think I felt superior. You know how someone doesn't like you and you don't know why. She came up to me at the embassy pool one morning and asked if I knew that you worked for the CIA? She called you a spook.

She wanted to embarrass me. I insisted you worked for the State Department – the lie *you'd* told me.'

Sara looked away from her father toward the chirping birds, but after a moment her eyes settled on him again. 'I didn't believe her. I didn't want to believe her.' She nodded at the living room's tall parlor windows, which faced P Street. 'Do the men in the car parked outside also work for the CIA?'

Gabriel left the kitchen and pulled aside one corner of the drawn drapes. In the narrow arc of window, he saw a neighbor's parked Volkswagen, and behind it he recognized another neighbor's Mercedes-Benz. A Ford sedan also caught his attention. On a street where residents preferred imported cars, the plain black Ford stood out. When the man in the passenger seat glanced in Gabriel's direction, Gabriel stepped back out of view and continued to watch the car.

'Who are they?' Sara asked. She had leashed Molly and was preparing to walk the dog.

'I don't know.'

'You don't know, or you won't tell me?'

'I don't know.'

'They're not police,' she said. 'Police drink coffee and eat donuts.' She arched an eyebrow. 'FBI.'

'*Really*,' he said.

'We were told how to spot them at anti-war marches.'

Gabriel appreciated the confidence of her boast.

'I'm walking Molly,' she said.

'I'll change and join you.'

Molly pulled Sara down the quiet residential street, a proud dog with a wolf's menacing snout, straining on her leash. Father and daughter followed behind the lunging animal, and they found themselves in a fragile peace. Molly's interest in neighborhood dogs' scents was a pleasant distraction.

Coming to the end of the block, Gabriel happened to look

back. The intuition he'd acquired in the divided city of Berlin, which he'd later put to good use in Saigon's narrow streets, the feeling of knowing he was being watched. There behind them, the man in the Ford's passenger seat had his head out the window. He wore a snap-brim hat, garroting tie, and dark glasses. He made no effort to hide his presence and spoke into a walkie-talkie.

'Go inside,' Gabriel said to Sara, pointing at the front door. 'I'll be right in.'

Gabriel started across the street, but when he approached, the parked car drove off.

# 9

## WASHINGTON HILTON HOTEL, WHITE HOUSE CORRESPONDENTS' DINNER

MRS PHILLIP TREACHER WAVED at reporters who surged forward when she stepped from the black Lincoln Town Car that had stopped at the festively lit entrance of the Washington Hilton Hotel. She emerged from the left side of the limousine, and her husband waited as she came around. Velvet rope cordoned arriving guests from onlookers and the numerous journalists, who leaned in from either side of the red carpet, shouting questions.

Treacher held his wife's elbow, and he escorted her toward the hotel's revolving door, which was guarded by Metropolitan Police and a few Secret Service agents wearing wireless earpieces. Tammy Treacher's chiffon gown swept the carpet, her blond hair was gathered in a sculpted updo, and her pink hoop earrings swung as she turned from one reporter to the next, waving and savoring the attention.

'Now, you're throwing so many rumors at me, I can't possibly answer all of them. My husband has assured me he was not involved. Couldn't have been.'

She was baited by a provocative question that was shouted at her.

Tammy Treacher stopped and faced the *Times* reporter, Neil Ostroff. He had his notebook open, poised to record her answer. She gazed at him, lips curling, and clutched her sequin purse. In stopping, she had also brought her husband to a halt. Tammy scrubbed her Georgia drawl when she was among friends, but lazy rounded vowels crept into her speech when she performed for the press. Her smile had the tart charm of an annoyed Southern lady.

'If he was,' she shouted back, 'I wouldn't know! He never talks to me about his work. Church and State. I trust and pray he was not part of any scandal. The CIA is a dirty business. But it's got to be that way, doesn't it? It's dangerous work fighting Communists.'

She had stopped to answer one question and suddenly found herself fielding another. 'Knew Wilson?' she said. 'God, no. I've never known anything about the CIA except that my husband had the privilege to work there and, of course, what you in the press write. I'm glad it's all coming out. All these terrible family jewels – nasty stuff. It's a big relief, isn't it, like opening a pigsty and letting the stink out.'

Treacher stood patiently at his wife's side, mildly exasperated but also cautious of the potential for cameras to capture an embarrassing moment. Stoic. Calm. Seething. Treacher nudged his wife forward to extract her from the reporters.

'Thank you,' he said. 'Thank you. Excuse us.' To his wife in a whisper, 'Let's go.'

'Careful,' she said tartly to her husband, smiling at the reporters.

'I don't have time for this,' Treacher said.

Tammy spoke in his ear. 'Don't forget, I'm the one who made you.'

'I'm afraid my parents had that honor.'

'They did the easy part,' she whispered. She allowed her husband's arm around her waist, and as she moved past the Metropolitan Police, she shouted back, 'Thank you, all!'

Tammy and Phillip Treacher joined the queue waiting to enter the International Ballroom. Treacher's white bow tie and paisley cummerbund set him apart from the dignitaries in black-tie tuxedos. He had let his hair grow to his neck, and he wore aviator glasses, in line with the current fashion. He acknowledged the British ambassador and his wife, a dry, withered flower with a sapphire diamond necklace, and she returned his smile with a condescending nod. The Speaker of the House was surrounded by men eager to bend his ear, and at his side, looking unamused, his plump wife.

Treacher and Tammy looked around to see who they knew or recognized.

'There's what's his name,' Tammy whispered in her husband's ear. 'Cute, isn't he?' Tammy stood tall, proud, glowing in the company of celebrity glamour. Her pale freckled skin set off her ruby brooch, which she touched with nervous fingers. Her head was turned at that moment, as she stared at a Marine officer in smart dress blue, conscious of her place in the social pecking order.

That's when the accident happened. Tammy didn't see two Secret Service agents opening a path through the thick crowd. Her head was turned, and when she swung back around, she bumped into one of the agents, and the collision sent her staggering sideways on her high heels. She grabbed her husband's tuxedo, and then tripped on the uneven stone floor and found herself falling into the rescuing arms of a tall, distinguished man. Her ankle had wrenched painfully, but she managed to keep a smile for the camera that recorded her moment of distress. Then she turned to face the man who'd caught her.

'Mr President,' she gasped.

The president stood beside the First Lady, and around the couple were three members of the security detail, who opened a small area. Guests who had seen what happened commiserated with Tammy's misfortune.

'Are you okay, Tammy?' the president asked, helping her stand.

She smiled through the pain. 'Yes, it's nothing. I'm fine. Really, it's nothing.' She smiled bravely at the president. *Idiot*, she thought. Her ankle was mangled. Dancing would be out of the question. There was tearing hot pain when she put weight on her foot. 'I'm fine. It's nothing.'

'I'm so sorry,' the First Lady said. 'We were being pushed along. Apparently, we're late.'

'I was distracted,' Tammy said. Her eyes sought the real culprit, the handsome major, but he was gone.

'They're with us,' the president said to the security detail, dragging Treacher and Tammy out of the queue. The president offered his deputy chief of staff a big, insincere smile. 'She'll be fine. You're doing a good job, Phil. Tough election coming up. We'll need all the oomph we can get.'

The president turned to Tammy. 'You look stupendous.' Then to the First Lady. 'Doesn't she look stupendous?'

*

Inside the International Ballroom, the Treachers stood alone beneath the magenta ceiling shaped like the underbelly of a sperm whale that hung over a vast sea of round tables with flower arrangements and numbered cards. Tammy suddenly turned to her husband. 'How did he know my name? I've never met him.'

'He perfected the skill of knowing names in Congress. He put it to good use every two years.'

'A common man,' she said, 'with an uncommon touch.'

Treacher smiled at the emphasis his wife put on the last

word, turning the ad hominem remark into a rude slander.

Everywhere elegance was on display. Women in strapless gowns stood beside husbands, or dates, who preened like displaying penguins. Everyone in the room was conscious of who was there and who was not, and guests glanced about, looking where others looked, thinking a celebrity had arrived.

The only completely stationary person in the room was the patient hostess behind the dais's microphone, miserably pleading for everyone to find their table. The huge banner behind her welcomed guests to the White House Correspondents' Dinner.

Tammy followed her husband as he pressed forward with an aggressive *excuse me*, and when he got no response, he cleaved an opening with his shoulder. She grabbed a flute of champagne from a passing waiter and hobbled after her husband, sipping as she limped.

They found their table, but as the last to arrive they found the two unoccupied seats were across from each other, not adjacent, so they sat beside strangers. The table was in the middle of the room, just beyond the row of tables reserved for broadcast network executives, television newsmen, and dowager big-money contributors. Tammy waved to get her husband's attention. 'Where are the Cheneys, the Rumsfelds, the Albrights? I don't know a soul.'

\*

Denied his wife's company, Treacher turned to the young woman on his left, whose wedding band linked her to a balding, older gentleman at her side. She had dazzlingly platinum hair and wore a low-cut strapless dress that provocatively revealed modest cleavage. 'I'm Blaire,' she whispered in his ear. She put a limp hand forward to shake his. 'Nice to meet you.'

She tipped her head back and laughed, and Treacher, not wanting to be rude, also laughed, a tolerant laugh. Treacher thought her face, with its bright eyes and passionate mouth, was lovely. It was only the slur in her speech that made her a sad, lonely thing. Her sober husband poked at his Bibb lettuce with his spoon. The couple reminded Treacher of the hell of marriage.

He looked up and saw Tammy staring at him from across the table with scolding eyes. Tammy nodded at the inebriated young woman and mouthed, *She's flirting with you.*

Again, the hostess pleaded for quiet. A chorus of shushing swept the room and struck crystal settled the crowd. 'Thank you. Thank you.' Then she looked to her right, where a stage door had suddenly opened.

'Ladies and gentlemen, the president of the United States.'

The president moved along the dais, greeting seated politicians and newsmen, stopping to shake a hand or pat a shoulder. A spotlight illuminated his bone-white hair. Open microphones on the dais caught his husky speaking voice, which added to his impression of friendliness, even toward those people he disliked. And there were a few known enemies of his new presidency that he ignored on his way to the lectern.

'I do appreciate Helen's kind and gentle introduction,' he said, removing his speech from his jacket pocket. 'As you know she has a reputation for speaking her mind. Seven years ago, when I was a congressman, Helen and I were walking down Pennsylvania Avenue when we passed one of those scales that gives you your weight for a penny and tells your fortune. Helen said, "Why don't you try it? I might get a scoop." So, I got on the scale and put in a penny and a card came out that said, "You are handsome, debonair, sophisticated, a born leader of men, a silver-tongued orator, and some day you will make your mark on history." Helen looked at me and said, "It's got your weight wrong, too.'"

Treacher felt a tap on his shoulder. He turned to find a waiter who leaned down and whispered loudly over the room's booming laugher. Treacher took the note the waiter offered. The waiter pointed to a far exit. 'There,' he said. 'That man asked me to give you this. He wants to see you in the bar.'

*

Two men stood at the far end of the empty hotel bar. That was Treacher's first surprise. Their backs were to him, but at the sound of the door opening, both men turned, and Treacher got his second surprise. Herb Weisenthal stood next to Michael Casey. The bar was quiet except for the president's voice piped through the public-address system. A waiter behind the bar looked up, his hands vigorously drying washed tumblers.

'Who chose this place?' Treacher said, when he joined the other two.

'It was the convenience of it,' Weisenthal said. 'It chose itself. I knew you'd be here so I arranged to come. I thought we should talk.'

Treacher gazed at his old adversary. He saw that Weisenthal's face had aged, his hair now grayer and longer, his face thinned, eyes softened, but he still claimed the authority of a former boss. What he remembered about the man came back, the odd tricks of memory pulling up the man's tics, his sayings. *People don't change. They only get worse.* Later, on the way home, Tammy would ask Teacher, *Did he look nervous? Did he look put out? He must have said something.* But as Treacher looked at Weisenthal standing in the bar, he didn't think he looked like anything. He didn't blink, there was no tremor in his hand, just the face of a man he hoped he'd never see again.

'Talk about what?' Treacher asked.

'Don't impugn my intelligence with your stupid act. You read the newspapers. Ainsley is dead. He always was a risk.' Weisenthal lifted the bottle of scotch the bartender had left. 'A troubled man, but a colleague.'

Treacher made no move to join the condolence.

'Not drinking?'

Treacher's eyes didn't respond to the offered glass. 'I gave it up.'

'You were a big drinker.'

'Things change. Sometimes for the better.'

Weisenthal laughed. 'When?'

Treacher looked directly at Weisenthal. 'Twenty-two years ago.'

Weisenthal threw back the liquor in his glass. 'I've made a few changes also. We live in Virginia on a farm.'

'I heard.' Treacher felt the old grudges stir up. The false pleasantries passing for real concern, the probing comments disguised as casual conversation. Treacher studied Weisenthal, looking for a sign of the man's conspiring intelligence weaving its web.

'Well,' Weisenthal said. He placed his glass on the bar and waved off the bartender, indicating they needed privacy. 'Ainsley's name was also on the invitation. His death is unfortunate, but he was an unsettled man. The Metro police detective who interviewed me called it a suicide, but he seemed to have some doubt.'

No one spoke, no one offered a kind word, no one discussed how he'd died. The collective silence of the group spoke for itself.

'We have nothing to worry about,' Weisenthal continued. 'I was careful. We scrubbed the documents, hid some, destroyed most. We put down a story that stands, and there is no record on Wilson.' He looked at each man. 'We did our job. There is no shame in that.'

'Bullshit,' Casey snapped.

Silence lingered for a long moment.

'You've been called to testify,' Treacher said. 'Not a pleasant thing to be summoned out of retirement and put on that stage.' He looked at Casey and then back at Weisenthal, eyes taking a measure of each man. 'If you are right and there are no incriminating documents, the danger is among us and what we say. That's obvious, but sometimes it's important to say the words.' Treacher looked directly at Weisenthal. 'You asked for this meeting?'

'I didn't volunteer to testify. I was subpoenaed. You need to know that I am not cooperating with them. Each of us has his thoughts about what happened, and maybe you have regrets, but there is no shame in our work.'

Treacher interrupted. 'You talk too much, Herb. We are beyond what happened. We are in the here and now, dealing in the present.' He turned to Casey. 'Anything yet?'

'His phone is wiretapped. He's called the Wilsons. He's being diligent, asking questions, probing until he excites a nerve. He spoke with Ainsley, and he tried to call you, Herb.'

'I didn't take his call.'

'Why not?' Casey asked.

Weisenthal's eyebrow arched. 'For the obvious reason,' he said caustically, then smiled. 'This sideshow will pass. It serves no one's purpose to dig up old bones.'

Treacher looked at Weisenthal. So sharp with his orders that Thanksgiving evening, now quiet in retirement. 'When you testify, keep your doubts to yourself and your answers short. Tell the truth – as little as you can get away with.'

The meeting ended. Treacher held back when he felt Casey's hand, and they let Weisenthal walk ahead.

Treacher turned to Casey. 'Do you trust him?'

Casey's eyes came off Weisenthal, who disappeared through the exit. 'Retirement has stirred up his ghosts.' He adjusted his cuff links and rose to his full height over the shorter Treacher, like a bronze statue, impressive and unimpressionable. 'Gabriel will try to get to Herb. Gabriel is the one I worry about. But I have an FBI contact with a grudge against the CIA. Gabriel will make a mistake, and when he does, they'll take him down.'

Treacher walked beside Casey and said nothing. His mind played out the reasons that Weisenthal might have asked for the meeting, going over and over the ways in which their acquaintance, which he thought was a thing long past, was now a present danger.

*

Treacher brooded about the word 'jeopardy' on his walk back to the ballroom. It had an urgent resonance. He didn't need to discover the precise meaning in a dictionary, but he had done so that morning out of curiosity. He got satisfaction in finding just the right word to describe a feeling: 'danger to an accused person on trial.' By that definition he was not in jeopardy, but events were unfolding and they were aligned against him.

*

Two hours later, Treacher sat beside his wife in the back of the Lincoln Town Car on their way home. She'd had several drinks, and her eyes were closed against swirling inebriation. He was clearheaded and stared out the window at the false peace the evening laid on the sleeping city. Government buildings along Pennsylvania Avenue were old and dilapidated, or new and soulless. All were dark. Far ahead lay the luminous cupola of the Capitol. The Statue of Freedom, in her aging glory, was shrouded in scaffolding, awaiting a facelift. Treacher gazed at the tableau and then looked out the rear window and watched the White House recede.

Washington had been his life, but he hadn't been born there, and he wouldn't die there. It was a city of transients: men and women drawn to public service and to power – its rewards, its privileges, and its corruptions. Here he was, he thought, on the far side of an old choice that kept him in its gravitational pull.

'You're awfully quiet,' Tammy said.

He turned to his wife. Her face was deep in shadow, but streetlamps punctuated the shadow with flashes of light, and in the moment of illumination he saw her concern. Treacher was aware of the driver, so he answered with a reassuring smile. He was aware of the first lie he'd told her that Thanksgiving long ago. That deception had metastasized in his soul. He felt more alone than ever.

# 10

## LINCOLN PARK

DAYS AND NIGHTS TESTED Gabriel's patience, and he agonized over the slow pace of his efforts. Questions followed questions, and he exhausted his few leads. It was about this time that he noticed a change in behavior among his colleagues. He found himself being ignored in subtle ways, which he dismissed as the light dusting of incivility toward a man who'd chosen to leave the Agency. Requests to have lunch were rebuffed with the usual excuse that pressing assignments required the colleague to work, but when he got the same response from different men over several days, he knew he was being cold-shouldered. And the slights got deeper. Without his having told anyone of his special assignment, everyone seemed to know. Coffin took Gabriel aside one morning and confided that case officers who disliked the director had transferred their animus to Gabriel. It was then that Gabriel put two chalk marks on the mailbox.

Lincoln Park attracted Washington's poor and homeless, and at night it drew a lively crowd of male prostitutes who flagged down cars with Virginia license plates. Gabriel felt deepening trepidation parked in his Volvo across from the sex trade waiting for the man he had come to know only as John. Claire had found a woman's stocking in the Volvo's back seat the morning after Gabriel's first meeting and confronted him.

He explained what he could, calling the man his source. Claire had called him his john. The name had stuck.

Gabriel glanced at his watch. John was thirty minutes late, and Gabriel saw he had attracted the attention of restless men standing in the shadows of the park's tree line.

A tall transvestite hustled across the street in her stiletto heels. 'Going out?'

She wore a blond wig and a leopard-skin shawl that barely covered her open blouse, and clutched a tiny rhinestone purse in her big masculine hand. She was missing a front tooth.

Gabriel closed his window.

'Honey, what are you doing in your car?' She rapped on the glass. 'Pay me twenty bucks and I'll do it for you.'

'Get lost.'

The transvestite put her face against the window and licked the glass. 'Don't be a dick. You're alone in your car. I know you're looking for a little fun.'

Gabriel stared straight ahead.

'Maybe I'm not your type, but I've got rent to pay. Be polite.' She continued to stare into the car. 'Look at me, honey!' Before turning away, she growled. 'Asshole.'

Gabriel watched her hop-step across the street and return to the far curb, presenting an exaggerated smile to single men driving past.

It was then that Gabriel heard his car door open. His eyes shifted to the rearview mirror, and he saw John settle into the back seat.

'Drive and let's talk. What's up?'

'Christ,' Gabriel snapped. 'You're half an hour late!'

'Something came up. I'm here. What's so urgent?'

Gabriel started driving. 'There's nothing. The files are missing. Weisenthal avoids me. So far the only person who seems to know anything is you.' In the rearview mirror, he watched John look for surveillance. 'I wasn't followed.'

'You wouldn't see them. They're good. Take a right, then another, and another.'

Gabriel turned at the next intersection and watched as the one car behind continued past the light, and then he completed the maneuver.

'Okay,' John said, looking forward. 'Clean. Head toward Constitution Avenue.'

'What am I missing?' Gabriel asked.

'Look at what doesn't make sense. Ask yourself why.'

'Nothing makes sense.'

'Jesus, you're a dumb fuck.'

Gabriel shot an angry glance into the rearview mirror.

'It's the stink theory of scandal. If it smells, there's something rotten. I smell something rotten with Wilson. Think about it. The *Times* story identifying Wilson as the unnamed LSD victim in the Rockefeller Report came out on a Tuesday, and the family was in the Oval Office ten days later getting a seventeen-minute apology from the president of the United fucking States. When does anything good in this town happen with wicked speed?'

John raised his hands incredulously. 'You've been looking in the wrong place. Forget about Ainsley. Look at 1600 Pennsylvania Avenue.'

The luminous White House lay ahead under a gloomy night sky. The voice in the back seat continued to lay out his case: scandals in the Agency crippled the president's efforts to claim a higher moral authority and get past Nixon's disgrace.

'Officially the White House is appalled by the Wilson case, but unofficially they want to shut it down and get on with the next election. Old shit is prologue to new shit. The president is demanding the director stonewall Congress.'

'What does this have to do with Wilson?'

'Everything has to do with Wilson. Pull that thread and the whole tapestry of deceit comes undone.'

They drove in silence toward the glowing citadel of power.

John suddenly tossed a document into the passenger seat beside Gabriel. 'You might want to look at this. I understand the White House apology. The poor man's death was covered up for twenty-two years. I get the money for the family's pain and suffering. But I don't get this.' He pointed at the document.

'You'll read it and make up your own mind. It's the release of claims that the family was required to sign to get the money. Wouldn't the White House have looked stupid if it paid a million dollars and then the family sued? Someone there wants this story to die. No one wants it to come out that he was murdered.'

'You don't know he was murdered. Maybe he was. Maybe he wasn't. Where's the evidence?'

'Dig him up. See what the body tells you.'

'The family has to authorize that.'

'Get their consent. They'll listen to you. It was a closed-casket service. Nothing happens by chance.'

Gabriel had pulled to a stoplight at the corner of Fifteenth Street. He was contemplating John's suggestion when he heard the back door open. John walked away from the Volvo with his back to the car, a tall man with an umbrella who had pulled off his nylon stocking mask and dropped it in a garbage can.

Gabriel looked past the Ellipse toward the well-lit South Lawn. The White House cast a long shadow over the circumstances of the case. The cover-up of Wilson's death, begun in 1953, continued.

Gabriel recalled the day Wilson had been buried. It had been Monday, November 30. He had flown twelve hours from Berlin and had gone straight from the airport to the cemetery. So quickly put in the ground, he'd thought. The casket had arrived from Washington by hearse that morning. He remembered his surprise when he'd been told that disfiguring injuries made it sensible not to have a viewing. Maggie had not been in her right mind – a distraught widow with two young children – and she'd agreed.

# 11

## A COUNTRY LANE
## FREDERICK, MARYLAND

GABRIEL'S WALK FROM HIS parked Volvo to the Wilson home on that humid summer evening was as much an act of penitence as it was a professional obligation. The setting of the one-story ranch house had changed little over the years. It sat at the end of a narrow country lane surrounded by a wide cornfield that belonged to a gabled farmhouse farther up the hill. A stand of majestic oaks still shaded the lawn, and the view was still dominated by Fort Detrick's water tower, which loomed over the sprawling Army complex in the valley below. The house was worn now. Its shutters needed paint, the hedges along the dirt lane were untrimmed, and Gabriel thought that it looked tired.

Every plot of land has its smells, tastes, and sights that evoke memories in the returning visitor, and for Gabriel, as he approached the ranch house, the breathing of the trees, the smells of freshly cut hay, and the sight of the distant water tower unlocked the memory of his first visit. It had been an unremarkable day except for his reason for making the hour-long drive from Washington. Wilson had saved his life a few weeks before, and Gabriel had finally found the one gift that would repay that debt. An ebullient Wilson had stepped from the front door with his wise smile, offering a quiet greeting in his learned speech, and made a generous invitation for Gabriel to come inside for cocktails. Gabriel's gift astonished Wilson, and he insisted on returning the favor, pulling a new book of poetry from his collection and handing it to Gabriel.

'You like Keats,' he'd said. 'You'll like this.' The book was *The Sand from the Urns*. Wilson said the author was a German-speaking Romanian who had lost both parents in Nazi concentration camps. 'You must read it,' he'd said. 'A new voice, just translated. A poem is like a hug. You can't be lonely in a poem.'

Gabriel remembered how surprised he'd been by the conversation and curious at Wilson's interest in poetry. He'd thought of Wilson only as a scientist who worked on weapons. He recalled how Wilson had held forth philosophically. 'Only one thing endures,' he'd said, sipping his martini. 'Language. Language endures across time and against all enemies except one: silence. You must never be silent.' Wilson had laughed, then raised his glass in a congenial toast, a nod to Gabriel's survival.

\*

Gabriel knocked once on the front door, and he knocked again when no one answered. 'Maggie?' He peered through the screen door into the darkened home, and finding the door unlocked, he entered. He moved through the vestibule into the living room. He looked to see if she was asleep, or fallen, curious why the door was open but no one home. He was immediately struck by how familiar everything in the room was – the hint of mildew, the large family photograph above the fireplace that showed the smiling Wilsons kneeling behind young children. A wedding album sat on the coffee table, and beside it there was a photograph of a proud Wilson and his smiling son, who sat on a bicycle with training wheels. Everything in the room was a shrine to a happier time.

'Hello?' Gabriel called out.

'What are you doing?'

Gabriel turned. He recognized the family lawyer, Seth Greenburg, who stood beside Antony Wilson.

'I knocked,' Gabriel said apologetically. 'I came to see your mother.'

'She's sleeping. Does she expect you?'

'Yes. We spoke on the phone.'

Antony nodded at the lawyer. 'Well, she's not feeling well.'

'Is she okay?'

'We'll see. Why are you here?'

'I'm investigating your father's death. The Agency has questions. The same questions you have.' Gabriel saw Antony's skeptical expression. 'Different men were in charge then. We want to understand what happened.'

'What happened!' Antony snapped. 'He died. Fell or jumped. That's pretty clear, clear as mud.'

Gabriel was impatient with Antony's testiness. 'We both believe someone needs to be held accountable.'

'Really?' Antony stared. 'He suffered the killing love of his friends.'

Gabriel pointed to CIA documents carefully arranged on the living room floor in a jigsaw puzzle, lengths of string connecting one document to another, like a spider's web. Gabriel challenged the two men. 'Have you found anything?'

Greenburg stepped forward, placing a restraining hand on Antony's shoulder, and turned to Gabriel. 'You're CIA.'

'I was also his friend.'

Antony scoffed.

Gabriel pointed to Antony's wristwatch. 'That's a Vacheron Constantin with tonneau crystal, dual time-zone dials, and a date aperture.' Gabriel pulled up his sleeve and revealed his own wristwatch. 'They are identical in every way but one. The back of yours is engraved, "In Gratitude." There is no name, no date, and no explanation. Only I know the circumstances of the appreciation because I'm the one who gave your father the watch.'

Antony's eyes moved skeptically from one watch to the other, making the comparison and confirming the similarity.

'Your father saved my life,' Gabriel said. 'In appreciation, I gave him the watch. He had always admired mine.'

Gabriel recounted the story. He had been called to a meeting in the basement of a restricted building in the Fort Detrick complex. He was walking in a tunnel that connected to the steel incubation tank in Building 470, and in the darkness he didn't see a high-voltage cable that had broken and lay in pooled water. Wilson had found Gabriel on his back in the electrified water, eyes open, face and hands twitching violently. Wilson pulled him from the water and started his heart with a blow to his chest, and then he administered CPR.

'We were different in many ways, but he risked his life to save mine. I owed him a debt, and we formed a bond. In the months that followed we got to know each other, and we shared opinions. Your father invited me to join him in Washington for lectures on civic duty and moral complexity. During the hours in his car we talked about a lot of things that were on our minds – Eisenhower, the Cold War, our Midwestern upbringing, the atom bomb.'

Gabriel paused. 'I remember one conversation very well. It startled me, because it was as close to talking about his work as we ever got. Oppenheimer had come out against the hydrogen bomb, and your father was quite interested in Oppenheimer's views about his work at Los Alamos. Scientists who developed the atom bomb had found ways to close their minds to what happened at the other end – when the bomb was dropped.

To impersonalize the bomb they called it "the gadget," "the device," "the beast," "the gimmick," or simply "it." Your father quoted Oppenheimer's Hiroshima remark, *the physicists have known sin*. It was only a five-minute conversation, and then we moved on to something else, but I could see that your father struggled with doubt, just as Oppenheimer had. Of course, we all knew what went on at Detrick. I asked what bothered him, and I reminded him what he'd told me: *You must never be silent.* He looked away and changed the topic.'

Gabriel looked at Antony. 'I left for an overseas post in July '53. He was dead in November. He never told me what troubled him.' He turned to the documents and said, 'Go ahead. Surprise me. Tell me what you've found.'

Antony nodded at Greenburg. 'Fill him in.'

Greenburg lifted an index card, making no effort to hide his frustration. 'There are fifty-four documents, a few from January 1954, another batch written earlier this year after the *Times* article came out, but most are from December 1953. There are many inconsistencies. One is dated January 5, 1953, and mentions the decedent underwent psychiatric treatment after the offsite weekend – which we have to assume the date is wrong, and it was actually January 5, 1954. That error is indicative of sloppiness in the documents. Many pages are heavily redacted, some are marked TOP SECRET or EYES ONLY, and they have reference to cryptonyms that mean nothing, even in context, and without a definition, the memos make no sense. Several were written by Roger Ainsley the morning Dr Wilson died, one by a man we assume is Dr Weisenthal, but his name is redacted, informing the General Counsel's office of the death.'

Greenburg nodded at Gabriel. 'We've spent several days with the documents, but we haven't come up with any satisfying answers. I asked Ostroff from the *Times* to review the files with a fresh eye. He also found the documents a jumble of deletions and conflicting statements. There is no overview, no personnel files, no fitness reports, no blood tests, no coherent account of the death, or any indication there was a credible investigation. Records from the Metropolitan Police and the coroner's office are sketchy and lack detail.'

Greenburg paused. 'In my view, the files show an Agency scrambling to understand what happened and then creating a postmortem record. One memo describes the inspector general's urgent efforts to discover the source of the LSD and to impound all of it in a combination safe in his office. Several documents offer the standard explanation of the death, repeating without question the unlikely physical feat of a man awakening from sleep and going through a closed window. There is a medical note from a psychiatrist that describes depression and paranoia, but the doctor's name is redacted, and there is no mention of his hospital affiliation.'

Greenburg abruptly dropped the index card to the floor. 'That's it. Something, but not enough. We tracked down Ainsley, but we arrived a day late.'

Antony turned away from the plate glass window with its view of the distant Fort Detrick water tower. 'Fell to his death,' he added sarcastically. 'Isn't that a coincidence.' He was quiet for a moment. 'Nothing in this case makes sense. You think, *There is a lead*, and then it shuts down. You get the feeling this is a story that someone doesn't want told.'

He looked at Gabriel. 'The documents are vague in what they don't say. There is nothing about his work or the work done at Detrick. They say nothing about the purpose of the meeting at Deep Creek Lake, or the conduct of the discussions, or who was there. Thank God for the invitation my mother found.' He paused. 'All we know is that your CIA went to great lengths to keep its involvement hidden.'

Antony lifted a document from the floor. 'Ainsley gave a

false ID to mislead the police. He wrote this memo to file that my mother was worried about my father and suggested that he get psychiatric help.'

'I never said any such thing.'

Maggie Wilson stood in the living room doorway beside her daughter, Betsy. They had entered without anyone noticing. Maggie's wig was gone, her baldness startling. She wore slippers and an old bathrobe loosely cinched at her waist. Anger stiffened her posture, and she refused her daughter's offer to help her walk to the sofa. Her voice was clear but soft, her eyes indignant.

'I never said that. That is a complete falsehood. I only met him once. I thought he was the driver. I had no reason to say anything personal to him. Why would I say that? I didn't think it. I didn't believe it.'

She looked at Gabriel with a tired, impatient expression. 'All the noise woke me. So, you came. Are you going to help?' She glanced at the documents on the floor. 'Did you find anything?'

Greenburg approached Maggie, who had taken a seat on the sofa. 'We have questions.'

'What about answers?'

'More questions than answers.'

Maggie looked at her son. 'You're quiet.'

Antony turned away from his mother and went to back to the picture window. Evening had come, and with it the red aircraft beacon on the water tower was a compass point in the growing darkness, pointing to the past. Gabriel felt the weight of family conflict in the long silence that followed.

'What's on your mind?' Maggie asked her son.

He turned. 'I want to sue.'

'We can't sue,' Greenburg said. 'You signed a full release.'

'I didn't sign anything.' Antony looked fiercely at his mother. 'You made that choice.'

Gabriel stepped forward. 'There is an alternative. You never saw the body.'

A gasped release of breath came from Maggie. She looked at Gabriel, appalled. Her face had drained of color, and her voice quavered. 'I can't bear the idea of disturbing him. I can't imagine what we'd find that is worse than what we know.'

Antony stared into the night – sullen and silent.

Gabriel would later learn that Antony and his mother had had this conversation before, and it had never gone well. She was not prepared to exhume her husband.

Antony turned to his mother. 'Fell or jumped. Wouldn't you like to know which?'

Maggie received her son's sarcasm defiantly. There was a long awkward silence. Maggie was comforted by her daughter, who spoke for the first time. 'It's time to move on,' Betsy said. 'We know enough.'

Antony threw his hands in the air, exasperated. He shouted, 'We don't know anything!'

Maggie stared at her firstborn, her eyes swelling with tears, then looked at Gabriel. 'What about you?'

Gabriel pointed at the collage of documents on the floor. 'These won't tell you anything. You've figured that out for yourselves. I think it's the right thing. I know a forensic pathologist who can do the examination.'

Maggie looked around the room. She was alone. 'Fine,' she said.

*

Gabriel drove back to Washington late. Rain had begun to fall, and the steady rhythm of the wipers sweeping the windshield numbed his unsettled thoughts.

*Jumped or fell.* The cadence of the phrase echoed in his

mind. The alternative explanations of Wilson's death were hard to reconcile. Each implied a vastly different man in the final moments of life. One a freak accident. The other the choice of a disturbed mind. Neither fit the man he knew. He stopped at a gas station on his way home and used the pay phone to make a call.

'We have a body to bring up,' he said when the voice came on the line.

# 12

## TESTIMONY
## RUSSELL SENATE OFFICE BUILDING

GABRIEL LOOKED TOWARD THE front of the packed Senate hearing room at Herb Weisenthal, who sat alone in an aisle seat near the front, a small, hunched man waiting for the hearing to begin.

It was ninety-eight degrees at 2:30 p.m. on that July afternoon, a record for the day. Inside the hearing room it was even warmer for the senators who sat on either side of the subcommittee chairman and fanned themselves or turned to the large standing fan that had been brought in to compensate for the failed air conditioning. Tall windows had been opened for air, but the tepid breeze did nothing to relieve the stifling heat. Someone had turned off the large pendant chandelier and the brass wall sconces to eliminate heat gain, giving the darkened room the illusion of cooling shade. Curious spectators had removed jackets and opened collars, and the national press seated at the base of the dais sweated profusely.

The chairman wore a charcoal gray suit that barely contained the weight he'd gained in his years of Senate service, but his bulk and jowls added to the commanding presence of a man known for his imperturbability. His dense eyebrows arched as he listened to an aide, and then he looked out to the crowded room, tapping his microphone.

Gabriel was seated away from the aisle near the rear, looking to see who he knew and who he should avoid. That's when he heard his name called. Three late arrivals made their way toward him, begging their way past seated men and women.

'I gave up on you,' he said, removing a newspaper spread across three chairs.

Antony took the chair next to Gabriel, and the next chair was taken by Seth Greenburg. Antony pointed to the third man who sat in the last seat.

'You know Neil Ostroff.'

'We've met,' Gabriel said. He stared at the man who'd published his photo on the front page of the *Times*. 'I thought your mother was coming.'

'She's in the hospital.'

Gabriel was surprised by Antony's callous tone.

'Serious?'

'We'll see.'

'Ladies and gentlemen,' the chairman said into his microphone. He brought down his gavel when he failed to get the room's attention, and he struck twice more, firmer and louder. His voice boomed, 'Ladies and gentlemen, I have just been informed that the air conditioning will remain out, but we will proceed. This is the Senate Subcommittee on Health and Scientific Research. We will hear the testimony of Dr Herbert Weisenthal. If that's not why you're here, you might want to leave for a cooler spot.' He saw two people make their way to the exit. 'Always a few,' he said, eliciting laughter. 'Dr Weisenthal, please come forward.'

Gabriel watched Weisenthal rise from his chair. He was a slight man and visibly uncomfortable at being so publicly on display, a difficult thing for any reluctant witness but especially hard for an old spy. The prospect of testifying before a television audience clearly weighed on him. His face was drawn, and his black business suit starkly set off his pale complexion. He was joined at the witness table by an attorney. There were the formalities of swearing in, the offering of written testimony, and the attorney's brief statement on behalf of his client.

Photographers were crouched at the base of the dais. Weisenthal didn't shy away from the cameras or hide his face, but nor did he smile.

The room was packed with congressional staffers; several men like Gabriel from the intelligence community, including George Mueller, who stood taller than many others taking seats; and conspiracy buffs, curious to get their first view of the spy whose Technical Services Staff had made the poisoned cigar intended to kill Fidel Castro.

'Mr Chairman,' Weisenthal said. 'I have placed a statement in the record. I want this committee to know that I am not here as the beggar Lazarus to plead understanding. I come unwillingly under subpoena, proud of my work record. But I will endeavor to answer any questions that will help clarify the circumstances surrounding the death of Dr Wilson.'

'Thank you. Yes, we have your statement. We appreciate your cooperation.' The chairman consulted his notes. 'Dr Weisenthal, when did you join the CIA?'

'1947.'

'It was the CIA then?'

'It was the Central Intelligence Group. The CIA was formed in 1948.'

'What were you hired to do?'

'I had received a PhD in agronomy from the University of Wisconsin. I joined the Chemical Branch and became its chief. We were concerned with biochemical weapons programs, and we evaluated psychotropic hallucinogens that could be used by our adversaries against us. Programs I ran, which have been identified by the press – and I might add, mischaracterized by

115

them – were Bluebird, Artichoke, and MKULTRA. I worked with the Army staff at Fort Detrick, where I became acquainted with Dr Wilson. I continued to work in the CIA in various capacities until I retired.'

'What year was that?'

'1973.'

'And then what did you do?'

'My wife and I sold our house, and we traveled for two years. We took up residence in India, where we volunteered our time in a leper hospital. We returned earlier this year, and we live on a small farm in Virginia. I provide speech therapy to children in the local public school.'

Gabriel felt Antony become restless. 'What's his point?' he whispered. '"I'm a good man now"?' Gabriel put his hand on Antony's knee to calm him, and in looking at Antony he saw that Neil Ostroff was looking around the room to see who he knew. Their eyes met. Only the senator's voice took Gabriel's attention back to the proceedings.

'Let's go back to 1953. You put LSD in Dr Wilson's after-dinner drink at Deep Creek Lake, did you not?'

'I did.'

'Ten days later, he committed suicide while under your care.'

'That's correct.' Weisenthal paused for a moment. 'I think you can understand that it was a difficult period for me. It was a great tragedy, and in the weeks that followed we consulted medical experts to help us decide whether to continue the program. It caused me a lot of personal anguish. I considered resigning from the Agency.'

'Dr Weisenthal,' the Republican senator from Missouri interrupted, 'I'm sure it was quite difficult for you, but why in God's name would you give an untested drug to a top scientist?'

'We were concerned, Senator, what would happen if one of our men was kidnapped and drugged while traveling overseas.

If so, what would he say? Could he be made to speak? The late 1940s and early 1950s were terrible war years. The Soviet Union and the Red Chinese had developed chemical agents to control human behavior. We knew the Soviets had tried to corner the market in LSD, which was then produced in one Sandoz plant in Switzerland.'

The chairman brought down his gavel forcefully to quiet the room. 'Sir,' he said. 'What was Dr Wilson working on? What could he betray if, as you feared, he was abducted by the Soviets?'

'I can't get into the specifics of that.'

Weisenthal's attorney pulled the microphone from his client. 'Senator, if I may, my client retired, but he continues to be bound by the Espionage Act, the National Security Act, the Defense Secrets Act, and various laws.'

The chairman raised a skeptical eyebrow. 'Did you ever lie in the course of your work?'

'Sir?' Weisenthal replied.

'Lie. Deceive people about what you did or what you knew?'

'We all lie, sir. It's a trivial thing, to claim at a party you've been to Beirut when you haven't. It does no harm, and it was part of my job.'

'Can we expect truthful answers from you today?'

'Where I can answer I will do so, but as my attorney attested, I am bound by law.'

'Good to know you abide by the law.' The chairman consulted his papers. 'I have here a newly uncovered letter of February 12, 1954, from the Director of Central Intelligence criticizing your judgment administering LSD to an unwitting Dr Wilson without proximate medical safeguards. The letter says you violated his civil rights. By this letter we know that the highest levels of the CIA knew of Dr Wilson's drugging after it happened, and you got reprimanded.'

'Sir, is that a question?'

'Were you reprimanded?'

'Yes.'

'Let's turn to the question of records. You destroyed your files before you retired. Can you tell us what you destroyed and why you felt it necessary to destroy them?'

Weisenthal adjusted his reading glasses and cleared his throat.

Antony leaned forward. 'I want to hear this.'

'It's a long answer, if I may. In late 1972 and 1973, I began to destroy files that I felt would not be useful to my successor or were superfluous. There were two reasons for this. The Agency had a burgeoning paper problem, and I destroyed those files that were no longer of any use. Second, there were sensitive files with names of prominent scientists and physicians whose work we'd confidentially funded. The careers of those individuals, and their reputations, would be severely damaged if their association with the CIA became known. I destroyed those as well.'

'Did you keep the destruction certificates?'

'No. It would defeat the purpose, wouldn't it, to destroy documents but keep destruction certificates with a record of what was destroyed?'

*Unbelievable*, Gabriel thought. So calm and so completely, implacably assured.

'You did this on your own accord?' the senator asked.

'Others were involved.'

'Who?'

'My associate Dr Ainsley was one. The deputy director was one.'

'Did he order the destruction?'

'Certainly not. I brought up the topic. I outlined the reasons that I just shared with you, and he concurred.'

'How did you do it? Burn, shred, bury?'

'The job was left to Dr Ainsley.'

'Where is he?'

'He's deceased.'

Gabriel heard Weisenthal's clever parsing, and he recognized how masterfully he'd shaded his actions. His seeming openness was a trick and his contrition an intentional subterfuge. *Untouchable*, Gabriel thought. There were no incriminating files, and none would be found. There would be no files to impeach his testimony. The only records of the past were locked in his mind. Gabriel saw a small man stuck in his beliefs, incorruptible. *Untouchable.*

'Just a few more questions, Dr Weisenthal.' The chairman's voice became folksy. 'You testified you were the one who put LSD in Dr Wilson's after-dinner drink.'

Weisenthal looked over his reading glasses. 'Yes, I said that.'

'I may be repeating myself. That's a condition of my age and a prerogative of my office.' The chairman raised a piece of paper and waved it. He looked directly at the witness, and his voice deepened. 'You knew everyone at Deep Creek Lake and everyone at the Hotel Harrington.'

Weisenthal seemed confused, and he hesitated.

'Dr Weisenthal, I am asking you if you knew everyone who was involved. You ran the project. You were reprimanded for it. Did you know everyone who was involved?'

Weisenthal turned to his attorney.

The chairman read from the paper in his hands. 'Can you tell me who Nick Arndt is? The name Nick Arndt. Does it jog your memory?'

'No. It doesn't.'

'You do not recognize the name Nick Arndt?'

'That's correct, sir.' Weisenthal was quieter and less certain.

The chairman lowered his reading glasses and looked toward

the witness. 'Mr Nick Arndt was in the Hotel Harrington that night. You testified you knew everyone involved, but now you testify you don't know who Mr Arndt is. You can't have it both ways. Either you knew everyone or you didn't. Would you square that circle for me?'

'I haven't seen the document you are holding. I don't know who the man is or if he was, as you say, a part of the project. Let me remind you, this was a very long time ago. May I see the memo?'

'It's not a memo.'

Antony looked at Gabriel and nodded at Greenburg. 'He found it.'

The chairman raised the paper. 'I have here a copy of the Hotel Harrington's guest registry of November 26, 1953. Mr Arndt was registered in room 918, adjacent to the room occupied by Dr Wilson. The two rooms were connected by one of those see-through mirrors. And we have this record. Did you forget to destroy it? Or perhaps someone in the hotel saw something and kept a record.'

Gabriel took a deep breath. Secrets are restless things. Secrets come out. The invitation in the Bible. A name in a hotel registry.

'You have no memory of this Mr Arndt?' The chairman's voice filled with rounded vowels, enjoying his capacity for mockery. 'No idea who he was or why he was in the safe house. No idea at all. Is that what you're saying?'

'Yes.'

'Is that a yes? We couldn't hear you.'

Weisenthal spoke louder. 'Yes, that's a yes.' He took a plain handkerchief from his pocket and wiped his brow.

'You may be excused, Dr Weisenthal. We have no further questions today. You remain under subpoena, and you should not leave Washington. Let me remind you, sir, we need to come to terms with our past. We are not a nation that rewrites its history. Ghosts of our past want to rest.'

Weisenthal leaned into his microphone. 'Mr Chairman, if I may. I would like this committee to know that I considered all my work, at the time it was done in the circumstances of the Cold War, to be extremely difficult, extremely sensitive, but, above all, to be extremely urgent and important. The Berlin airlift showed us the danger posed by the Soviet Union. We urgently sought ways to know if our people, in the event of capture by the enemy, could resist interrogation. What was happening in the early 1950s was a dangerous replay of what happened in the late 1930s. The Soviet Union was ruthlessly intent on expanding its totalitarian power and taking over the world as the Nazis had a decade earlier. I realize that it is difficult to reconstruct those times and that atmosphere in this hearing room today.'

Weisenthal placed his reading glasses in his jacket pocket and gathered his papers. He rose from the witness table, reclaiming his dignity. Sympathetic applause from a few in the room was met by loud honking scorn from a larger number of people, and in that moment the supporters of the CIA and their numerous indignant opponents were a snapshot of American public opinion.

Antony Wilson had jumped from his chair and planted himself in the aisle, blocking Weisenthal's path to the exit. Antony was a head taller than Weisenthal, but the intensity of their expressions was the same and attracted a few people who stopped to look.

'I'm his son.'

Weisenthal allowed a smile. 'I see a resemblance to your father.' He nodded at Antony's hands. 'I'm so glad you haven't brought a gun. Last night I had a dream that you came to the hearing and shot me.'

Antony was momentarily speechless.

'This is my wife,' Weisenthal said, pulling forward a tall, kindly woman. 'Mary Thomas. Dear, meet Charlie's son.'

The woman's hands were gnarled from gardening, her hair bleached porcelain white. She wore simple sandals and a saffron-colored sari she had cinched with a knotted string belt. A likeness of Buddha hung on her neck.

'We were big fans of your father,' Weisenthal said. 'He was a committed scientist, a pleasant man, but those were difficult times. We all made mistakes.'

Antony resisted the seduction of the man's affectionate tone. 'You expect me to believe you gave my father a powerful, untested drug to see what would happen? He was a scientist, for Christ's sake. The whole idea that you would put a top scientist at risk to test a hypothetical makes no sense.'

'That is what happened,' Weisenthal replied.

Antony snapped. 'The whole story makes no sense.'

'Look,' Weisenthal said calmly. 'Your father and I were alike. We cared about our country. We were concerned about our survival. We found ourselves in a war effort applying science to new weapons. Our work was urgent and sometimes unpleasant. The Korean War showed us how much was at stake, and we may have gone too far.'

Weisenthal's wife pulled him forward, uncomfortable with the crowd that had gathered, but her husband resisted. He looked at Antony.

'I can see your father's death is still deeply troubling. Clouds hang over you.'

Antony looked at Weisenthal. His voice was thick with sarcasm. 'How could that be? A quarter century gone and my father not yet forgotten?' Antony wiped concern from his face. 'See how easily I move from shade to sun.'

*

Gabriel accompanied Antony and Greenburg out of the Russell Senate Office Building. They stood at the top of the wide marble steps under a brilliant blue sky. Antony slipped on his dark glasses, adjusting their fit against the glare, and then gave his judgment.

'He played the room. How much of what he said was true? How much was intended to present him in a good light? And his conversion, playing Saul on his way to Damascus. Now he raises goats and plants organic vegetables. *Givemeafuckingbreak.*'

Antony looked at Gabriel. 'He is trying to distance himself from what happened. How often did he use the phrase *those times*, as if there was that world, and now there is this world, and the circumstances then justified what today looks like carelessness, or a crime? Well, that's bullshit. The man flew to the fucking Congo with poison toothpaste to assassinate Patrice Lumumba.'

Silence lingered among the three men after Antony's outburst.

'He put me at a disadvantage from the moment I confronted him,' he continued. 'The idea that I would bring a gun. I didn't know what to say.'

Antony's eyes had drifted to the nearly empty street, where fierce heat melted the asphalt, but then he turned and faced Gabriel. 'Everyone says it's a black hole; we may never know what happened. That's bullshit. Total bullshit.

'They say it could be this, or it could be that, and everything in your CIA is a hall of mirrors. When people say that, what they're really saying is that we'll never know what happened.'

Antony pointed across the park at Pennsylvania Avenue and the Hotel Harrington, twelve blocks away. 'Something did happen in that hotel room. And it *is* knowable.'

\*

Gabriel's Volvo was parked two blocks away, near the Folger Shakespeare Library. He started the car, which had been baking in the sun, and let the air conditioning cool it down. Washington's heat wave had emptied the sidewalks.

What was next? He'd taken the assignment thinking he'd get an answer quickly, but nothing was easy in this case, nothing played out as he expected.

And then the unexpected happened.

Gabriel heard tapping on the window and turned to find Herb Weisenthal standing on the passenger side, alone. His face was close to the window, lips moving but soundless. Gabriel opened the window.

'Can I join you?' Weisenthal asked. 'It's hot out here.'

Gabriel nodded. 'Door's open.'

Weisenthal slipped into the passenger seat, glancing around to see if anyone was watching.

'We haven't met,' he said, 'but I know who you are. You were in Berlin after the war; then you left Operations and rejoined after the Bay of Pigs. Someone was smart to get you back. Those were dark times. Surprising that we never worked together.'

Gabriel said nothing. *Let the man talk.*

'This isn't a particularly convenient way to have a conversation,' Weisenthal noted.

'No, it's not,' Gabriel said. 'I'm late. It's hot. We're parked in the sun.'

Weisenthal looked at Gabriel. 'Wilson was a colleague to both of us. A decent man. The family suffered.'

Gabriel wondered what Weisenthal was doing in his Volvo. 'Yes, he was a good man.'

'Somehow my name came out in all this. First, it was the invitation. Then other documents appeared under FOIA requests. Every name but mine was redacted.'

'How does that make you feel?'

Weisenthal shook his head. 'Of course I am being set up. Sacrificed. I gave the Agency twenty-six years of loyal service.'

Weisenthal's lips tightened, and his eyes narrowed, and his voice now had an indignant vibrato. 'Trust,' he said. 'There's a word that I could devote an hour to. In our work, trust was expected of us, and we expected it in return. I could give you a whole lecture on trust and its possibilities for disappointment.'

He looked away for a moment, but his eyes returned to Gabriel. 'We put our trust in Japanese war criminals after VJ Day for their knowledge of biochemical weapons they'd used in China. We trusted Nazi doctors who'd recorded the time it took for prisoners to succumb when immersed in vats of freezing water. Trust, you see, in those cases, was our ability to set aside scruples to work with war criminals in order to better prepare ourselves for war.

'There is another kind of trust. Can you trust a man who has the power to harm you? We trusted our colleagues in MI6, but only up to a point. We trusted our Soviet double agents because their lives were at risk. That trust had nothing to do with whether they were good or bad men. It had to do with fear. Fear engenders trust. We trusted our colleagues in the Agency, but not enough to do away with the polygraph. Trust. A simple notion and yet a complex idea with shading and nuance.'

Weisenthal looked at Gabriel. 'I know you have doubts about the Wilson case. The circumstances are bizarre and strain our ability to accept them. Do you trust the official story? Do you trust me when I tell you that I have nothing to add?' Weisenthal continued to meet Gabriel's eyes. 'I have done my part. Now it is up to you to believe it, or not.'

Weisenthal's eyes drifted to the Statue of Freedom atop the Capitol, wrapped in her scaffolding. A helicopter hovered overhead with a huge sling that would carry the symbol of democracy away for much-needed restoration.

'We trust in God,' he said. 'But trust among men takes work. It can be exhausting to calculate the degrees of trust. I'm tired.'

Gabriel heard a deep release of fatigued breath. He saw a small man, quiet by the window, burdened. Gabriel said nothing.

'Faith can help us trust,' Weisenthal said. His tenor voice had turned surprisingly pleasant. 'This brain of ours, how ingenious it is, able to deceive, hope, regret, and trust all inside its thick skull.' He tapped his head, then smiled kindly. He opened the Volvo's door, stepping into the afternoon heat. Before closing it, he lowered his head and added, 'I don't know you very well. This is our first talk. I understand you like to row.'

Gabriel hesitated.

'That's what I've been told. Is it true?'

'I do.'

'I'll call you. Let's meet one morning and talk again. The Potomac Boat Club.' He smiled. 'Yes, I am a member. The first Jew.'

# 13

## THE OVAL OFFICE

IT WAS WARM AT 7:30 p.m. across Washington, and in the Oval Office it was even warmer for Phillip Treacher and two other senior staff sitting on either side of the president, suffering the ire of a man known for his calm demeanor. At that hour once a week, the president convened his last meeting of the day to review the week's schedule, discuss pending matters, and bring up concerns that didn't otherwise fit into his crowded calendar. A deep russet sun glowed through the curved wall of windows behind the Resolute desk.

The president wore a white shirt, gray suit, bold red tie, and a small American flag lapel pin. He had the temperament of a Midwestern gentleman who found himself suddenly thrust into the White House, having been pushed forward with the hope that his reputation for common decency would keep the White House free of scandal. They had just finished discussing the Mount Kenya Safari Club and had turned to next year's election. His brow knitted when he came to the end of a memo that described his falling approval ratings. He violently crumpled the paper and tossed it at a wastebasket by the desk, missing.

'I've got the pulse of a corpse,' he snapped. 'I've dropped thirty-two points in six months.' He looked at his three staffers. 'Get me something to campaign on.'

The meeting ended.

Phillip Treacher heard his name called as he was walking out.

'Got a minute, Phil?' The president opened a cabinet in the credenza under the Remington sculpture. 'Drink?' He held out a bottle of gin. 'I forgot, you're still on the wagon. Mind if I do?'

Treacher was numb to the temptation. Twenty-two years. But it never got easier. 'Go ahead, Mr President.'

'You okay? Job okay? And your wife?'

Treacher acknowledged the three questions with a single nod. 'Fine, thank you. All good.'

'The First Lady still thinks I was to blame for tripping Tammy at the Correspondents' Dinner. I didn't want to be late, and we were pushing through the crowd. Tell her that we're still looking for a way to make it up to her.'

The president took a generous taste of his gin. 'You don't look well. The job gets to you if you let it. You need to find a way to push forward.' He toasted alone. 'To keeping calm.'

Treacher raised an empty glass in solidarity. 'Amen.'

'I leave the meshugaas here in the office and walk to the family quarters with a clear head. Doesn't work all the time, but it's a strategy. You need a strategy so you're not overwhelmed.'

The president pointed, indicating they should exit the French doors that led to the South Lawn. As they approached, the vigilant Marine guard on duty outside opened the doors, and the two men passed through to the warm night.

'Presidents never open a door,' he said to Treacher. 'It took me months to get used to that.'

A tepid evening breeze was a pleasant change from the stifling atmosphere in the Oval Office. Dusk was rapidly falling, and with the evening came the alien sound of cicadas and a degree of relief from the seasonal lethargy that descended on the capital during summer months. It was Thursday, but the city's population was preparing to flee the heat for the coolness of Chesapeake Bay.

The two men ambled along the portico. Treacher stopped when the president paused to look over the expanse of freshly mowed lawn, and farther away, the low government buildings that fretted the tree line – unbroken except for the Washington Monument's dark spire. Treacher felt the president's preoccupation, which had settled in with his gin, and he knew there was something on the man's mind. The impatient honking of cars detoured around the construction that was tearing up downtown Washington drifted toward them.

'Goddamn subway,' the president said. 'Today I got word the digging severed the hotline to Moscow. For six hours we didn't know if it was incompetence, sabotage, or war.' The president shook his head at the dark comedy of an accidental nuclear holocaust.

'Nobody knows what it is like to sit in that office,' he said. 'The burdens, the crises, the worry, the nonsense. Everyone who gets past Dorothy wants something – a favor, a demand, a decision. It's a big job with big headaches. You feel the pressure, too. I can see it in your face. You should get out. Not out of the job,' he quipped, laughing. 'Out for fun. Take Tammy to the theater. There's a production of *Richard II* at the Folger.' He winked. 'A timely choice. I prefer *South Pacific*, but I allow the First Lady to drag me to Shakespeare once a year. Our treat.'

'Kind of you, Mr President. I'll ask Tammy.'

'It won't make up for the ankle, but it will make us feel better.'

Upon passing a second Marine guard, the president threw back the dregs of his drink and handed him the empty glass. 'Too much comes across my desk,' he said. He tapped his skull twice in an exaggerated show of emptiness. 'There is only so much room up here. I can't fill it with nonsense and crap. I wish we lived in Jefferson's contained world, but we don't. He was the last president, maybe the last man, to believe – not arrogantly, but in an enlightened way – that he could know everything important about the world. He filled his library at Monticello with every important book ever written. You could hope to know everything then. That world is gone and perhaps it never existed, but the explosion of information has wiped out even the contemplation of that idea. That one man could know everything, or should. Some information is needed, much of it is useless, all of it takes up space. I don't need to know everything.'

The president turned to Treacher and lowered his voice. 'Understand?'

The men continued to walk onto the lawn away from the White House. Freshly cut grass was fragrant in the warm air, and moths circled the portico's pendant lamps.

'Nixon made a lot of mistakes, but the one I find hardest to understand, particularly for a paranoid man, was the whole tape fiasco. How could he not know that his every word, every curse, every insult, was being recorded? All those private remarks that were never meant to leave the Oval Office brought him down.' The president continued out of earshot of the Marine guards. He stopped suddenly and faced his deputy chief of staff.

'Let's talk here, Phil.'

Treacher met the president's eyes.

'The Wilson family.'

Treacher nodded. 'You did the right thing, Mr President.'

'I hope so. It's what you recommended, what you pushed for.' The president studied Treacher. 'I understand there was another hearing. The family was there?'

'The son.'

'The one who didn't shake my hand?'

'Yes.'

130

'I didn't like him. He didn't smile. Too angry. Anything I should know?'

'No, Mr President. The Director of Central Intelligence is on board.'

'Not a bad man. Probably as good as you get for that job, but he needs to understand his loyalty is to this office. I can't have him genuflecting to those senators.' He looked at Treacher with a grim expression. 'I can't find myself defending, or even talking about, our use of biochemical weapons a quarter century ago. Understand?'

'Yes, Mr President.'

The president's eyes had drifted to the brightly lit White House, but they settled again on Treacher. 'A man takes his life. As regrettable as that is, and it is a sad thing, particularly for the family, the act of one unbalanced man long ago can't be the undoing of this presidency. We are going to Beijing in November to meet the new guy, Deng.' He looked at Treacher.

'Deng Xiaoping.'

'Yes, and Mao. It would be supremely awkward if I had to cancel the trip because it came out that we dropped anthrax on North Korean villages in that goddamned war. I don't know if we did or didn't. I don't want to know. But if it was the case and Wilson was involved, then it's very unhelpful now – for diplomacy, for hearings in Congress, for voters. For this presidency.'

'Yes, Mr President.'

'You're handling this?'

'Yes, I am.'

'We are not having this conversation, understand?'

Treacher knew the president's apparent simplicity masked an uncommon sophistication, which made it easy for adversaries to dismiss the man, but only at their peril. 'Yes, sir.'

The president looked toward the festively illuminated marble fountain on the South Lawn. 'Nixon was a son of a bitch. My pardon has cost me votes. Another public relations catastrophe would put a kibosh on the election.' He turned to Treacher. 'Understand?'

# 14

## WEST WING

THE CALL TO VISIT the West Wing came late on Tuesday as Gabriel was leaving his Langley Headquarters office. He thought he misheard his secretary, but she repeated Phillip Treacher's request to meet. He offered two appointment times the next day, but in the demure manner of an efficient career secretary who wouldn't permit her boss to slip away, she replied, 'Tonight. He wants to see you now.'

Gabriel stopped at his office door, raincoat in hand. His first thought was that he had promised Claire he would be home for dinner.

'You can be there in thirty minutes,' his secretary said. 'There isn't much traffic at this hour. Shall I confirm?'

He closed his eyes against his bad choices. 'What's the subject?'

'She didn't say.'

'Get me the Mount Kenya files. I need to take a look before I go. And call my wife.'

'What should I tell her?'

'I was called to the White House. She'll be upset. I would rather you made the call.'

'You're a coward, Mr Gabriel,' she said, smiling.

Gabriel was the designated CIA contact who initiated wire

transfers requested by the White House. Money came from Saudi banks into a special numbered account Gabriel had set up at Riggs Bank, and when instructed, he wired the funds to numbered accounts in Zurich or Paris. Gabriel wasn't told who got the money or what it supported, but he knew the White House had found a way to go around the CIA, and he suspected it funded the White House's pet projects in Africa. These covert operations were off the CIA's books and invisible to Congress. Gabriel was the ignorant errand boy.

\*

Gabriel moved through the narrow West Wing hallways following the security guard's directions, but he had missed a turn or misheard the guard, and he found himself wandering past the small closet offices coveted by every political hack in Washington. Men dressed in navy blue suits, wide ties, and starched white shirts, but a few defied the conforming fashion with muttonchop sideburns and aviator glasses. There was an urgent air about these men as they darted past Gabriel or emptied from a conference room, comporting themselves as if what they were doing mattered more than anything else in Washington. Ad hoc meetings in the hallway were held in clipped voices, and Gabriel sensed that the place was in permanent crisis.

Gabriel paused at a glass-enclosed work area where young staffers sat hunched at their desks. The dual and dueling demands of life and work were on display. It was long past the end of the normal workday, and these ambitious young men and women were sacrificing their Friday evening for the insular energy of the West Wing. Three televisions were turned to CBS, ABC, and NBC, and occasionally one of the staffers looked up and stared at the live sports coverage.

'Where can I find Phillip Treacher?' Gabriel asked. A woman pointed to a desk at the end of the corridor, and he thanked her.

Gabriel loomed over Treacher's conscientious secretary and gave his name, startling her.

'Mr Gabriel! Go right in,' she said. 'He'll be right back.'

Gabriel entered the office, taking in everything at once. Gabriel's previous meetings with Phillip Treacher had been in conference rooms, and this was his first visit to his office. The full calculus of power was prominently on display: three ground-floor windows with a view of the South Lawn, a large desk telephone with parallel columns of preset numbers, three televisions, framed photographs of Treacher golfing with the president, and a picture of an ebullient Treacher, arms raised high in victory, crossing the finish line in his racing shell.

Gabriel stepped to the wall opposite the credenza where a trio of Hudson River School paintings hung. Gabriel's fascination with the Romantic era had begun freshman year of college. He'd been drawn to the calming images of dreamy naturalism, and his fascination deepened when he learned they'd been painted during the carnage of the Civil War. He'd spent one summer driving to the locations that inspired the paintings, and he had discovered, to his disappointment, the rude, sprawling, nasty character of those places. Nature itself was chaotic, bug-infested, humid, and hard to match against the bucolic serenity on the canvas. Art usurped the essential truth and left behind the tormenting black flies.

'Like them?'

Gabriel turned, startled. He was embarrassed to discover that his quiet contemplation had been rudely observed.

'Don't look so surprised,' Treacher said. 'Who else would it be? You're in my office. I'm returning your call.'

Gabriel hesitated, caught off guard by the mention of the old message, left two weeks before.

Phillip Treacher smiled. He pointed to the middle painting – the tamed beauty of fully leafed trees shading domestic animals grazing by a calm river. '*Pastoral Landscape* by Durand. Borrowed from the Smithsonian. Perk of this office. This is *Scene in the Catskills* by Weber. I remember you set out that summer to find the spot that inspired the painting, but failed. You always have been a dogged investigator. I admire that in you, but I also thought your trip was a ridiculous waste of time.'

'You went sailing, if I remember, and got very drunk.'

Treacher laughed. 'But you did find this office.' His arm swept the room. 'Five months since I moved in. Feels like a lifetime.' He pointed at the scuffed paint on the walls. 'This was Haldeman's office. He called it his bunker. People were angered by what went on here, so we're not painting it just yet. We don't want to give reporters an easy shot at a bad joke.'

Treacher directed Gabriel to the sofa and took a high-backed armchair, promptly putting his feet on the glass coffee table, displaying his polished cordovan wingtips.

Gabriel saw a man content in his life, happy to be a few steps from the Oval Office. He'd always been ambitious. Gabriel knew his story: pushed by his parents, mentored by their close personal friend, Cardinal Spellman; a young man openly motivated by success but privately ashamed of it. His privileged upbringing made it unseemly to want status too much or to covet power too openly, and yet he did – which was his conflict. To want success, but not to appear to want it.

Gabriel and mutual friends made fun of Treacher for this, nicknaming him Reacher Treacher. They had celebrated one of his promotions in a private room at Harvey's and had given him a varsity letter sweater emblazoned with a large blue A. Treacher resented having his insecurity put on public display and had blamed Gabriel for the joke. The two didn't speak for years.

'What's up?' Gabriel asked.

Treacher dropped his shoes to the floor and lurched forward. 'Jesus fuck, Jack. Wilson. Wilson is what's up.' Treacher settled back in his chair. His eyes turned to the night view of the South Lawn; then he looked at Gabriel again. 'We need to move on. We had the family in the Oval Office. There was a need to show decency, to put money in their hands, but now it's time to put this to bed.'

Treacher's fingers were a steeple on his lips. For a moment the two men were silent.

'You know,' Treacher said, 'we Americans are the only nation in the world that believes we have a monopoly on morality. The French, the Soviets, even the English practice common sense. But we get all knotted up in right and wrong. We think of ourselves as idealistic, which of course we are, except when we aren't, something that happens from time to time. And when it happens, we are consumed by chest-beating hypocrisy. The married senator, a family man, who is always seen in public with his wife but dies in the arms of his mistress. It's fine when no one knows, but when it becomes public, there is sanctimonious outrage from other congressmen, themselves secret adulterers. This, Jack, is the American paradox. We are a nation that sets a high ethical standard, but we lapse into cycles of disclosure, umbrage, outrage, and mea culpa, followed by recidivist behavior that brings on another cycle of outrage and mea culpa.'

Treacher paused. 'It's unique to us. The Soviets have prisons where they send political prisoners. They are public about it. It's their reality. You don't hear the Soviet intelligentsia complain, *Oh, how could that happen here?*' Treacher's voice had acquired a sarcastic bravado.

Gabriel waited for him to continue, but the outburst had exhausted itself. The civics lecture surprised Gabriel, coming as it did, out of the blue. He said nothing. There was nothing to say.

Treacher stood abruptly, signaling the end of the meeting. The men stood briefly at the office door, close enough for Gabriel to sense Treacher's disquiet. He was now settled from his outburst.

'I hear you're asking questions,' he said. 'You've talked to the Wilson family. That is decent of you. He was your friend, as I remember. It plays well in the press. I understand you've been asking questions about me.'

'Where are you hearing that?'

'Where does anyone hear anything in this town?' Treacher smiled. 'You need to practice some common sense. It's time you wrapped this up.'

Gabriel had always found it hard to respect Treacher's willingness to accommodate convenient answers and march to the tune of men he worked for. His expression became conciliatory. 'Good advice.'

'Your colleagues are angry at you for asking questions. Don't do anything stupid.'

Gabriel had moved past the secretary's desk when he heard Treacher call lightheartedly, 'How's Claire? Give her my regards.' Then he added, 'You still row? Day after tomorrow. Potomac Boat Club.'

*

Dense fog on the Potomac River shrouded two men pulling hard on the oars of their one-man shells. They traveled through a cottony mist that was beginning to lift under the waking sun's streaking rays. Dawn's chill fogged their breath as they moved down the middle of the river. Each labored effort came with the sucking breath of fierce exertion. They moved in tandem toward the looming stone arches of Key Bridge, bows breaking the calm water and leaving little waves that propagated toward the dark shore. The quiet of the empty river was broken by the steady rhythm of dipping oars and throaty grunts.

'Tired, Jack?' Treacher asked, glancing left.

Gabriel didn't answer.

'You look tired. You could beat me once.'

'I still can.' Gabriel made his claim but felt his age. He was the taller one, but height wasn't an advantage on the water. His sweat shirt was wet with perspiration and his sight blurred, but he didn't wipe his forehead. He knew he would lose a stroke and drop half a boat-length behind.

Treacher laughed caustically. He pulled harder on his oars to keep the lead.

'Wilson,' Treacher said.

'Wilson what?'

'What's the director's interest?'

Gabriel looked straight ahead. 'Yes.'

'Yes, what? That's all you've got to say?'

Gabriel felt the ache in his shoulders, but he pulled harder on the oars. He glanced across the ten feet of water separating them. *Innocent question? Probing?* He put his shoulders into a heroic effort and made for the bridge with a quickening pace.

'Put it to bed, Jack.'

'What?'

'I said put it to bed.'

'You're repeating yourself. So unlike you. It's the third time you've said that.'

'There are things you don't know.'

'That's supposed to make me less interested?' Gabriel's voice had become husky with fatigue, and he tapped reserve energy to try for the lead.

'Not less interested, Jack,' Treacher said easily, glancing

sideways. 'What's on your mind? Who's put you up to your little investigation?'

'Weisenthal.'

'Weisenthal?'

'He's been on my mind. Hard to understand him.'

Treacher grunted. 'You're flagging, Jack. Three miles is your limit. You are covered in sweat. I didn't expect you to keep up. I do this three times a week. What about Weisenthal?'

'His testimony. I was there. As I recall, you worked with him.'

'We were one big team.'

'He approached me. He's angry. His name was left on FOIA documents when other names were redacted.' Gabriel had Treacher's attention. Silence settled between the two men moving on the water.

'He's in the boat club, you know,' Treacher said, nodding past the approaching bridge to the white-frame boathouse on the river's edge. 'I got him in a few months ago. It was a tough sell. Wrong pedigree, wrong appearance. I can get you in too, if you want. It's a two-year wait for anyone else.'

Treacher added, 'Ellsworth. Remember him? Clement, Hadley, Butterfield, Whitten, Faehter, Bigelow. All of them on the board with me. A good bunch of old WASPs.' Treacher laughed lightly. 'You're one of us. Sort of.'

Gabriel had always looked for a reason to like Treacher, but he invariably found his sense of entitlement distasteful. And yet his unlikable entitlement gave Gabriel a thing to mock, and that made him tolerable.

'Be careful of him,' Treacher said.

'I'm careful of everyone, including you. Those are the rules of the game.' Gabriel turned to Treacher. 'Who is Nick Arndt?'

The two men were moving swiftly when Gabriel asked his question. Gabriel, who'd let the conversation diminish his effort, pulled hard again, unwilling to concede the race. The two men were later-aged athletes, and their muscles had lost tone. Treacher was the confident competitor, Gabriel the dogged adversary. Treacher was fitter, stronger, and shorter, with a sinewy neck, and he had drawn ahead, putting great effort into each arm stroke. His face was grim with victory.

Gabriel too raced hard, and each man was silent in his determination to embarrass the other. Two sleek shells skimmed the dark water, making for the finish line on the near side of the bridge. Gabriel's chest tore with each hard pull, and streaming perspiration stung his eyes. The space between the boats had narrowed, and each man's desire to win brought the boats to a sprint finish.

Then they were there, crossing the imaginary line. The shells glided quietly, and both racers slumped forward, exhausted. Neither man claimed victory. Each drew deep, labored breaths that drifted across the silent river. The boats moved through the shadow of the bridge and out of sight of any casual witness standing on shore.

Gabriel felt the blow to his head. Momentarily stunned, his hand came off the back of his skull, and he saw a scarlet stain on his palm. He woke up to the shocking cold all around him. Suddenly, he was aware that he was underwater, sinking into the heaving darkness below. His hair floated loosely above, and his arms extended out like those of a crucified man. He saw death rise up and pull him down to her labyrinth. He felt cold but also calm, surrendering to luxurious sleep. Then his active mind awoke. He kicked fiercely and worked against the water, pulling himself to the surface with long, reaching strokes.

He gulped air when he broke through the water's surface. Sucking breaths came one after the other until danger lost its claim on his consciousness. He put his hand to the stinging pain on his head, and he saw the dark stain again.

'You're bleeding,' Treacher said. 'Here, take this.' He extended the long oar and swung it for Gabriel to grab.

Gabriel ignored the offer and swam the short distance to his shell, which had drifted in the current. He pulled himself up, working against the weight of his soaked sweat suit. He shivered from the cold and the shock and pulled his sweat shirt over his head.

'Here.' Treacher drew near and offered his dry shirt.

Gabriel looked at Treacher warily.

'You came too close, Jack. You were greedy to win and you forgot to look out for my oar.'

Gabriel pondered the truth of the statement. 'Right. My fault.'

'Let's take a look. A little blood, that's all. You'll live.' Treacher maneuvered his boat. 'I had to pull my oar from the water. It was a race, Jack, a gentlemen's contest that you made into a blood sport.'

Gabriel again took his hand off the back of his head. More blood. He squeezed water from his soaked sweatshirt and bound his head in a makeshift bandage. Gabriel took up his oars and made for the boathouse ramp. The two men rowed in silence, but as they approached the ramp, Treacher pulled alongside Gabriel. He leaned toward him. 'Nick Arndt doesn't exist. Never existed.'

Treacher rested his arms on his oars and spoke pleasantly. 'I could make a case for not telling you, but you'd find out sometime. You might already suspect. We were asked to create an alias for the hotel. There is nothing to learn from him, and there will *never* be anything to know about him, except wild suspicions that your fevered imagination invents.'

Early-morning traffic had begun to cross Key Bridge and the rising sun burned off the mist. Treacher looked at Gabriel. 'Wilson was distraught. Did we handle it as well as we should have? No. He was gone before we could help him. The family deserved their apology. They deserved their money. Money doesn't change the tragedy, but it's better than not having it. Nothing good will come from getting close to this. Understand?'

Gabriel said nothing.

'I'm telling you this in confidence,' Treacher said. 'If you repeat it, I will deny it. My word against yours.'

*Untouchable*, Gabriel thought. *All of them.*

Treacher smiled. 'We've known each other a long time. Nothing is going to change if suddenly the world knows that Phil Treacher knew Wilson back then. You care. The family cares. No one else cares. It's a cold case. Wilson took his life. I did the decent thing and got them an apology from the president and a ton of money.' Treacher looked at Gabriel. 'Let it go.'

*

Gabriel was at his desk in Headquarters early. He had covered his wound with bandages from the boat club's medical kit, and he wore a hat to hide the wound from his secretary. It was Treacher's admission that bothered Gabriel, because it was so easily offered, so inconsequential, so at odds with the viciousness of his attack. Gabriel spent the morning looking through the Wilson files for Treacher's name, and he wasn't surprised when he found no mention of it. But he was surprised when he found nothing to indicate how Treacher knew Nick Arndt was an alias. There was nothing to connect Treacher to Wilson's death, and yet Treacher wanted to disassociate himself. Perhaps Treacher felt remorse, but that wasn't the Treacher he knew.

# 15

## AN EVENING AT HOME

GABRIEL STOOD HATLESS IN the vestibule of their Georgetown home, facing Claire, who'd opened the front door as she often did when he was late.

'What happened?' she gasped, staring at the white gauze wrapping his head. 'Come into the light. Let me look.'

He followed her into the kitchen and allowed himself to be seated at the table, where she took a scissors to the gauze dressing, moving his hand out of the way. She stared at the angry wound matted with dried blood, and in the moment, they assumed their roles. She became the competent doctor and he the compliant patient.

'Be still. You need stitches. What happened?'

'How does it look?'

'Terrible. It's open, drying poorly, and I need to debride tissue to get at debris inside. You waited too long. How did this happen?'

'Does it matter?'

'It matters to me. You come home with a gash in your skull. How can it not matter?'

'I said it was an accident.'

'You didn't say that. You're lucky it's not infected. When did it happen?'

'This morning.'

'*Jesus!*' She met his eyes. 'Maybe you forgot about it. Is that possible?' she said sarcastically. '*Oh my, I'm bleeding. How could that be?* Maybe it knocked the sense out of you.'

'Don't make me laugh. It hurts.'

'I'm sure it does.' Claire had pulled out her black leather medical bag and arranged several surgical instruments on a clean towel on the kitchen table. Overhead light illuminated her tools, and bright red blood flowed from her probing.

'You've been walking around all day with this bloody bandage. I guess I don't have to call the police.'

'No, that wouldn't be a good idea.'

'You saw the person who did it?'

'It was an accident. I was with Phil Treacher. His oar came out of the water.'

'I don't believe it.'

'Which part?'

'That it was an accident.'

Gabriel didn't protest, but neither did he elaborate. Over the years Gabriel had complained about Treacher, and while he had never been totally honest, he had mentioned Treacher's ambition. In a moment of candor, he had told Claire how much he disliked the man, and he'd said they'd always been competitive. Claire had resisted Gabriel's suggestion that the two couples meet socially. *For what?* she said. *To watch the two of you go at each other?*

Claire met Gabriel's eyes. 'Why would he hit you?'

'He didn't. It was an accident.' He touched his wound. 'Are you worried?'

'Of course. I'm a doctor. I worry about my patients.' She displayed forceps holding the slivered wood she'd removed from his scalp. 'It's clean now.'

'I don't want you to worry.'

'Should I? About him?'

Gabriel winced. She flushed the wound with peroxide, and he gritted his teeth against the sharp sting, but he heard her through the pain. 'Did you really go all day like this? No one in the office pointed out, "Oh, Jack, there's a gash in your head?"' He ignored her sarcasm.

Claire rendered her opinion. 'You'll live. Four stitches and you'll be whole again.' She made him sit still while she closed the wound with needle and thread.

The wall telephone rang. She was poised with a penlight examining his pupils, and they listened to a second ring and a third. It was past 10:00 p.m.

Gabriel lifted the receiver after the fourth ring, but the caller had already hung up. Gabriel answered the question that he saw on Claire's face. 'I'm expecting a call from Herb Weisenthal.'

Claire wrapped her medical instruments in a towel and placed them in her bag. She had grown quiet, and he knew there was something on her mind. She opened an upper kitchen cabinet that their daughter would have no reason to look in and took down his 9mm Hi-Power. She held it out like an offering.

'I found this in your jacket. Why do you have it?'

'I've always had it.'

'You keep it locked in our bedroom.'

'Why were you looking?'

'You've been acting strangely. Late hours. Meetings with John. Quiet and sullen when you get into bed. Now this injury. You want to tell me what is going on?'

He took the pistol, checking the safety, and put it under his belt.

She pointed to his scalp. 'That was not an accident.'

'I can't talk about it,' he said.

'You haven't said anything.' She stared. 'You sneak out and put chalk marks on the mailbox. Men sit in a parked car in front of the house. You come home with a bloody gash in your head. It's Wilson, isn't it?' His silence was her answer. 'You have to let it go. Your daughter needs you. *I* need you.'

Again the telephone. Claire lifted the receiver on the third ring. 'Who is this?' she demanded. She handed the phone to her husband. 'It's a woman.'

Gabriel took the telephone. Betsy Wilson announced herself and told him the news that her mother was in the hospital again. Maggie had undergone chemotherapy in the morning and had not felt well. She'd unexpectedly developed a pulmonary edema that went to her heart, and she'd suffered cardiac arrest on her way to the hospital.

Gabriel placed the telephone in its wall cradle. He sat at the kitchen table, stunned.

'What is it?'

'Maggie is in a critical condition and not expected to live.'

Claire drew him to her chest with a comforting hug.

*

Gabriel arrived at Maggie's bedside in Frederick Memorial Hospital the next day in the early afternoon, joining Claire, who had come earlier from her clinic. Betsy was there with her two young daughters, who pulled at her hand to leave. Maggie's first-floor room was free of the life-support medical apparatus inflicted on dying patients. Her large window looked on a shaded flower garden with tops of trees warmed by the deepening glow of a summer sun. Well-wishers' potted flowers sat on a windowsill. The room had no air of emergency.

Maggie lay on the elevated hospital bed under a thin cotton sheet that was loosely contoured on her depleted body. She wore no wig, her skin had become jaundiced, and there was an oxygen tube in her nostril. She looked pale and fragile, but her eyes fixed on Gabriel when he entered, and she smiled. She joked about something that he wouldn't remember and gifted each of her guests with her calm. Claire kissed her forehead. Gabriel embraced Betsy and shook hands with her daughters, who fidgeted, smiling shyly.

Maggie thanked Claire and Gabriel for coming. Claire said she wouldn't miss it for the world, which made Maggie smile again. No one talked about things of consequence. There was nothing, which if not already said, was going to make a difference now. They chatted about Claire's work, about little things, and Maggie asked after Sara, as she always had, considerate to take an interest in the person visiting. There was something in the news that interested her, so they also talked about that, but the only purpose to talking was to have contact, to be close. Talking tired her quickly. Her eyelids closed while Gabriel spoke but snapped open to hear him finish a sentence.

'When does Antony arrive?' he asked, and saw her sad eyes look away.

At one point, Gabriel followed Claire out of the room and took her aside. 'Where's Antony?' he asked urgently. 'Is he coming?'

She shook her head. 'He is in New York. He told Betsy he'd be here tomorrow.'

'Tomorrow will be too late.'

Gabriel looked in Claire's tearing eyes. They both understood that it was Maggie's final moment and Antony would miss it. All the words that were to be said between mother and son – the full text of their lives – had already been said. The unsaid feelings, the uncompromised resentments, all the heartfelt pain, would live on. Gabriel's mind filled with a collage of Maggie's life – the tall, intelligent woman who didn't ask for help and was too proud to accept it; the widow who tried to protect her children from hurtful gossip in the close-knit Army community; the lonely woman who never remarried. For all her strength, she had no defense against her son's anger.

Maggie died late that evening. Gabriel and Claire were en route back to Washington, driving with the numbing sound of windshield wipers working against a steady rain. Betsy called the next morning to tell them that Maggie had slipped away fitfully around 10:00 p.m.

# 16

## MOUNT OLIVET CEMETERY

A MIDDAY MOLTEN SUN bore down on a clutch of witnesses standing beside an open grave. Gabriel wore sunglasses against the glare, and a woman in uniform stood to one side and incongruously held a black umbrella under the clear sky. She was from the county sheriff's office and had come to observe Dr Wilson's exhumation. Seth Greenburg was there with Antony Wilson.

A backhoe clawed the red earth, and finally two workmen slid into the hole to secure a rope harness around the casket. It was slowly raised by the machine operator. Water stains discolored the wood, and dried earth clung to the sides. It swayed in its harness as it was lowered onto a wood pallet, and then a forklift carried the casket a short distance to a waiting hearse.

Gabriel turned from the open grave to view the new headstone in the adjacent plot. Abundant flowers from Maggie Wilson's interment the day before had wilted in the sun. Her sudden death, coming as it appeared that she was recovering from cancer, contributed to the atmosphere of melancholy. Old wounds of the past were accompanied by bad memories, and fresh wounds recently opened made the soul weep. Grievous injustice had defined her life, and shortened it.

Gabriel gazed across the mowed lawn arranged with rows of bleached headstones and a few grander mausoleums. He contemplated these feeble efforts of the living to honor the incomprehensible.

'No one should have to suffer as she did,' Gabriel said. His hand was on Antony's shoulder, urging him to leave.

*Wicked speed*, Gabriel thought. Exhumation of the father following hard upon the mother's burial. Maggie would never know what happened to her husband. Perhaps she hadn't wanted to know.

*

Wilson's casket was opened in the biology lab at nearby Hagerstown High School, where Gabriel had arranged access. Matthew Kosinski, professor of law and forensic science at the University of Maryland, supervised the work. At Gabriel's request, he had placed a team of specialists on call, and the team was now quietly assembled. They were experts in X-ray imagery, toxicology, and crime scene analysis and were cleared to work on Agency business. Gabriel had helped Kosinski obtain the required state and local permits to disinter Wilson's remains.

Kosinski and Gabriel stood opposite Greenburg and Antony in the small lab, separated by the casket on a dolly. Bright fluorescent lights filled the room and highlighted the rust of the iron drains and the gray of the concrete floor. Kosinski wore a white lab coat, protective glasses, and a surgical mask that was lowered to his neck.

'I obtained the Washington medical examiner's report from 1953,' he said. 'Usually these are dozens of pages long, particularly in a case like this, so you can imagine my surprise finding this.' He held up two pages. 'No autopsy was performed.

In my experience, in this type of death, where there is a question of how death occurred, that is unusual.'

Kosinski drew Gabriel's attention to the first paragraph. 'Here it describes facial lacerations from glass of the window that he went through. His disfigured face was the reason cited for a closed-casket funeral.'

Two workmen eased open the casket's hinged cover with crowbars, exciting a screech in the joinery. Circular hand saws were used to cut away the sides, dust shooting into the air, and the lab's confined space amplified the shrill buzz. The work went quickly, and all that remained when they finished was a cadaver preserved in a yellowed linen shroud. Harsh light and impersonal workers, Gabriel thought, made this a terrible setting to experience the complex emotions of a son's reunion with his father. Kosinski's general rule was to keep family members away from the autopsy room, but Gabriel had asked him to make an exception.

Kosinski stepped up to the cadaver. 'We are fortunate. I can see that the tight seal and care taken to preserve the body in 1953 has kept the remains free of mildew and mold. I expect we won't see putrefaction, which will greatly help us.'

Kosinski put on surgical gloves, stretching his arms to pull the latex tight over his fingers. He proceeded to cut strips of the old cloth, lifting away linen to reveal the mummified remains. Wilson's skin had blackened with age and was pulled tightly over the skull, giving prominence to the amber teeth.

Gabriel easily recognized Wilson even after nearly a quarter century. As he watched Antony step forward and gaze at his father's mummified remains, Gabriel saw the uncanny resemblance between father and son. And he saw fraught emotions – apprehension and sadness – on the young man's face. Antony appeared uncomfortable, but he couldn't look away.

Gabriel looked down at the skull that once held a tongue. What would it say if it rose up suddenly and spoke? Fell? Jumped? Foul play?

'What can we know from this?' Gabriel asked, looking up.

'First, I do a visual inspection,' Kosinski said. 'Are there injuries that suggest a set of actions in the room?' He pointed to a sutured chest wound. 'This is where embalming fluid was injected. It's normal and, forensically speaking, uninteresting.' He pointed to the legs. 'He fell nine floors after going through a glass window. If he landed feet first, I would expect to find multiple leg fractures consistent with a fall from that height. We also have the concierge's account that Dr Wilson's femur protruded from his thigh.

'We will X-ray the body and the skull. Toxicology tests will tell us if there were drugs in his body at the time of death. Most drugs dissipate over time, but we can macerate the flesh and test for residue. It means, unfortunately, that we remove skin and take apart the body.' He looked at Antony. 'Are you okay with that?'

Antony nodded.

'Good.' Kosinski looked down at the remains. 'There are already hints. The medical examiner's report, as I said, described multiple lacerations on Dr Wilson's face and neck. Of course, that makes sense for a man in underwear and a T-shirt who threw himself through a closed window. The idea that he fell through a waist-high window sitting above a radiator is preposterous.'

Kosinski leaned down and touched the mummified face, wiping the surface with his latex glove, pushing, pressing, seeking evidence of old scars. He had the photographer turn his arc lamps on the dolly to better illuminate the skull. The skin was blackened, parchment thin, and brittle.

'What I notice,' Kosinski said, standing up and removing his gloves, 'is that there are no cuts on the face. You don't throw yourself feet first through a closed window. That would be the act of a contortionist. I would expect to see lacerations on the cheeks and forehead, and perhaps the neck, but there are none. No marks. No breaks in the skin. We will confirm this with a microscopic evaluation, but for the moment we have an important inconsistency.'

*

Gabriel walked with Antony to the parking lot. Antony stanched his keening sorrow with quiet indignation.

'For me,' he said, 'there was always a feeling of shame that my father had abandoned me. Shame that he had committed some kind of inexplicable suicide, but also shame that I didn't know how to speak about his death. When I was twelve, I made up a story so I would have something to say when I was asked what happened. I said he died of a concussion. Not knowing how he died was a trauma. No one understands that.'

Antony's eyes had reddened, and he looked off when he spoke. 'If you are nine years old, you are identified with your father. You look at your father and you see yourself. It's not just affection or love. You are that person. It's like looking in the mirror, but in my case the mirror disappeared. He didn't die. He vanished. Then my mother wouldn't talk about it. It was all taboo. There was no viewing, no resolution.' He added sarcastically, 'No five stages of grief.'

Antony's eyes turned back to Gabriel. 'She never understood. She wanted to move on with her life, just like everyone wants to move on from this story. She would look at me and say, "Why don't you stop staring out the window and take out the trash?"'

*

Professor Kosinski presented his team's finding to Gabriel privately. Gabriel had arranged a conference room in the Hotel Harrington, where he was known and could expect discretion. They convened the day after Kosinski visited the fateful hotel room, in the final stage of his investigation. The long-serving manager, a proper woman in her late fifties, provided a projector and screen for the slides Kosinski had brought. Gabriel ruled out bringing the team to Langley. Even inside the Agency, the exhumation was known only by the director, Coffin, and a few others. Gabriel had considered having Seth Greenburg at the first meeting, but he demurred. He didn't know what would be presented, and instinct told him to guard the findings closely, and then, if needed, widen their release. At the last minute he invited Antony.

Kosinski stepped to the head of the conference table a few minutes after 2:00 p.m., waiting for his full team to arrive before he addressed Gabriel. When not in the lab, he dressed with flair. He wore a bow tie, tan slacks, and a navy-blue blazer with a canary pocket square. His well-trimmed, full beard completed his professorial appearance and he stood with the confidence of a man sure in his knowledge and pleased with himself. He carried a telescoping classroom pointer.

Gabriel sat at the far end of the table, alone. Someone had ordered a tray of coffee for the three experts who'd joined the meeting, who sat quietly on one side of the table. Antony sat across from them. Gabriel had slumped in his chair as Kosinski pulled down the projector screen and began.

A graphic of Dr Wilson's skull appeared on the large screen, and Kosinski used his pointer to circle a fist-size hematoma on the forehead. 'We found this in our examination. A blood vessel hemorrhaged under the skin above the right eye. The flesh was intact and had not been cut or incised. There was no fracture of the skull or other injury that might have caused the hematoma. It stands out and apart. It should also be noted that the hematoma was not mentioned in the medical examiner's report.'

Kosinski shifted to his next finding. He had established from the size of the hotel room and the angle of the fall from the window, based on where Dr Wilson hit the sidewalk, that his exit velocity could not have been more than 1.5 miles per hour, a speed half the rate of a normal walker's pace. That speed would not be sufficient for Dr Wilson to throw himself through a closed window.

Kosinski displayed a Freedom of Information Act document he had obtained. The *Times* published an excerpt from a just-declassified CIA manual on assassination techniques written by the Agency in 1953. Kosinski had gotten a copy of the manual, which had been released under a Freedom of Information request filed by two of Kosinski's colleagues who were researching the CIA's involvement in Guatemala's 1954 coup d'etat. Kosinski passed out portions of the nineteen-page document to the group.

'The manual's language is spare, matter-of-fact, simply written, and I don't see the slovenly word choices or avoidable ugliness that characterizes most government documents. The tone is literate and informal. It calls the "contrived accident" the most effective assassination. If done properly, it is only casually investigated. It says the most "efficient accident" is a fall of seventy-five feet or more onto a hard surface. Elevator shafts, stairwells, unscreened windows, and bridges will serve. If the assassin immediately sets up an outcry playing the "horrified witness," no alibi or surreptitious withdrawal is necessary.' He read, '"It will usually be necessary to stun or drug the subject before dropping him."'

Kosinski put down the document and looked at Antony, who stared at his copy. His face was drawn and pale.

Kosinski added, 'The manual's step-by-step prescription

matches the circumstances of your father's death.' He concluded: 'The hematoma was from a blow to the head used to stun. Your father was tipped out the window, glass already broken. Scientific fact, investigative fact, and the probabilities unerringly point to the death of Dr Charles Wilson as being a homicide – deft, deliberate, and diabolical.'

Antony was quiet, face ashen, as if experiencing his father's death again.

Gabriel had questions, which he threw out. Was everyone in agreement? The expert in crime scene analysis was less definitive and explained that the evidence of foul play was suggestive but not conclusive. Circumstantial but not certain.

The meeting ended, and Gabriel joined Antony outside the hotel on the sidewalk. A swatch of white blemished the uniformly blue sky. They walked in silence for half a block, but upon reaching the end of the street, Antony suddenly turned. 'What was the motive? He died. He's still dead. He died under a cloud. The cloud hasn't lifted.' He looked at Gabriel. 'What do we do with this?'

*

Gabriel got home late. He slipped into bed beside Claire, and they lay side by side in the warm evening heat.

'What happened?'

'He was hit on the head in the hotel room.'

She rolled over on her elbow and looked in his face, startled out of her slumber. Gabriel met her eyes. 'He was murdered.'

They gazed at each other for a moment, surrounded by silence and the unsaid implications. 'Let's talk in the morning,' she said.

He knew it was futile to sleep. His mind filled with the images of Wilson in the hotel room, and his imagination re-created the final moments of Wilson's struggle and his fear as he fell nine floors. The images kept him awake.

Finally, he heard Claire's soft breathing and he knew she'd fallen asleep. He lay in the quiet room listening to crickets outside, and suddenly, in his imagination, he heard the sound of a man hitting the pavement. He sat bolt upright, as if a giant hand had reached down from the ceiling and pulled him up.

Gabriel was trained to consider the unthinkable, but he found the facts hard to accept. Had the CIA killed one of its own? He calmly considered the possibility, testing it, rejecting it, considering it. But there it was – an immutable fact.

What was a long-serving, high-ranking CIA officer to do with his belief? What in God's name did a man loyal to his job and his colleagues, who believed in the Agency's high purpose, do now? Should he ring alarm bells and play into the hands of its enemies? *My God, you've gone off the reservation*, he could hear the director say. And what was the motive? Questions needled him, the end of one became the beginning of another, and in time he exhausted himself. He lay back down in bed, eyes wide open.

# 17

## A SECRET ARCHIVE

GABRIEL MET WITH JOHN the next day. Following their established pattern, Gabriel was in his car near Lincoln Park when he heard the back door open.

'This is our last meeting,' John said, breathless, as he closed the door.

Later, when Gabriel was trying to figure out who John might be, he reflected on the changed tone in John's voice in the moment. Something was different. He was abrupt and anxious.

'Wilson was murdered,' Gabriel said.

'Are you surprised?' John snapped. 'You're getting a lot of attention inside. You've made people nervous. It's becoming dangerous for me to meet you. Someone suspects you're getting help.'

'Every murder needs a motive. Point me in a direction. Where do I look?'

'Use your nose. Smell the lies. Weisenthal testified that Ainsley destroyed all the records, but Dora Plummer told you Ainsley brought 450 boxes to be processed. "Destroyed" is very specific, but "processed" implies a variety of outcomes.'

*So John was in the room when Weisenthal testified.* Gabriel remembered the half-dozen intelligence officers he'd seen in

159

the packed Senate hearing room, but he couldn't place John among them.

'What if you wanted to dispose of documents but didn't want to destroy them because one day the incriminating evidence could become exculpatory – or used for blackmail? In the meantime, you want the files to be archived but not discoverable. What would you do? Where would you send them? There is only one place.'

*

Gabriel had accomplished one thing during his twenty minutes with the chief archivist at the National Archives. He had established where Record Group 263, the CIA's archives, was held. The archivist refused Gabriel's request to browse the stacks, but he'd gotten the talkative man to let him peek in, using the excuse that he was a fan of John Russell Pope, the building's architect, and he was curious how the original interior courtyard design had become floors of stacks. While the archivist gave a commentary at the open door, eager to show off his knowledge, Gabriel's sleight-of-hand fixed a two-inch swatch of duct tape over the heavy metal door's spring latch bolt.

Gabriel closed the metal door and stood absolutely still, glancing in both directions to be certain he was alone. In the event of some chance encounter, he was prepared to account for his presence, and he had an explanation ready for why he was in the off-limits stacks.

Gabriel's first sensation was the tomb-like quiet – no sounds from the outside world penetrated the windowless space, leaving only dense, velvet silence. The floor was illuminated by dim pendant ceiling lamps hanging at regular intervals. Beyond the circles of light there was only darkness. Pervading everything was a sense of warehoused documents – a vast historical record of a million incidents all locked in sealed containers, dead to the present except when a researcher, by reading the pages, brought them to life. Aisle after aisle met the long hallway at right angles, and the hallway disappeared in a distant vanishing point. There was none of the grandeur of an old library, only row after row of floor-to-ceiling steel shelving that bulged with fat cardboard boxes, thin green folios, and leather-bound books. A cold and charmless place.

Gabriel now heard a very faint hum that he traced to the many dim electric lights. As he stood just inside the closed door, evaluating his next move, he became aware of footsteps nearby. The sound had no provenance in the muffled space, and he turned in one direction, then in the other, looking for someone approaching. Gabriel stepped into the nearest aisle, and not finding a place to hide, he climbed a ten-foot rolling stepladder, his head rising above the horizontal plane of light. The person paused to look up at the dark figure on the ladder, but then Gabriel heard the footsteps continue down the hallway. He waited until they were faint and distant.

Gabriel took the stairs one flight down and found a section of the floor separated from the main area by a chain-link fence. There was a brightly lit table inside with boxes of files waiting to be returned to shelves. Here it was: the locked crypt of buried secrets stored in a forgotten catacomb.

Gabriel pulled the keyed doorknob twice, rattling the cage, and found that someone had left it carelessly unlocked.

Gabriel quickly discerned the logic of the filing system. Printed signs on aisle ends described record subgroups with inclusive dates for the shelved boxes and general descriptions: Berlin Tunnel, Bay of Pigs, National Intelligence Estimates, Iran, Guatemala, and the boxes on the shelves within the aisle were more particularly described – Vol. 3, Bk. 1, Confidential

War Diaries, 1945. The pattern repeated itself through the one acre of storage. The card file for Record Group 263 had not indexed 'Dr Charles Wilson,' or even a vague reference to his work, which left Gabriel to browse the stacks. As he strolled through the aisles, glancing at the descriptions, hoping something would jump out, he quickly saw the challenge: 450 boxes or folios attributed to Ainsley, nine hundred linear feet of documents, over two million pages. The grim prospect tested even Gabriel's determination.

He sat on the step of a rolling ladder and pondered. He looked at his watch. He'd already been in the building an hour and he had no clue how to begin or even if his suspicions were correct. Doubt crept into his thinking. What in God's name was he doing, believing he could solve this puzzle? A fool's errand. John's comment came back to him. *What would you do?* He thought: name a file with a label no one would ever connect to the actual content. The whereabouts of a deliberately miscataloged file would be known only to the man who mislabeled it. A simple deception. The idea settled in. Of course! People were lazy. Memory was lazy. Men picked passcodes that included their birthdate, or home address, or license plate number, because they were easy to remember. The real danger for the code maker was to create a passcode that was hard to remember and therefore easily forgotten.

Gabriel stood. He gave himself another hour to test his hypothesis. He started at one end of the aisle and systematically scanned each box and folio for an idiosyncratic description. The unusual label, the odd description, and nothing so general that it would attract attention. He looked in several. There was a box titled 'Pont St. Espirit,' another '81 Bedford Street,' and a third labeled '225 Chestnut Street, San Francisco.' But the contents had nothing to do with Wilson. Gabriel proceeded diligently, but when the hour was up, he'd had no success.

Gabriel sat down on a chair by the table that held boxes waiting to be returned to the shelves. He wasn't ready to give up, but he saw no path forward. He thought about Wilson as he sat there in the vast collection of secret history. He owed Wilson his life, but his debt wasn't open-ended, and perhaps he'd come to a reasonable conclusion.

Gabriel saw that his shoelace was untied. As he bent over, Wilson's face appeared in his mind's eye, an image so startlingly real, so vivid, that it took his breath away, and in that moment he had the very real sensation that he was on his back on a gurney being taken down the tunnel under Building 470, passing under bright ceiling lights. Between the intervals of blinding lamps, he saw Wilson's ghostlike apparition urging Gabriel to keep his eyes open, coaxing, demanding, berating. But Wilson's voice was silent, his lips moving soundlessly. And suddenly Gabriel heard Wilson's voice boom loudly: *Don't close your eyes. Look at me. Look at me. Look at me.*

Premonitions are strange things. So are feelings, and so are impulses. And the three combined into one for Gabriel at that moment. He had finished tying his shoe when he suddenly looked up, following the voice, and on the table in front of him there was a green folio labeled, 'dei opus est scriptor.' Where had he seen that phrase? Then he remembered: Ainsley had said it in their phone conversation. The Latin words, and their connection to the Knights of Malta, had stuck with Gabriel.

Gabriel opened the folio. He lifted one document, put it down, lifted another, and in a moment realized it was a treasure trove of Wilson's missing records, things he'd been told were lost: fitness reports, letters of commendations, numerically scored personnel evaluations, and Wilson's unredacted psychiatric evaluation with the doctor's name. And there were also Wilson's trip reports and summaries of covert weapons projects that he had managed. Gabriel felt the nerves on the back of his neck tingle. Patience, rigorous attention to detail, an intelligent approach to a problem. These were essential for a good case officer. But Gabriel also knew that stubborn assignments didn't succeed unless there was also luck involved, and this was his lucky break.

Gabriel saw the folio was among cardboard boxes that were waiting to be returned to the shelves. Someone had recently retrieved the folio, Gabriel thought. Someone else knew the code.

Gabriel read the documents hungrily, scanning one and moving to the next, letting information on the pages form a picture of Wilson's work. He was halfway through the folio when he stopped. A memo from November 12, 1953, with the subject line 're: Security Violations' was addressed to Phillip Treacher from Herbert Weisenthal. Someone had written in the margin, 'Trips to Berlin?' Gabriel recalled Treacher's emphatic denial he'd worked with Weisenthal.

Gabriel looked up and listened. Loud cries came from somewhere in the vast stacks, and in the quiet of his mind he knew that someone had found the duct-taped door and had put out an alarm. There were excited sounds of people running everywhere, shouting.

Gabriel placed the inch-thick file next to his stomach, and he drew his shirt closed, making sure the file was under his belt and unseen. He calmly walked out of the cage and pulled the door closed, locking it. He knew that security guards were now involved. A breach of the inner sanctum would draw a quick police response to protect stored originals of the Bill of Rights and the Declaration of Independence.

There was no place to hide. Voices were coming from the floor above, where the door had been found forced open, so Gabriel took the stairs down one flight. He walked down another flight, stepping quickly, hearing the gathering yells.

The voices, which had been distant, were closer now, and there were too many to count.

Gabriel spun around, unable to find a place to hide, and saw an exit door: 'Emergency Use Only.' There was a fire extinguisher on the wall next to the door and above it, at eye level, a manual fire alarm, with the instruction 'Pull Down.' He broke the glass and yanked the handle, and the stacks filled with fierce, high-pitched sounds and pulsing strobe lights.

Gabriel slowly leaned against the security bar, opening the emergency exit, and he carefully pulled the door closed. He found himself in a hallway on the main floor of the building. It was a chaotic scene. Staff ran in different directions, hustling tourists toward the building's main entrance, and security guards led stunned researchers from the main reading room, most clutching papers. Gabriel joined the exodus.

Chaos was everywhere in the rotunda, and the building's population evacuated through the tall bronze doors. Gabriel saw a video surveillance camera peering down, but he ignored it. In the unlikely event his face was identified among the many people being evacuated, he would say he'd been with the chief archivist. He passed two security guards at the door, but they were uninterested in a well-dressed man offering up a look into his attaché case. Gabriel joined the crowd outside, who looked up at the magnificent Corinthian columns, gaping in disbelief, looking for the fire.

Gabriel slipped into his parked Volvo two blocks away. He removed the documents and placed them on the passenger seat. As he pulled into traffic, his mind was already beginning to frame the first paragraph of the report he would write.

# 18

## LANGLEY HEADQUARTERS

'HE'LL BE RIGHT IN.' The director's secretary held open the door, guiding Gabriel into the small conference room. Nothing in the room had changed since his last visit. The portrait gallery of former DCIs was the same, the spot on the wall reserved for the current occupant was still empty, the brace of flags on either side of the thirty-eighth president's photograph hung limply, and there was still no air conditioning and no sense of day or night behind the drawn curtains. Nothing had changed, but Gabriel knew from the late hour, and the sudden request to meet, that something was different.

'Jack,' the director greeted. 'Sit, sit.' They took seats across the table from each other. The director clasped his hands prayerfully and got to the point.

'Wilson,' he said. 'It's late, I know. Time gets away from me. Where are we?'

Gabriel had put the final touches on his report that morning, and while pieces were still missing, he had enough to make his case. It was done. As done as he could make it.

'We keep great volumes on things we do,' Gabriel began. 'We have many cubic feet of files on the Berlin Tunnel and the Bay of Pigs, but until yesterday we had very little on Wilson.' He handed the director a manila folder with the fifty-four documents the Agency had given the family, and he included the Notification of Personnel Action that described Wilson's quiet transfer to the Agency. The documents were the thickness of a no. 2 lead pencil. 'This is everything we gave the family and missing, of course, are the documents that Weisenthal destroyed. We don't know what was in those documents. I discovered Wilson's personnel records in the National Archive, where they had been miscataloged – wrongly labeled.' Gabriel paused. 'I stumbled upon them. They were on a table waiting to be put back on the stacks.'

The director didn't show any reaction. 'You got lucky. The magic of chance.'

'Perhaps. But it begs the question: Are there more files that I haven't found?'

Gabriel suspected the director wouldn't know the answer, but he would understand the question. Questions were more helpful than answers – which, by their nature, were often incomplete or unreliable. Questions were open-ended, rich with possibility. Answers closed down inquiries.

Gabriel presented Wilson's psychiatric evaluation. 'This is an example of what I found – obviously a fake file concocted to keep an investigator from discerning the facts of the incident. It's dated January 5, 1953, but that's an obvious typo. It should be January 5, 1954. You can see the forgery in the carelessness. It describes Wilson as suffering from depression and being a risk to himself. I tried to track down the doctor, but there is no record of him. No medical license, no address, no hospital affiliations. It makes sense if you see it as a cover-up. And there are no names – except for Weisenthal and Ainsley – associated with the chain of custody of the documents. Follow the fingerprints is the usual game, but where the prints vanish, the trail ends. Documents were destroyed, or intentionally miscataloged, and others may be lost for good. All support the intended impression that Wilson committed suicide.'

Gabriel paused to let his conclusion settle in. 'But he didn't kill himself. He was murdered. He was struck in the head, stunned, and dropped from the hotel window.'

'Motive?' the director asked.

'I'll get to that.'

Suddenly, the door opened and the director's secretary interrupted. 'They're here.'

'I've asked James Coffin and George Mueller to join us,' the director said. 'I want them to hear this.'

Coffin sat on one side of the director, while Mueller sat on the other. All three were opposite him with the same drawn expressions, the same tolerant skepticism, the same studied silence. He thought, *Something has changed.*

Gabriel pushed his report across the table, and he took the carbon copy that he had reserved for himself and slid it to Coffin. Gabriel had typed the report himself on his Remington manual. 'There are only two copies.'

The director shared his copy with Mueller. 'Let's proceed.'

Gabriel had assembled a chronology of the events from 1949 to 1953 and added a narrative that linked known facts, filling out what was known about Wilson's death with information he'd found in the miscataloged personnel file, shaping a theory. He had written the ten, single-space pages in careful, spare prose – a dry report except in its explosive subject, stamped: Eyes Only.

'Dr Wilson,' Gabriel began, 'worked in a restricted zone in a building complex at Fort Detrick that housed chemical, biological, pathological, and bacteriological laboratories. Aerosolized anthrax was tested on rhesus monkeys in a sealed cloud chamber. Effective toxicity levels were determined by measuring how many monkeys died and how quickly. Anthrax was weaponized using bomblets as a delivery system, but tests of lethal delivery were also made with anthrax-contaminated combs, toothbrushes, feathers, and fleas.'

Gabriel pointed at the memo, which the three men opposite occasionally consulted, but otherwise they listened.

'Wilson participated in Operation Harness in 1949 off the coast of Antigua. Anthrax, brucellosis, and tularemia were released into the air over several thousand animals that were held in cages floating on barges offshore. Most of the animals died. In September 1950, Wilson participated in Operation Greenhouse, a Navy-sponsored simulation of germ warfare in San Francisco Bay. *Serratia marcescens*, a harmless bacterium physiologically similar to anthrax, was released over the bay to measure the rate of dispersion on an urban population. A similar test was done in the New York subway system when a lightbulb filled with contaminated material was dropped on the tracks.'

Gabriel slid a photograph across the table. It showed a hospital room crowded with sick children. 'This was among the documents that I found. I don't know how they got this or who took it. It's captioned "Pingrang, 1952." Bacterial weapons were deployed on the Korean Peninsula that year, and classified documents show that germ warfare was organized under the rubric "psychological warfare" – a few cases of plague and anthrax to strike fear in the general population. Railroad stations, public buildings, and schools were targeted. There were hundreds of reported deaths from sudden, acute respiratory failure.'

Gabriel waited for the director to look up from the photograph before he continued. 'In mid-1952, Wilson was promoted to Deputy Chief, Special Operations, and his new administrative duties gave him greater visibility into all Special Operations projects. He joined the Artichoke Committee, a joint Army–CIA group that reviewed extreme interrogation techniques, some that used behavior-altering drugs. Artichoke interrogations were done in teams of three, and they were performed on subjects in the basement of the CIA's Berlin Headquarters – Soviet double agents and ex-Nazis who'd become security risks. Interrogations used sodium amytal, sodium pentothal, and LSD in conjunction with waterboarding and electric shock. Artichoke interrogations explored whether a drugged individual could be made to overcome moral scruples. They hoped to find a way for the prisoner to assassinate a target and then wipe out the man's memory of the murder with hypnosis and electric shock.'

'Where is this going?' the director interrupted. 'You're straying.'

'This goes to the question of motive,' Gabriel said. 'Weisenthal recruited Wilson to the Artichoke Committee in 1952. He was a key part of the committee's work. Wilson was brought into the CIA the same year – a fact withheld from the subcommittee.'

Gabriel hadn't intended to raise the director's perjury, but the words had come out, and he saw the director's eyebrow raise. Gabriel looked at one man, then the other two, judging their complicity. He continued in a respectful voice. 'We know he worked with Weisenthal, and we know Phillip Treacher was there, too. I know others were involved, and I believe they're still in the Agency. We know what Wilson did, where he traveled, and I know from my conversations with him that summer that he was disturbed by his work and by what he saw in Berlin. Connect the dots. Harsh interrogations. Anthrax. Korea. Wilson's doubts.

'If Wilson knew we used anthrax in Korea, it would have been a state secret. We had signed the Geneva Protocol, which banned biological weapons in armed conflict. If in the process of doing his work he is given LSD and becomes unstable...' Gabriel paused. 'We have a motive.'

'You're speculating,' Coffin said.

'That's what we do. We take a hypothesis and test it. We now know from forensic analysis of Wilson's remains that he was dropped – thrown – from the window. We know the means, and, gentlemen, let me suggest, we have the motive. We need only the murderers.'

Gabriel looked at the quiet faces across the table, senior men with long careers in the Agency. He tried to look into their minds to judge who was surprised and who had already known.

'Good work,' the director said abruptly. 'It's what I wanted.' He took his original of the memo and Coffin's carbon copy and ran them through the shredder.

The director cleaned his glasses, rubbing the lenses with his yellow silk tie. His eyes were tired from the late hour and the burden of the job. He replaced his glasses and leaned toward Gabriel. 'I think you've done enough.'

Gabriel heard an order.

'Look,' the director said, 'you've done what I asked you to do. I am grateful, but we're not the FBI. We collect intelligence. It's the FBI's job to investigate criminal activity and prosecute wrongdoing. I can't put the Agency at risk. You can't let your friendship with Wilson corrupt our work.' The director paused. 'Are there copies?'

'No. No copies. Is this the White House speaking?'

'Does it matter? Our world has changed. So many shapes of crimes confront us, and everywhere right and wrong change places. I'll handle it from here.'

Gabriel had considered this moment, prepared for it, and he'd come to terms with the possibility that there was a limit to their tolerance for truth. He was not prepared for what happened next.

The director pushed an envelope across the table.

'It's your letter of resignation. You gave it to me before you agreed to stay on. I rejected it then. It's time to accept it.'

Gabriel looked at Coffin and Mueller, and their flat affect proved them complicit with the decision.

'You're firing me?'

'It's best you leave the Agency. It's what you wanted.'

'It's not finished.'

'It's finished for you,' Mueller said. 'Let it go.'

'We need just one man to speak up, and the whole rotten cover-up will unravel. We'll know who authorized it.' Gabriel looked at the three grim faces. 'Weisenthal is ready to talk.'

The director brought his eyes back to Gabriel and considered his claim. 'I asked you to stay on, and I'm grateful that you did.' His hand swept across the portrait gallery of his predecessors. 'They were all fired. I'll be gone too one day. I've studied each of their departures. You know what I learned? It's better to choose the timing of your leaving than to be forced out. So, let me repeat what I said. I accept your resignation. James and George will see you out of the building. I'll handle it from here.'

The director stood, Coffin and Mueller followed, and Gabriel rose slowly. He didn't take the director's offered handshake. At the door he felt no obligation to hold back. Dismay. Disappointment. Anger. His voice had a prosecutor's indignant conviction.

'Once they drugged him, they put themselves in a corner. They destabilized him, and they made him angry. He wanted to quit. We couldn't exile him or put him in prison.'

Gabriel looked at the three men. 'That was the story of the Agency then. We could do whatever we wanted because we were fighting the Soviet Union. The Western notion of conscience is that you live your choices and you can't hide behind an institution. You take responsibility for yourself. Wilson went into the office that Monday and said, "I'm quitting." Instead he was taken to the Hotel Harrington. We killed one of our own.'

*

Gabriel entered his small office to retrieve his raincoat and hat. He paused at the threshold and looked back. The sum of his work lay in his locked file cabinet and combination safe. It was no longer his to worry about.

'One minute,' he said to Coffin and Mueller, who chatted with his secretary, just out of view.

Gabriel took his Yale diploma off the wall and removed the cardboard backing. From the wastebasket, he took the carbon paper he'd used to type his memo and he folded the carbons behind the onion skin, replacing the backing.

'All set,' he said to Coffin, raincoat over one arm, diploma in hand. Nothing else was his to take. He leaned toward his secretary, and he could tell by her concerned eyes that she knew he was leaving the Agency.

'You'll be fine,' he said. 'Everything stays except this.' He tapped the diploma. 'It will hang in my office at home.'

*

'I won't need this,' Gabriel said to the guard at the lobby's security desk, handing over his badge. He allowed himself to be patted down.

He turned to his colleagues while the guard's hands felt the seams of his cuffs and the inside of his raincoat. He had made the final crossing of the lobby with its huge CIA shield set into the polished stone floor. A vigilant eagle perched on a crimson field decorated with radiating compass points. Every day he'd come and gone through the lobby without considering its reaching height, but now on his final passage, he looked back. The biblical quote chiseled into the sheer wall of Vermont marble came to him with numbing irony.

*And ye shall know the truth and the truth shall make you free.*

'It's something to aspire to,' Gabriel said dryly to Mueller.

The security guard, whom Gabriel had greeted in a friendly manner each evening, and had comforted when his son was killed in Vietnam, was respectful in his duties but less thorough than he should have been.

'Hope to see you again, Mr Gabriel.'

\*

Gabriel agreed to attend a small farewell gathering to honor his long, loyal service. A private room in the Army and Navy Club was taken a few days later. Glenlivet flowed generously among the dozen intelligence officers who'd come to toast Gabriel. Beneath the boasts and casual banter there were gripes about low morale, the new rules, and the Agency's shabby treatment in the press. The many indignities formed a defensive bond among the hard-drinking old guard. Stories were told, exaggerations called out, and the small private room filled with the camaraderie of men who shared a secret life. Everyone felt the changing times – and they lamented the closing of Harvey's, where they'd always drunk recklessly.

Coffin struck his glass to start the speeches, and he went first. He was not known for his wit, and he didn't surprise the men in the room, all of the same generation who shared the same jokes, the same fears, the same Cold War outlook. Everyone knew that James Coffin possessed an understanding of the Soviet Union's intelligence operations that was superior to anyone else's in Washington or London. He understood the nature of *threat*.

Coffin went on too long, and his ad hominem remarks were more warning than toast. A sermon of sorts. 'Ends don't justify the means,' he said, repeating what they'd all heard him say before, 'but they're all we have.' It was a dark speech.

George Mueller spoke next. He said very little, but unlike most of the officers present, he was stone sober. He cleared his throat and raised his glass of water. He spoke with the calculated bonhomie of a man reasoning with a drunken friend. 'Don't hold it against him that he's leaving us to cash in on his Agency years. He's smarter than all of us.'

'What's the best thing you can say about Jack?' someone interrupted.

'The best thing?' Mueller smiled. 'He's a sanctimonious, self-righteous son of a bitch.'

Gabriel felt the heat of attention in the laughter, and he twice waved off a request to speak, but at the third goading chorus he reluctantly stepped up to the bar. He smiled wearily at the boozy crowd, wearing their attention uneasily, and nodded at Dora Plummer, who held her own among the hard-drinking men. Gabriel gave a brief speech that without it being his intention became a grim warning about the White House's prediction that détente was a new era. 'The only new thing,' he said, 'is our naiveté.' He had their ears. He chastised Washington politics for corrupting the Agency's noble mission, and he warned that vengeance rose from the rubble of the house of justice.

*

It was Gabriel's party, so he stayed to the end. When he went for his raincoat, Mueller went for his as well. He looked at Gabriel formally, standoffishly, and he wore his sobriety comfortably. Their eyes met, but neither said anything for a long moment. Mueller held his umbrella in one hand and offered advice in a caring voice, 'You're out in the cold now, Jack. Be careful.'

Mueller left the restaurant and went into the night, a tall man in his mackintosh.

When Gabriel was ready to leave, Coffin accompanied him. Rain had begun early and been steady for hours, and the bleak day had become a dark, brooding night.

The two colleagues walked along the sidewalk, shoulders hunched against the drizzle. Neither had an umbrella, yet they endured the weather till they reached Coffin's black Mercedes. Water fell on their hats, but neither wanted to accept the end of the evening. Two souls joined by secrets, giving up the past for some unknown future. Once outside, Gabriel would become a stranger to everyone who'd come to see him off. The two men chatted, not because they had anything to say but because they were reluctant to separate.

'Morale is low. His new rules to make us a modern Agency are changing our world for the worse,' Coffin said. 'Good men like you, Jack, are leaving us. We came here to make a difference in the battle against Godless Communism and to fight enemies who bide their time waiting for an opportunity to strike. And you were right when you said détente is a fog of false optimism. The good men who would come here to work, like we did, now go to Wall Street, or management consulting, or the State Department.'

Coffin spoke the rival Agency's name with disdain. His voice had a noticeable English affectation that he had acquired in London during the war years. Nor had he given up his bespoke English suits, or his black Homburg, which shaded his face and kept off the rain. Gabriel had always found Coffin a quirky man, a dangerous man, but his ability to hold forth fluently in five languages always charmed.

'Perhaps we'd think better of Wilson if he'd left behind a few words about his doubts,' Coffin said. 'We made a hero of Nathan Hale, and he was a lousy spy. He arrived at his rendezvous in

Manhattan late and the British quickly found his secret writing in his shoe. We'd call him incompetent today, but he was well-spoken – and it's his words that inspire us – even if he was a lousy spy. *One life to give*, or *lose*, depending on what you want to believe. We look for our heroes in the most unlikely places.'

Gabriel thought Coffin looked infinitely tired and sad. He saw him glance behind to see if they were alone.

Coffin smiled at Gabriel. 'The Wilson case is over. You are wise to move on. Wise not to attempt the impossible.'

Coffin again looked to make sure they were alone. 'There is something you shouldn't have, but if you found it accidentally, it would be yours.'

An envelope fell to the sidewalk. Gabriel stooped and put the envelope in his pocket. The light drizzle had gotten heavier, and it brought the meeting to a quick end.

\*

Gabriel was seated in his Volvo when he opened the envelope. It was a copy of the director's letter recommending Gabriel for the Distinguished Intelligence Medal.

Self-righteous indignation came over him, which even days later, when he had reflected on the moment, irritated him. The gentle push out the door, the good words said like a eulogy to a dead man, and now the medal. Perhaps it was nothing more complicated than his desire to know who pushed Wilson out the window, and certainly that was part of it, but as he reflected, another answer came to him. It was a simple case of pique. He was being pandered to by men who wanted him to stop.

Gabriel crumpled the letter in his hand.

# 19

## BARTHOLDI FOUNTAIN

THAT IS WHERE JACK Gabriel should have left it, but he didn't. Once pique had taken him in her angry embrace, he couldn't ignore Weisenthal's request that they talk again. It was that simple. Curiosity and irritation struck him when he was reading the morning newspaper, or while he tended his flower beds. The feeling came to him suddenly, without warning, on the toilet, or when he concentrated on stubborn chickweed among his dianthus. He looked up suddenly, angry.

It was for this reason that he also took Coffin's call late one night and agreed to meet the head of Counterintelligence away from Langley. 'The Botanical Gardens,' Coffin had said. 'I believe you know the place.'

Claire had answered the phone and presented it to him with a skeptical expression. 'He says you know him, but he won't give his name.'

Gabriel was in his backyard garden struggling with a stubborn, deeply rooted dandelion when he remembered the querulous conversation from the night before. He was kneeling on the hard-packed soil, trowel in hand, feeling the rain begin. This was now his morning routine. He got up early in the predawn darkness, as he had done every morning during his career, and when the hour to leave for the office approached, disquiet settled in. He felt a flatness to his day, an emptiness after Claire left for work and Sara ran for the school bus. He pondered what it meant to be fired. Yes, his resignation had been accepted, but he'd been escorted out of the building.

Gabriel tugged at the root, loosening the soil with his trowel. *I have what you want*, Coffin had said on the phone. Afterward, Claire's questions. *What does he want?* 'To talk.' *Talk about what?* 'Business.' She had gazed at him disbelievingly. *You're out of work.*

Gabriel took the uprooted dandelion and tossed it on the compost pile. He got great satisfaction from the simple tasks of gardening, and the work put his mind at ease. He enjoyed ridding the beds of choking weeks. All around him there was delicate flowering beauty. *What's up?* The question echoed in his mind, as did Coffin's response. *I'd prefer not to talk on the phone.*

Gabriel stood and brushed earth from his pants. At the kitchen door he kicked off his work shoes and glanced at the wall clock. One hour before he was to meet Coffin.

Gabriel sat at the kitchen table and took the index card from his wallet. Black lines scored Dulles, Wisner, Edwards, and Ainsley, which left Treacher, Coffin, Mueller, and Weisenthal. He looked at the card for the first time in weeks. First the call from Weisenthal and now from Coffin. He added another name at the bottom in careful block letters: the director's. It was wrong to leave him off even if he had been stationed in Berlin in 1953. Denials and cover-ups flowed from Wilson's death, and the director's mission to protect the Agency was reason enough for him to be complicit in the crime.

He left a note for Claire. *'I'll be home for dinner.'*

Gabriel glanced at himself in the vestibule mirror on his way out the front door. He almost didn't recognize the man he saw, face gray with determination. He breathed deeply to calm himself. He didn't know what to expect from Coffin. He put his 9mm Hi-Power under his belt in the small of his back.

\*

Gabriel found Coffin on a secluded bench protected from the light rain by a stand of Norwegian pine, and farther along the stone path, there was the conservatory's tarnished glass dome. Swampy daylight brought out the intense purples, pinks, whites, and yellows of the ranging peonies, azaleas, and roses in the untended plantings, each bordered with bricks. Vibrant colors were a gift to the visitor's eyes, but everywhere the unweeded beds had gone to seed, and in front of Coffin stood Bartholdi Fountain. Gabriel wasn't surprised he been asked to meet by the fountain. A man who patterned his mind also patterned his day. Every Tuesday Coffin held a breakfast meeting at the Agency's Navy Hill offices so that he could spend his lunch hour in the orchid collection in the nearby Botanical Gardens.

'Once beautiful, wasn't it?' Coffin said to Gabriel when he approached. Coffin took in the expression of French Empire Romanticism, now neglected, with rust spots showing through the aging bronze veneer. Three busty nymphs in the fullness of desire stood atop a pedestal of seashells; water dribbling from the mouths of tired-looking dragons mixed with the rain. Several of the opaque glass lamps had been vandalized.

"Dreamt glory toward which our imagination leaps," Coffin said. 'Jack, good to see you. I'd invite you to sit, but you've invited yourself. Always a rude man, aren't you, sneaking up on me like that.'

'Well quoted. 'The dreamt glory.' A bad day to be outside.'

Nothing was said between the two men for a moment. Coffin looked quizzically at Gabriel. 'I didn't know that you had interest in poetry. You surprise me with the things that you know.'

Coffin pointed at the fountain. 'It hasn't been restored since the 1930s. A few tourists come here, but they won't be here today. If they're out at all, they'll visit one of the main attractions – Washington, Jefferson, Lincoln. Our recent presidents won't be honored with a big marble monument.' Coffin laughed caustically. 'We get the presidents we deserve. Narcissistic blowhards, smug liars, whiny bastards.'

He turned directly to Gabriel. 'We'll have this place to ourselves. I suspect you understand that it's no coincidence that I asked to meet now that you're outside.'

'Chance has its own design,' Gabriel said.

Coffin smiled. 'Now you're talking like me. Yes, I believe in the design of chance. Coincidence can hide an intelligent design – like nature. Have you visited the orchid collection? They don't have many species, but the ones they have are remarkable. They are natural adapters, the embodiment of chance as its own design.'

Gabriel watched Coffin, comfortable in his head expounding on his hobby.

'We collectors prize rare orchids for their showy colors and their complex relationship to habitat. Some are dependent on fungi in the soil; others use fungi that attach to trees. As habitats change, fungi change, and orchids can lose fungi they depend on. Orchids are the first casualties of environmental collapse. They are like truth that way – fragile like truth.'

Coffin smiled. 'I understand you're still looking for the truth of Wilson's death.'

'Is that why you asked me here? To test what I know?'

Coffin paused. 'The whole truth isn't known and should never be known. What have you got?'

'A source inside. He has the names.' *A lie.* 'Is it you?'

Coffin laughed. 'It was safer when you were on the inside.' Coffin sat quietly and took his eyes off a laughing couple sharing an umbrella, who had briefly gotten his attention. He looked at Gabriel. 'Truth in life is like truth in art. It's something that you never quite find, but we seek it like a greedy miner prospecting for gold. You think you've found it – a line of poetry that feels true – but you discover there is no such thing as *the* truth. That is why understanding the allusiveness of poetry is important for the spy. We think life is different because there are facts and an endless text, but it's not different. We fool ourselves thinking that with conscientious effort we can find *the* truth.'

Coffin paused. When he spoke again his voice was politely disparaging. 'Wilson died. How he died should be knowable. Others were in the room. A man in the Agency authorized it. But no one wants to speak. All we have is the official explanation. Our Cold War was an artful victory of language. We used language to create ambiguity, to shift meaning, and we used it to hide the truth. We wrapped ourselves in glorious, dissembling phrases. Our atrocities in Vietnam were "peace with honor" and suborning Mohammad Mossadegh a "victory for democracy." Our current history is written with our official denials, and with each denial comes *a* truth, which defeats *the* truth. Of course, you'd never get anyone to admit that, but there it is. We've used language cleverly and systematically to make it hard for anyone to say there it is, there's *the* truth.'

Coffin looked directly at Gabriel. A long silence settled between the old acquaintances. Gabriel didn't detect a note of irony in Coffin's voice, just a grim accounting. *Jumped or fell. A* truth.

'You'd be wise to live with the official explanation,' Coffin said, coming to the point of the meeting. 'Don't be blinded by what you'd like to see.'

*Just like him*, Gabriel thought. *The man's labyrinth.*

'The truth of Wilson's death will be hard to establish. Ainsley is dead. Dulles, Kelly, Edwards. All of them. It's a puzzle locked in the skulls of the dead.'

'Why did you want to me see?'

'You've been in contact with Weisenthal. Don't ask how I know. It's my job to know. Men in the Agency are threatened by you. They have careers at stake.'

Coffin interlaced his fingers, long and gnarled like roots. In spite of the humidity, Coffin wore his bespoke English suit, the color of undertaker's black, and his face had the pallor of a lifelong chain smoker. He was looking at nothing when he spoke again.

'You no longer work for the Agency. If you did, I could help you verify what Weisenthal tells you, but I'm not much loved by the Boss. He is looking for an excuse to retire me. He inherited me, and I suspect I'll be out in the next housecleaning – unless he goes first.'

Coffin raised an emphatic eyebrow. 'Was Wilson murdered? Yes. Is the man responsible still inside? Yes. Does Weisenthal know who he is?'

Coffin's eyes returned to Gabriel. 'You have a wife and a family. You would be wise to let it go.'

Coffin stood abruptly. He removed his Homburg and swept back his thick, graying hair. He opened his silver-handled umbrella and walked off with a measured stride. Upon coming to the edge of the pine's protective covering, he turned. 'There was really no reason that I wanted to see you. I just wanted to make sure you're doing okay. Being on the outside can feel very lonely. What I'm telling you is coming as advice, not as a warning. I'm not the only one who knows this.'

Gabriel looked at the tall, dignified head of Counter-intelligence, bent slightly from his long career, but still inscrutable with a hawk-like visage.

Coffin gazed at Gabriel. 'What gets you excited about this?'

'To make the men who inflicted terrible suffering also suffer.'

Coffin permitted himself a weary smile. 'A noble ambition. How will you make your catch?'

Gabriel flicked his wrist with a fly fisherman's practiced arm. 'Patience. Still water. A good lure.' He added, 'It all began with Mueller and Wilson in Berlin, didn't it?'

Gabriel waited for a protest, a nod, a hint, but all he got was the man's dull gaze.

# 20

## LINCOLN MEMORIAL DRIVE

EVERY CIA CHIEF OF station should have his own Jack Gabriel, they used to say in Saigon, for how could any chief of station in that war zone have managed without this diligent, unflinching fifty-two-year-old officer, with his quarter century of covert operations experience? It had been his job to find a good story that explained how a high-ranking Viet Cong officer died in captivity, and he'd explained pacification umpteen times to skeptical congressmen touring the country. Gabriel pulled off the extraordinary and the mundane, which added to his reputation for being good at outwaiting the other side in the spy's patient waiting game.

But Gabriel's patience was exhausted that morning. He'd done as instructed and sat in his Volvo at the address Weisenthal had given. Gabriel had read the newspaper listlessly, looking up when a pedestrian passed, thinking it was Weisenthal, and each time he glanced at the stately Victorian house across the street. How long would he wait?

\*

Gabriel stepped back from the Victorian's side door, having rung the bell three times. He looked up at the forest-green windows, which were a stark contrast to the canary-yellow flourish of a gabled roof, which set it apart from plainer homes on the street. Gabriel thought no one was home, but just as he went to strike the brass knocker again, an older woman appeared at the corner of the wraparound porch. Her hair was dyed dark brown, and she wore low heels and a conservative ankle-length dress. Her expression was polite but severe, the fussy expression of a verger directing a parishioner to a seat. She motioned Gabriel forward to the front door.

'I am looking for Herbert Weisenthal.'

'Yes, yes, of course. It's always someone. We don't use the side door. This way.'

Gabriel was inside the vestibule when she pointed to a black leather guest book. 'You can sign if you like. We keep a record of everyone who visits.'

Gabriel saw three signatures at the top, each an indecipherable scrawl. He tried to make out the names, but their penmanship was a sort of secret handwriting, and he added his name to the group with an unrecognizable scribble.

Abundant flower arrangements adorned the dark, wood-paneled sitting room that was immaculately free of the clutter of everyday life.

'Come this way,' she said sternly. She extended one hand, inviting him to move through the sitting room to the parlor.

Gabriel knew instantly this was not Weisenthal's home. Bouquets graced a breakfront and the fireplace's hearth, and he recognized within the flowers' fragrance another smell that tickled his nose – something familiar that he had trouble naming. He thought for a moment that he'd come to the wrong address, but the matron confirmed the name. The gaudy flower arrangements, the guest book, the respectful hush. His unconscious made the association even before his rational mind caught up with the word that described his suspicion.

Gabriel stopped at the French doors that opened onto a larger parlor, where he saw two women and a man sitting quietly. The front row of folding chairs faced a modest catafalque. On it, decorated in white silk bunting, sat a casket.

One mourner in the second row looked back at Gabriel but, not recognizing him, returned to her respectful silence. The usher extended her hand to an empty chair near the front and offered a copy of the printed funeral service.

Gabriel walked down the aisle and made his way to the half-couch casket. The pallor of death was shocking, but then came a sort of relief to see that the embalmed body wasn't Herbert Weisenthal. That possibility, absurd to contemplate, had rattled him briefly and still reverberated in his imagination.

The deceased, Gabriel read in the order of service, was Mr Patrick Kelly, veteran of the Korean War, graduate of Temple University, and a former employee of the CIA's Office of Security. Gabriel gazed at the face, drawn to its lifelessness. The eyes were closed, cheeks slightly sunken and touched up, and he had a lopsided jaw. Even in death he was a big, brawny man with shoulders like a rhinoceros, and he completely filled the casket.

Gabriel paid his respects to the wife, who sat in the front row. He felt an obligation to politely acknowledge her even if he didn't know the deceased. She wore her grief bravely, he thought, but also comfortably, and he thought how the death of a partner in a bad marriage could leave the survivor rapturously alone. He tried not to read too much into her sad smile when he offered his hand and a vague condolence.

A throng of people had begun to gather beyond the French doors waiting to join the viewing. Gabriel saw that the queue stretched out the front door onto the lawn, and in just a few minutes a crowd had gathered waiting to sign the guest book. He saw his mistake. He'd gone to the side door, where there was no sign for O'Malley's Funeral Home, and he'd arrived a few minutes early for the viewing.

Many of the mourners knew one another, and men and women in black nodded or shared a whispered confidence. Gabriel was on his way out, moving past the arriving guests, when he felt a hand on his shoulder. He turned and saw Herb Weisenthal.

'So, you are here,' Gabriel said. 'For a moment I thought you were in the casket.'

'Well, I'm not, but I could be.'

'A friend of yours?'

'I wouldn't admit quite so much.'

'What does that mean?'

'I knew him years ago.' Weisenthal nodded toward the casket. 'It's shocking, but then you move on. I thought you should see what you are up against. My wife is parked around the corner. Let's talk outside.'

Gabriel followed Weisenthal to a Volkswagen bus parked on a side street a half block away. Its rounded, bulging orange shape stood out against the black sedans, and a roof rack was loaded with suitcases. Gabriel recognized Weisenthal's wife sitting behind the wheel, watching for their arrival.

'Get in the back,' Weisenthal said.

Gabriel hesitated.

'Do as I say. It's not safe for us to be seen together. Get in. Mary will drive and we will talk.'

Gabriel hopped in and sat beside big duffel bags, a lunch box, and a stack of highway road maps. Without instruction, as if they had rehearsed the next steps, Weisenthal's wife pulled away from the curb and proceeded to the end of the block, turning into heavy traffic. Mary gripped the steering wheel tightly, and Gabriel thought she had the frowzy appearance of someone who'd left home in a hurry.

'Mary knows everything, Jack, everything relevant to this situation.' Weisenthal had turned around and faced Gabriel in the back seat. His voice had enormous calm and reasonableness. 'We talked about trust. There is a type of trust that I didn't mention. Mary and I have discussed what happened, and I told her the detail that interests you. Our plan to go forward changed two days ago when I saw in the newspaper that Patrick Kelly had drowned. There was an old photograph of him in uniform, and if it hadn't been for that photograph, I don't think I would have made the connection. Then I remembered the name. You meet a man once and it's not likely you'll remember the name, but we are visual creatures, and an image stays with you, particularly his face – that nose, that jaw.

'I wouldn't have stopped to read the news item, but the manner of death got my attention. The way it was described. A healthy man, a good swimmer, is found dead, washed up on a beach in Chesapeake Bay. His canoe was found a mile away, abandoned. Of course, he drowned, but the police couldn't tell if it was an accidental drowning, suicide, or murder.'

Weisenthal paused. 'What you don't know is that Patrick Kelly was in the hotel room the night Wilson died. I know that. Three other men know it. And knowing that set off alarms. I began to put things together. Ainsley was also in the hotel room, and he died in a fall from his balcony. Two deaths with no connection except that each man was in the hotel room with Wilson.'

Weisenthal directed his wife onto Twenty-Third Street. 'We left Washington two years ago and came back hoping that the city had changed, with Nixon gone and the protests ended. But it's not safe for us. This town doesn't let you change, and against our will, we were drawn back into my past. We're leaving again, this time for good. We were in self-exile in India, and during that time I learned that exiles feed on hope. Another month comes. Another year comes. But still there is hope.' Weisenthal swept his hand past the dull government buildings. 'Here are only monuments and corruption. Did I make mistakes? Yes. Leaving is the right thing to do.' He looked at Gabriel with a pleasant smile. 'Kelly died with his secret. I don't want that to happen to me.'

The old spy brought out a tape recorder. 'You'll want a record. There are no files because I was good at my job and I destroyed them. So, all you will have are my recorded words.' He paused. 'Am I afraid? Yes. Not for me, but for Mary. She didn't choose this life, and I am blessed to have her. Don't ask me where we're going. You would risk having to lie, and I would risk betrayal. I don't trust you to protect us, but I trust you with the truth.'

The Volkswagen bus was approaching Lincoln Memorial Circle. Afternoon light winked and sparkled on the broad Potomac beside the Lincoln Memorial. The marble staircase that led to the seated Lincoln gazing at the Capitol was hidden from the angle of their approach, but even from the north the memorial was a stunning monument. White marble columns were illuminated in the pallid light and crowned with a frieze of garlands that consecrated the memory of an assassinated president. Gabriel's eyes were drawn to the colonnade.

'There,' Weisenthal said, pointing. 'We'll sit there. We won't be more than an hour,' he said to Mary. 'I'll wait for you.'

'By the bench?'

'Yes, there, on the left,' he said.

Gabriel had gotten out of the Volkswagen at the end of Arlington Memorial Bridge, and he dodged cars crossing the street toward the sidewalk that circled the memorial. He heard Weisenthal's club foot limp behind, slowing him. Then Gabriel heard the explosion. A beat later, the force of the blast knocked him to the sidewalk. The massive concussive blast set off car alarms a block away and threw tourists assembled at the memorial to the ground. A hint of sulfur mixed with the afternoon heat.

A profound quiet settled around Gabriel. Startled tourists, some with small children, rose in shock. And then the knob in his brain that controlled hearing turned up and everywhere anguished faces screamed and stared. Gabriel had lost his glasses, and he crawled on his hands and knees, searching the sidewalk. His blurred vision amplified the chaos and confusion around him. His hands found the glasses in the grass and put them on, turning to look at the blast's origin.

Flames coming from the Volkswagen bus made thick, acrid black smoke. Windows had been blown out by the bomb, and the vehicle had risen in the air and come down in the opposite lane, stopping traffic in both directions. Stunned drivers stood outside their cars, gaping.

Weisenthal had returned to the Volkswagen and fought flames to pull his wife from the driver's-side door. A second blast came, creating a fireball, and engulfed Weisenthal in flames. He fell to the road, writhing horribly in a lake of burning oil until life left him and he was motionless, blackened, and smoldering. Flames continued to consume the scorched and mangled vehicle.

# 21

## P STREET

Even in the shade of the mature oak trees on P Street, the heat of early afternoon was sweltering. Casey fanned himself with his snap-brim fedora and watched as Gabriel's daughter locked the front door and proceeded down the sidewalk to walk her dog.

After parking two blocks away, Casey had come opposite Gabriel's home, and to avoid drawing attention, he had Barber and Martinez take up positions across the street on either side of the house. The call to visit the house had come shortly after 11:00 a.m. Casey had been in his office in downtown Washington when his secretary said a man needed to speak to him urgently. Not much was said in the telephone call. An understanding had been reached and the decision had been taken. New qualms about the old business. It was time to act, the caller had said. Casey put a service revolver in his holster, took a false identification for himself, and gave FBI badges to Barber and Martinez. 'Just in case,' he'd said.

Casey waved the two men to converge at Gabriel's front door. All three climbed the curved cast-iron steps, and Martinez quickly had his pick in the lock. Patient, expert probing opened the door in under a minute. The three men entered.

Casey assessed the challenge from the vestibule and turned

to Barber and Martinez. 'Fifteen minutes. That's all you've got. We're looking for stolen documents, a gun, anything to use against him.'

Casey directed Martinez to the master bedroom upstairs, and he assigned Barber to Gabriel's study. He gave himself the task of looking in the kitchen and the living room. He knew that everyone had their own eccentric ideas about where to hide things – and often it was counterintuitive. The amateur sleuth looked for hidey-holes or false bottoms, when in fact the psychology of the sophisticated criminal would hide things in plain sight. Casey surveyed the living room, testing his theory, but there were no suspicious files on the credenza, no envelopes slipped into a magazine, no paper taped to the pictures hanging on the wall. Casey kicked the dog's chew toy and watched it roll under the sofa. He knelt and looked under the box springs. Where does a man in the business of espionage put something he doesn't want found? Casey lifted a glass vase and looked inside. He opened the freezer. He unzipped a pillow.

Casey made his way upstairs, bringing to mind the profile he'd created on Gabriel – intelligent, clever, and arrogant.

Casey stood in the master bedroom's doorway and glanced around the room. Martinez had a burglar's expert touch. The dresser's rank of drawers was tipped fully open. Burglars opened bottom drawers first so they didn't have to waste time shutting one drawer to get to the next. He was on his knees at the vanity, and his fingers moved quickly along the edges, feeling for a hidden panel. When he was done, he looked in the boxes that filled the top shelf of the clothes closet.

Martinez nodded at Casey, but he focused on the work. Casey's eyes settled on the obvious in case Martinez missed something. The room had the color and smell that Casey associated with a woman – lavender fragrance, hints of perfume, and matching pale green pillows on the perfectly made bed. Casey looked at the framed photograph of a younger, happy Gabriel and wife at the helm of a large sailboat. There was nothing taped to the back of the photograph. He poked through the trash in the wicker wastebasket, unfolding a scrap of paper, then checking an envelope's return address.

That's when Casey heard his name called. Urgency in Barber's voice brought Casey to the study at the end of the hall. He saw a large combination safe against one wall, but this wasn't what had excited Barber. The man was at the window, standing to one side so that he couldn't be seen from the street. He pointed down the block. 'She's coming back.'

Casey looked at his watch. Twelve minutes had gone by.

Barber leaned forward to get a better angle on the sidewalk. 'She's not alone.'

# 22

## ESCAPE

GABRIEL SAT IN THE back of a taxi, his eyes closed in exhausted shock at the spiraling implications of another murder. Repeating patterns of danger settled in like rude relatives. He tried to bring shape to the threat, but no matter how he explained the bombing, a line was drawn from one murder to the next, connecting Wilson to Ainsley to Kelly, and now to Weisenthal. In the dark corner of his imagination that processed fear, he saw a labyrinth leading to a castle courtyard never penetrated by a ray of light. He turned one way, then another, and he saw that the door he'd entered was now a stone wall. He was surrounded by skeletons.

He opened his eyes. Searing memories of the blast dissipated, and suddenly he was aware he was in the back of a taxi, driving through Washington's traffic. He looked back and heard the sirens of police cars headed in the opposite direction.

\*

Gabriel stopped the taxi when he spotted Sara walking Molly a half block from home. He paid the ten-dollar fare with a twenty, foregoing change, and jumped out. He approached her quickly and tried to look calm.

'What's up?' Sara greeted. 'Home early?' Then she caught herself and stared.

Gabriel knew that his shirt was spotted with bomb ash, and he saw her glance at his torn pant leg and bloody knee. Pebbles had embedded in his palm when he'd been thrown to the pavement by the blast.

'What happened to you?' she asked.

'I'll explain later. Let's go inside.' Gabriel allowed Molly to jump on his chest in a sloppy greeting, and he gently petted the dog's head.

Sara pulled hard on the leash, scolding the dog and pulling her off. 'I'm trying to train her.'

'Is your mother home?'

'Her beeper went off. There was an emergency at the clinic.' Sara looked at her father. 'Is something wrong?' Her voice deepened. 'What happened?'

'Car bomb.'

Sara's face blanched.

'Two people died on Arlington Bridge.' He stopped himself from giving more details. One answer would lead to another question, and other questions would follow. He had not yet tempered his mind to the implications of telling his daughter of their jeopardy.

Danger announced itself without warning. Gabriel saw three men emerge from his home's front door. He didn't recognize the first man – tall, in a dark suit, wearing aviator glasses that reflected the merciless sun and giving a hint of menace, but he did recognize the two middle-aged men who followed. Gabriel stared at the stranger – he was certain he'd seen the man's face before.

'Quiet, quiet,' Sara said to Molly, who barked excitedly and strained at her leash. To her father, 'Who are they?'

'Stay here,' he said.

Sara shortened the leash on Molly and put her hand on the dog's head.

'Can I help you?' Gabriel shouted, assessing the men.

'You live here?' the man asked.

'Yes. Who are you?'

'We got a complaint of a theft,' the man said brusquely. 'We're investigating a break-in.'

The two men took a measure of each other.

Gabriel nodded at the open door. 'A burglary? Here?'

'I locked the door,' Sara said. She had followed her father and offered her judgment, defensively. 'I always lock it when I go out with Molly.' She petted the dog's head. The Malamute bared her teeth.

'It's okay, Molly.'

'Let's go inside,' the man said. 'We have a few questions for you.'

Gabriel glanced down the empty street and then looked at the three men, searching for their intentions. He faced the stranger in aviator glasses. 'And who are you?'

'Federal Agent Casey. FBI.' A wallet appeared in his hand, which he flipped open to reveal a shield. 'Inside, please.'

Gabriel felt a tremor of doubt. Had his face been recognized from the National Archive's surveillance video? He looked at the man. He could make a scene, but that would give them the excuse they wanted. Or, he could cooperate and hope for an opportunity to talk his way out of the jeopardy. His mind was already forming a plan.

Gabriel entered first. Sara followed with Molly, who paced anxiously on her shortened leash when she saw the men come inside. Sara had gone to the kitchen and commanded Molly to sit, but the dog was up again in a moment, nervously eyeing the strangers. Sara spoke again, but the pattern of rebellion and command repeated itself.

The kitchen's bay window looked onto the lovingly tended flower garden separated from adjoining yards by a tall lattice fence, and a graceful oak shaded the plantings. Bright afternoon light warmed the immaculate room. Everywhere order and cleanliness. Everywhere the loving touches of a happy kitchen.

Gabriel led Casey through the living room, and he kept an eye on the other agents loitering by the kitchen, keeping their distance from the nervous dog.

'Lived here long?' Casey asked.

'Two years. How can I help you?'

'What's upstairs?'

'Bedrooms. A study.'

'Can we look?'

*Stay polite*, Gabriel thought. He glanced at Sara, who had managed to calm the dog. *Don't leave her.*

'I'll be okay,' she said.

'We need a few minutes with your father,' Casey said, taking hold of Gabriel.

Gabriel pulled his arm away and clenched a fist.

The men's hands were on their holstered pistols.

'I'll be okay,' Sara said. 'Molly's with me.'

*

Gabriel's study door at the top of the stairs was open, and he never left it open. Gabriel followed Casey inside, looking to see what they had already searched, and his eyes were drawn to the large combination safe, which held the Wilson documents. First editions and mystery paperbacks overflowed floor-to-ceiling bookcases, and texts that no longer fit on shelves were stacked on the floor. Framed photographs of visits to an old French plantation in the Mekong Delta hung on one wall, and there was memorabilia from his years of service – the Luger acquired in Vienna, vintage bolt-action Springfield rifles from Cuba, and a sheathed Montagnard long knife.

Gabriel watched Casey poke through his desk, but his ears were tuned to sounds from the kitchen.

'Telephone work?' Casey asked, lifting the rotary phone. He listened for a moment and placed the receiver off the hook, producing the static hum of a disconnected line. 'What's in there?' Casey said, pointing to the combination safe. 'You keep files in there? Documents?'

Gabriel heard the dog bark. 'It's locked.'

'Can you open it?'

'Do you have a search warrant?'

'What about this?' Casey opened the desk's drawer. 'It's not locked.'

Gabriel's fist clenched, and he abruptly closed the drawer. 'Let's stop this, okay. What's going on? What are you looking for?'

Casey pushed Gabriel's hand aside and opened the drawer again, removing Gabriel's 9mm pistol. 'Whose is this?'

'Mine.'

'Do you have a permit?'

'I'm with the CIA.'

'Can I see your ID?'

Gabriel hesitated. 'I left the Agency last week. They haven't sent anyone to collect the gun yet.'

Gabriel heard the dog growling in the kitchen, a threatened animal baring its fangs. Snarling barks followed in a loud confusion of sounds and above it all Sara's screaming pleas. Gabriel took the staircase three steps at a time.

Gabriel found Sara in the kitchen struggling to restrain Molly, who lunged at the thinner man, snapping viciously. The white-tile kitchen floor was stained with a wide arc of scalding blood. The Cuban's face was mortally gray, and his hand was limp and had a deep gash that bled profusely.

Martinez stood just beyond the perimeter of the dog's leash, numbed by the sight of his wound. White tendons were visible inside the torn, gaping flesh. Violent energy disturbed the kitchen's peace.

Gabriel was at his daughter's side, lending a hand on the leash. 'What happened?'

Sara struggled to hold her dog, working hard against the force of her agitated pet, and her face was alive with dread.

'Fucking dog,' the Cuban said.

'Hold still,' Barber said, binding his belt on the wounded man's arm to form a makeshift tourniquet. He had taken a kitchen towel to stanch the flow, but blood continued to pulse from a vein on the wrist. 'You need the emergency room.'

'Fucking beast,' the Cuban snarled. He pulled his holstered revolver and raised the barrel toward the dog's snapping mouth.

Gabriel saw the drama in slow motion, and his mind imagined the end at the same time that he saw its beginning. He was aware of vague protests, and later he wouldn't remember if the words he'd heard were an order to desist or an encouragement.

Gabriel stepped forward. His right hand firmly gripped the man's revolver and twisted sharply, so the gun came out of his hand just as the elbow began to snap. Martinez let out a deep-throated scream, which rose above the dog's barking and drew everyone's attention.

Gabriel felt a blow to the back of his head. Stunned and dizzy, he looked into Sara's face, so full of fear. He thought, *I'm okay. I can see you. I'll be okay.* Her scream startled him, and suddenly everything in the room sped up in wild rotation. His legs were weak. He crumpled to the floor.

*

Gabriel didn't know how long he was unconscious. He had blacked out, but in the dim, primitive memory that resisted the temptation of death, he had felt his limp body being dragged from the kitchen. Men's voices above him had been garbled, but he had recognized a pragmatic calm in their instructions.

His first waking moment was uncertain, and dizziness and nausea followed. The pain in the back of his head throbbed and dulled his senses. He blinked against the harsh light, disoriented, and didn't know where he was, how long he'd been out, and, even for a moment, what had happened. He was on his back, looking into the bright ceiling light that seemed to sway. He sat up. In the course of looking around, he realized he was in the half-bathroom off the kitchen. *How long have I been out?*

He stood unsteadily and tried the door, but found it locked. He stepped back and kicked, but he was weaker now and the door solid, and his second effort also failed, as did his third. Beyond the door there was only quiet.

'Sara?'

He put his ear to the wood, but still no sounds from the kitchen. In the seconds that followed he felt an excruciating uncertainty and an overwhelming need to be reassured his daughter was safe. He could only imagine her fear – but he banished the terrible thoughts that entered his mind.

He felt dull pounding in his ears and dryness in his mouth. His only child in the hands of those men. Nothing in his life had prepared him for this. Without warning or pausing Gabriel threw his shoulder against the door. He saw two degrees of breach and knew the door was not locked. The men had blocked the door from the outside. He kicked the bottom panel twice, but the wood resisted. He ripped the towel bar from the wall and turned it into a fulcrum, leveraging the tool against the narrow gap at the floor. Grit and muscle joined with the laws of physics to snap the door's panel. He crawled through the small opening.

The dog lay on the tile floor just inside the kitchen. Molly was so still he thought she might be asleep, but then he saw pooled blood under her head. Thick gray fur on her neck was matted and dark where the whetted blade of the Montagnard knife had made its long crescent cut. The dog's eyes were open and vacant.

'Sara!' Gabriel shouted.

He listened through the silence in the house, hearing only birds chirping in the garden, and the tyrannical ticking of the wall clock. He took the staircase two steps at a time and came to her bedroom. He tried the door, but it was locked.

'Sara? Are you in there?'

His shoulder hit hard against the door, and the mortise lock popped. He found his daughter under her desk, knees wrapped in her arms, quiet and still. Gabriel knelt and took her in his arms. She leaned in and gave a great heaving sob, weeping uncontrollably. He held her tight, and he felt her trembling fear.

'They're gone,' he said.

Sara let herself be comforted, and she cried on his chest. He held her until she settled, and he remembered how he'd hugged her as a little girl when the adult world disappointed her. Her pain and sadness exhausted themselves in time.

'We have to pack,' he said.

'Where will we bury her?'

*

Gabriel covered the dog with a bath towel and carried her to a shallow grave he'd dug in the backyard. When he'd filled in the grave, he laid a flower on the turned soil. Sara watched from the kitchen's bay window.

Gabriel asked Sara to gather a change of clothing from her room and to pack the book she was reading, her diary, and whatever other important things she could fit into her school backpack. They would be leaving the house for a little while, he said. 'Take only what you need and pack quickly.'

'How long?'

'I don't know.'

'Where are we going?'

'You'll be safe.'

'School?'

'You won't be going to school. We'll figure out something.'

'Are we in danger?'

'Yes.'

She had been out for her afternoon walk with her dog and then the world was abruptly torn apart, the day's innocent beginning vanished into violence. He saw that she didn't understand what was happening.

'Are we coming back?' she asked.

'They'll be looking for me. The house isn't safe.'

'What about Mom?'

'She'll be here shortly.' He pointed to the sofa. 'Wait there when you're done packing.'

Gabriel surveyed his study. They had ransacked the room. A hacksaw, a hammer, and a broken chisel lay in front of the large safe. They had failed to open the combination lock, but in an effort to force it, they'd damaged the tumbler, rendering it inoperable. They hadn't gotten the Wilson documents, but Gabriel couldn't get them either. They would return soon with proper tools. He saw they had broken into his locked filing cabinet, disgorging its contents to the floor, and his desk drawer had been removed and stripped. They may have connected him to the National Archive, or maybe they were searching for Agency documents, providing a pretext to arrest him. Gabriel put his framed diploma with the carbon paper inside his Army duffel bag, adding his 9mm pistol.

Gabriel called Neil Ostroff at his *Times* office, but he got a recorded voice. He hesitated, but then left a message. 'It's me, Jack Gabriel. We need to talk.' In the silence that came after the recording, Gabriel became aware of a weak but distinct tone on the line, and he recognized the telltale echo of a listening device. He unscrewed the mouthpiece and saw the tiny transistor spliced to four colored wires that conveyed his phone conversations to a listening post.

It had been hard for Gabriel to see the beginning of the danger, but it was easy now to see the end. As he looked at the bug, he lost hope that there would be a civilized way out of his jeopardy. The clarity of his predicament made the muscles in his neck constrict.

It didn't take Gabriel long to find the beacon in his Volvo. Once he knew what he was looking for, he quickly inspected the logical locations. The black device was taped under the dashboard exactly where he would have put it. The beacon was smaller than the ones he had used in Saigon – a better microprocessor technology, he thought, as he examined it. He went to remove it but changed his mind.

\*

Gabriel established a new order for the family in the minutes that followed Claire's return. It was a difficult conversation. He didn't remember how he started his explanation, but it was after she'd entered the living room, either when she saw blood on the tile floor or the ghostly expression on Sara's face. Gabriel took his wife's shoulders, as he had done the night of the Tet Offensive, and he held her. He saw that she had already prepared herself for terrible news. She was calm, as she always had been in their marriage when the stakes were high. It was only the little things that required drama.

Gabriel gave a list that explained itself. Molly was dead. Men had sacked the house. Weisenthal – *remember him?* – he and his wife died when their Volkswagen bus exploded near the Lincoln Memorial. *The men who did this are not FBI.* Gabriel had come to that conclusion quickly. He expanded on what he knew, using the names of men who were unfamiliar to her, but the names didn't matter. Claire saw only her husband's eyes, his worry, and his concern. He might be arrested for having the gun without a permit; they would return to open his safe. They would find a convenient excuse. *I will be next.*

Their eyes met. 'How is this possible?' Claire asked.

Fading sunlight shadowed the yard and darkened their mood. Claire brought her family together in an embrace. 'We survived Tet. We will live through this.'

They had discussed this contingency before, but always during a foreign posting in a dangerous city, where his unmasking, or unexpected civil violence, put them in danger. They had memorized the inventory of things they needed – passports, change of clothing, telephone numbers of trusted friends, false identification, and money. Their planning had helped them survive that night during the Tet Offensive, and as terrifying as the night had been, he never expected their evacuation through the confusion of Tet to be a rehearsal for an escape from Washington, D.C. He never expected to find himself at risk in America.

Saigon. Gabriel had been awakened by his Marine guard shortly after 3:00 a.m. in the bedroom of his CIA residence a few blocks from the embassy. Viet Cong had attacked the main American compound, and all personnel were being ordered to a predesignated evacuation point. Gabriel had grabbed the rucksack he kept packed for this possibility. It contained gold coins, maps of the city, his 9mm Hi-Power, black-market Canadian passports, and telephone numbers of safe houses they could seek out if their route through the streets was blocked. Outside, frantic people rushed through darkened streets, no one taking notice of Gabriel and his family, and in this way they moved cautiously, one street at a time, stopping, peering from the sheltering corner, venturing forward. Chaos everywhere. Gabriel had been frightened and calm, the two opposite emotions helping them survive the terrible night.

\*

Gabriel joined Claire and Sara in the Volvo. He pointed to the homing device under the dashboard and drew a cutting finger across his throat. He didn't know if the device had remote recording, but he did not want to chance that their conversation could be picked up and compromise their next move. Gabriel raised an eyebrow, confirming that Claire understood, and he nodded at Sara, who acknowledged that she too understood. All three sat quietly in the car.

Gabriel took Claire's hand, and his expression conveyed the gravity of the moment. They looked at the graceful town house they'd lived in for two years. The brick façade had enchanted them when they first saw it, and slowly they had warmed to the modest home set between grander structures on the pleasant tree-lined street in Georgetown. It was the home they'd hoped for and dreamed of. Its windows were now dark. He had a deepening sense that they would never see the house again.

Gabriel pulled away from the curb, but upon coming to the end of the block, he suddenly stopped the Volvo. He tore the beacon from under the dashboard. He knelt beside a parked Chevy and fixed the device to the car's gasoline tank.

He got back in the Volvo and turned the ignition. 'That will buy us a few hours.'

# 23

## THE FOLGER THEATRE

PHILLIP TREACHER AND HIS wife were seated in aisle orchestra seats in the Folger Theatre, watching as King Richard in Act IV was asked by Bolingbroke if he was content to resign the throne. Treacher found the casting of a whiny actor for Richard an odd choice to play the somber, sullen king, the light shading of mood eviscerating the inherent comedy of the petulant tyrant struggling with self-doubt. Treacher had hoped for irony but found only flatness and sincerity.

His Pageboy began to buzz. It began as a simple note, indistinct and forgettable, like the first chirp of a smoke alarm. Treacher heard it, and then it continued to buzz, drawing the attention of a bald man directly in front, who whipped his head around and hissed violently, '*Shhhhhhh.*'

'I'll be right back,' Treacher whispered to his wife.

He'd told Casey he would be at the theater that evening if there was any news. He didn't find Casey outside the building, but his second choice paid off. He found him in the men's room. The two men stood next to each other at the bank of urinals. Casey was the first to finish, and he stooped down to see if any of the stalls were occupied.

Treacher followed Casey to the porcelain sinks, running hot water over his hands, and caught Casey's eye in the mirror. 'Have you found them?'

'Not yet.'

'What about Charlottesville?'

'I don't think they went there. We checked the sister's home, but she knew nothing.'

Treacher looked sideways at Casey.

Casey ignored Treacher's gaze. 'He knows we have the Volvo's license plate. He's not an idiot, and he'd expect us to alert police. I think they're still in Washington. We're going on that assumption.'

'Where?'

'We don't know. She withdrew the entire balance from her bank account. Six grand. They won't get far on that. Money will be their problem.'

'What did you find in the house?'

'His gun, but we left it. We informed the FBI, and he's now considered an armed fugitive and dangerous. We went back with an acetylene torch to open his safe. There were no carbons.'

Treacher reproached quietly, 'They weren't in his office, so they had to be in the house. I don't have to remind you that if his memo ends up in the *Times* we'll find ourselves buried in scandal.'

'Don't lecture me,' Casey snapped.

Treacher scrubbed his hands vigorously in the sink and cast a scalding look at Casey. The two men stood side by side, separated by a gulf of mistrust. 'What's next?'

'Assume the worst,' Casey said. 'We picked up a conversation from the wiretap. It went to voicemail. He has called the reporter twice.'

'You need to quash that. Understand?' Treacher's voice was querulous and demanding. He closed the hot and cold faucet handles firmly and repeatedly wiped his hands with a paper towel. Treacher glanced at his watch and, conscious of his hostile tone, added in a conciliatory manner, 'You were right about Weisenthal.' He faced Casey. 'Do they know who set the car bomb?' Casey's silence was his answer. Treacher considered what else to ask and what he didn't want to know. 'A man dies. It's a sad thing. What happened to Kelly?'

'Drowned,' Casey said.

Treacher pondered and nodded. 'Weisenthal. Ainsley. Kelly.' Casey said nothing.

Treacher balled the paper towel and dropped it in the wastebasket at the door. When he turned to face Casey, he saw grim impatience. 'Where will Gabriel go? Hotel? Airport? Union Station?'

'He won't get far. He doesn't have a gun permit. Police want him for questioning in the theft of federal documents.'

'You're on top of this?'

'Of course,' Casey grunted. He fixed his eyes on Treacher. 'He saw me. He'll place my face soon enough.' Silence opened between the two men, standing at opposite ends of the bathroom. 'He is well-trained. Well-trained and clever. That will be our challenge. He won't be taken into custody.'

Treacher heard Casey while he was opening the bathroom door, but he didn't stop, and he continued through the lobby, stunned.

*

Treacher was alone at the bar in the theater lobby. His head spun dizzily with the quickening implications of his growing jeopardy. Suddenly, everything was speeding up. Everything was heading toward catastrophe. *Jesus fuck.*

'Sir?' the bartender asked.

Treacher looked up. He had the face of a man who had seen his ghost. His eyes burned with the searing heat of treachery and the closing doors of time. Old grudges against Weisenthal rose up, and hard feelings were fresh.

'What will it be? Scotch? Beer?'

*Double fuck.*

'Sir?'

Treacher saw the bartender's pleasant smile, and he was seduced by the man's offer.

'Double scotch.'

Treacher smelled the alcohol before he tasted it – the familiar fragrance. He took his drink to the periphery of the empty lobby, where the silence mocked his predicament. He stood at the door, open on the hot night for the tepid breeze. He took one sip from the glass, then a longer pull, and he breathed deeply as the alcohol hit his stomach. The old heat of the scotch took hold and brought clarity to his thinking and settled the twitch in his neck.

How had he gotten to this precipice? He stepped outside. He was alone under a menacing sky that spread across the darkened city. He imagined the brightly lit windows of his office in the West Wing and, a few steps away, the curved brow of the Oval Office. He saw jeopardy in everything he had worked for. No words fully expressed his contempt for human frailty. Terror's drumbeat filled his head, and old resentments came alive with fury.

All he had worked for was glowing brightly in the night, and he couldn't get it out of his mind that all of it could vanish.

His hands tried to grasp the moment, but colorless, formless, tasteless time didn't yield. None of what he'd become was his to own, only his to lose. He looked at his palms, pale as milk, but he saw only staining blood.

# 24

## HOTEL HARRINGTON

GABRIEL UNDERSTOOD THAT THE best choice to escape danger was often the least obvious one. For that reason, he chose to spend the night in room 918 at the Hotel Harrington. Police would be checking guest registries at hotels across the city, which made the obvious choices risky. He presented his business card to the pleasant Southern girl at the front desk, who understood that guests requesting room 918 were not to be questioned. It was a normal thing to offer his card, which had been a source of quiet gratification to him during his years of service, and he showed it automatically.

The long-serving manager emerged from the back office. She was conservatively dressed in a ruffled blouse buttoned to the neck. He didn't have to ask for the key. She simply presented it. They had never exchanged a word in this transaction, not even to chat, but he felt her disapproving eyes.

A half hour later, Gabriel opened the room's door for his wife and daughter. He'd advised Claire to wear scarlet lipstick, hike up her skirt, and try to give a convincing appearance of an adulterer's girlfriend with daughter in tow.

*

Gabriel sat on the closed toilet seat and let Claire inspect his scalp wound.

'It's the same spot,' she said. She teased blood-matted hair away from the wound and gave her judgment. 'People keep hitting your head, but they don't knock any sense into you.'

'Spare me the sarcasm. Stitches?'

'A Band-Aid will do. How did you know about this room?' she asked, dabbing with a wet washcloth. 'Don't move,' she admonished.

'I'm not moving. You asked a question.'

'And?'

'It's an Agency safe house.'

'The two-way mirror? The film camera?'

'You can guess.'

'Safe house. What an appalling euphemism.' Claire faced him and contemplated his grim expression. 'While we were waiting downstairs Sara asked if you'd ever killed anyone. Don't pretend you haven't.'

Gabriel grunted. 'Good to know.'

'What's next?'

'The Band-Aid.'

'What's next in our *lives*?'

Gabriel frowned. 'We have a choice to make. It's not my choice. It's ours.'

Claire's eyes had drifted to the street below the bathroom window. Men and women who lived normal lives were leaving normal jobs, going about their day with normal concerns. She was no longer one of the ordinary people thinking of her daughter's school and the petty crises of work.

She turned back to her husband. She was indignant. 'You haven't done anything wrong. We need to leave the city. We need to leave the country.'

Her suggestion startled him. It was an unthinkable choice

that he wasn't prepared to reject, and he let its implications settle.

'This isn't going to blow over,' she said. 'Twenty-two years ago, something terrible happened. The men responsible are still at work. You are the least naïve man I know, Jack, but your admirable desire to avenge a friend's murder puts all of us at risk – and it will put you in jail or get you killed. You owe it to me and to this family to move beyond this.'

Her voice had risen to an angry vibrato. She took Gabriel's hand and placed it on her chest, looking calmly into his eyes.

'You don't want to be a lost bleating voice in the wilderness sacrificed to the corruption of this town. We don't want to visit you in federal prison or grieve at your grave. We have a choice to live our lives as we had planned.' She looked at him fiercely. 'Move on. Don't look back. Let the bastards win. You'll have time to think, time with your daughter, time, if you want, to write a novel.'

He began to protest, but she stopped his mouth with a kiss. 'We move to the Caribbean,' she said. 'Not Cuba. They don't need doctors, and I couldn't stand the idea of living in a Communist country. I don't want to be called a defector. Someplace in the West Indies. I can set up a practice. We've always talked about sailing around the world.'

'On six thousand dollars?' he said.

She kissed him again. 'We're clever. We'll figure something out.' She placed the Band-Aid on his scalp. 'Done.'

\*

'What are you reading?' Gabriel asked Sara, who sat cross-legged on the sofa wearing bulky Koss headphones, carelessly flipping the pages of a magazine, and then he saw that the headphone's plug-end was loose on the carpet.

She pulled a headphone from one ear. 'What?'

'Were we talking too loud?'

'Arguing too loud.' She lifted the cover of *TV Guide* and looked at him with an air of sufferance. 'There's a drawer full of porn in the TV cabinet.'

Gabriel confirmed her discovery. Months-old copies of *Hustler*, *Playboy*, and *Penthouse* were stacked in the drawer with paper cups and a half-empty bottle of bourbon. He could only imagine what she thought of the hotel room – spare furnishings, gaudy velvet paintings, bordello lighting, a carpet with cigarette burns, and the 16mm film camera pointed at the two-way mirror and the adjoining room.

'Mom said you've killed people.'

Gabriel's eyes were averted when he heard Sara, and he turned his attention to her. 'Yes, I have.'

He surprised himself with how easily the words came. He had rehearsed this moment many times, and always he'd come up short. The many hollow explanations had all been wrong.

'Tell me when to stop,' he continued. 'What I say might anger you. Some of it might surprise you. Most of it won't change your mind.'

'I don't need to know everything. But I don't know *anything*.'

Sara's eyes reddened, and she folded her arms on her chest. She glared at him and said nothing. He resisted an urge to comfort her, knowing that she would reject his offer. *Why is this so hard?* The moment of his testing had come.

'I ended one life to save another,' he began. His memory was a kinescope of bloody images that came in chaotic succession – a crowded street in Cholon filled with black-pajama-clad Viet Cong advancing on Gabriel and his wounded ARVN colleague after a firefight left them behind enemy lines. Heavy enemy fire had left dead on the street, and Gabriel surprised a Viet

Cong when he pulled the wounded ARVN officer into a shop doorway. Two armed men surprising each other, but Gabriel was the better trained, the more frightened, and he was the first to raise his pistol and fire.

Something happened between father and daughter as Gabriel spoke, and in the pauses between words where the mind shaped thoughts, the unintentional happened. He got her attention. His willingness to speak brought them together and opened an intimate window onto the dark shadings of his work. He finished his account, and they were joined in an extraordinary silence.

Gabriel gave his wife and daughter the queen bed, and he took the sofa. He had turned off the lights and stood bedside, looking down at Sara, who'd pulled the covers up to her chin. Their eyes met, and she blushed. 'What?' she said.

'Nothing.' He kissed her forehead. 'Good night.'

*

No one slept well in the unfamiliar room, and Gabriel had suffered doubly on the lumpy sofa. Phantoms had come to him during the night, and his mind tried to expel the faces of men and women whose lives were shattered in the safe house's adjoining rooms. His dreams were a montage of desperate, crying men taken down by a weakness for sex or money, and the horrified faces came like jerky newsreel footage in a darkened theater, causing him to turn restlessly, covering his head with a pillow to escape the haunting images.

He freed his mind by making lists, but the lists were always unsettling and always the same: anthrax, tularemia, brucellosis, Q fever, Venezuelan equine encephalitis fever, enterotoxin B. Wilson's bacteriological agents came as words and then became the disfigured Korean victims of the deadly toxins. In fitful sleep that wasn't sleep at all, he came to understand what he needed to do.

*

The next morning, Gabriel stood in the telephone booth at the corner of Pennsylvania Avenue and Fifteenth Street, across from the Ellipse, gazing at the White House, and then, when he'd overcome his hesitation, he deposited the coins. He dialed the emergency number John had given him. A woman's voice came on the line.

'I need to speak to the man who this number belongs to.'

Gabriel heard a muffled conversation through the line's static, and he knew she'd placed her palm on the phone.

'Who is this?' a man said.

'Jack Gabriel.'

There was a long pause.

'You aren't to call this number.'

Gabriel heard the man's voice deepen in an effort to disguise himself. 'This an emergency,' Gabriel snapped.

'What's happened?'

'Weisenthal was murdered. They are looking for me. I need to get out of the country.'

'I can't help you.'

Gabriel stared at the receiver in his hand, and he had the sudden realization that he was talking to his adversary.

'Look,' John said, backtracking, 'maybe I *can* help. Where are you? I can have a car meet you and drive you south. I have contacts in Florida.'

Gabriel stared at the telephone in his clenched hand. He slammed the handset into its cradle. *Fuck.*

Gabriel took a deep breath, and then he took another. He tried to wrap his mind around the treachery that had been used

217

against him. Remorseless anger welled up in his chest, but he let it dissipate. It was no good to get angry. Nothing good came from indulging his anger. He stared at the White House, and his mind settled on a plan. He remembered how he had been hounded by Ostroff to meet, and when he'd finally gone to his office, the boastful reporter had pointed out his front-page scoops taped to the wall. One six-column headline had broken the news of the CIA's illegal domestic spying and the other broke the Wilson LSD story. He'd disdained his competition at the *Washington Post*. Gabriel remembered Ostroff's rant. *You guys don't understand we are a country mordantly curious about the CIA – the assassinations, human drug experiments, moles. What the hell happened to Wilson? You'll tell me over lunch.* I don't talk to the press. *You're talking now.*

Gabriel dialed the reporter's number from memory and got voicemail. 'It's Jack Gabriel again. I have a story for you. I will call back in two hours.'

*

Gabriel announced his plan to Claire and Sara in the Hotel Harrington's coffee shop. They were not hungry, but eating was a ritual, and rituals helped make life easier. They had arrived at the coffee shop at 10:30 a.m. It was empty at that hour because tourists had already left for the city's attractions, eager to start their sightseeing. Warning signs had gone up in the lobby that Hurricane Eloise would arrive that evening. Gabriel sat across from Claire and Sara, sullen and slumped in her seat, fingers turning a loose silver bracelet around and around her wrist.

Claire waved off the waiter offering a menu. 'Just coffee.'

'That's perfectly okay, dearie. I'll be right back.' The waiter sashayed off.

Sara leaned across the table and lowered her voice. 'We don't know him. Why does he find it necessary to be so familiar?'

Claire looked at Gabriel. 'What did you come up with?'

He explained the first part of the plan he had developed in the hours since rising at dawn. He had left the hotel room at 8:00 a.m. and found a nearby travel agent that opened early. 'The hurricane arrives early tonight. Flights will be cancelled for two days, maybe three. No one knows how bad it will be.' He handed Claire black-market Canadian passports for herself and Sara and an envelope.

'Here are your plane tickets and the rest of the money. Your flight leaves at 4.00 p.m. this afternoon from National to San Juan, and you'll make a connection to Martinique. I'll follow when I can.'

He explained that by now Metropolitan Police and FBI would be casting a wide net for him. Their home had been broken into, his telephone bugged, and he was being implicated in two suspicious deaths. Their town house would be seized, bank accounts frozen, communications with relatives monitored. Their life as they had known it was shattered, and now they had to think about their safety. A sailboat, if that is what they would live on, would cost more money. 'Do you understand?'

'No. I don't know what you're saying.'

'You need to travel today. You'll fly to the Caribbean.' He saw Claire's frightened eyes receive his suggestion and weigh its implications. Gabriel leaned forward. 'But there's one thing I need you to do before you leave. It is *very* important.'

'Ready?' the waiter asked. He held his carafe poised to pour.

Sara covered her cup with her hand.

'Okey dokey, dearie. And you?'

Gabriel tapped his cup's lip, and the waiter chatted as he poured. 'It's going to rain today. Take your umbrellas. Hurricane Eloise is on her way. Big storm. Best to stay indoors or go to the

Smithsonian. They have a fabulous Native American exhibit.' He looked at Claire. 'And for you, dearie?'

Gabriel produced a sheet of hotel stationery when the waiter was out of earshot, and he pushed the written instructions across to Claire.

'We will need a lot of money,' he said. 'Money to buy a sailboat and live for a long time.'

He explained that he had access to a restricted account at Riggs Bank a few blocks away. She would visit the bank after breakfast and wire funds to a foreign bank account that they would access from Martinique. The paper in front of Claire had two columns, one titled 'Riggs Bank' and the other 'Bank of Commerce and Credit International,' and under each column, in corresponding rows, there were account numbers, account passwords, bank addresses, and three answers to questions that validated a unique identity.

'Memorize these.'

He told her the name of the bank manager to ask for, how to conduct herself, and that she would be requesting funds in one numbered account be electronically transferred to a second numbered account, making the transfer untraceable.

'How much?' Claire asked.

'Ten million dollars.'

Sara looked up from her bracelet. 'That'll pay for breakfast.'

'Where's the money coming from?' Claire asked.

'Dirty money. No one will report it missing because officially it doesn't exist.'

Claire was skeptical. 'And you?'

'I'll be fine.' His face was resolute. 'I have to finish what was started.'

She paused. 'When will you join us?'

'When the airports reopen.'

Claire saw resolve in his face. 'You're a lost, bleating voice,' she said. 'A goddamned bleating voice.' Her eyes moistened, but she smiled through her tears. 'Don't die on us.'

Gabriel wrote down the phone number of a telephone booth. 'Call this number at 1.30 p.m. when the wire is done. I will answer. Let's pack.'

As they made to leave, an unmarked black van pulled up just outside the plate glass window. Both van doors opened, and heavily armed SWAT agents jumped out. Each of the six men had 'FBI' emblazoned in yellow on his bulletproof vest, and they were weighed down with black Kevlar helmets, utility belts, and UZI assault rifles. Electronic crackle from open mics, labored grunts, and the slap of boot leather punctuated the coffee shop's quiet. Two teams of three each rushed through the hotel's revolving doors and took up positions in the lobby, startling one woman, a jogger, who'd just stepped out of the elevator.

Gabriel looked at Sara, knowing he'd forgotten to warn her. 'Did you turn on the television this morning?' More than once he had watched the room through the closed-circuit monitoring lens embedded in the screen.

'Yes,' she said.

Gabriel rose slowly and took the rucksack at his feet. He directed Claire and Sara toward the kitchen's swinging doors. 'Don't run. Look casual.' His voice had the same calm urgency that he'd used to guide the family to safety in Saigon.

The waiter appeared at the kitchen door and stepped aside to let the family pass. 'Take your umbrellas,' he said tartly.

Gabriel nodded at the startled short-order cook who looked up from the flaming grill, but Claire looked right past the white-hatted chef.

Gabriel had already pressed the freight elevator's call button when he heard excited voices through the kitchen door. He heard a volley of angry threats and the brusque exasperation of men challenged by a witness who didn't speak English. Gabriel punched the call button twice more, but his impatience had no effect on the elevator cab's slow descent from an upper floor. Without pausing, he kicked the exit's self-locking door, sending it wide open onto a courtyard of dumpsters.

'Follow me.' He pointed at a narrow alley. His mind was a tuning fork to danger, primed and calibrating the deceptions of their escape. 'Listen,' he said when they were at the street. His face was gray with worry. They would proceed as planned, he said. Nothing had changed. But even as he spoke, he felt his confidence weaken, and in the primitive part of his brain where inchoate thoughts form, he knew their prospects had dimmed.

\*

Twenty minutes later, Gabriel stood under an angry sky across Pennsylvania Avenue from Riggs Bank's stately façade and watched his wife and daughter dodge traffic, making their way toward the bank's stone columns. He waited until they were safely across and then stepped into the public telephone booth that faced the Ellipse. He lifted the receiver and felt an old fear tightened his chest.

Metamorphosis is a painful process for a deep-thinking deskman who wields power with the stroke of a pen, and deep inside he was conscious of a carapace cracking open like the caterpillar turning out of its skin, shedding caution to become a man on the run. Old instincts returned, and once again he was a solitary case officer, registering danger, alert to surveillance, ready with his gun. For the first time since he had settled on his plan, he understood how reckless it was.

Gabriel punched in the telephone number of the *Times*' office and got Ostroff on the third ring. He had rehearsed how he would broach his topic, but noise on the street and Ostroff's unpredictable nature conspired against what he had planned to say, so he got right to the point, and suddenly there were Ostroff's rapid-fire questions, punctuated with obscenities. Gabriel gave an answer, and in the silence that followed, he knew the hook was planted.

'Which entrance?' Ostroff asked. 'There are two. What's in it for me?'

Gabriel exploited the reporter's competitive nature. 'For you? An exclusive. A front-page trophy to hang on your wall. You'll finally make it across the East River to the Emerald City.'

'Fuck you.'

'Charm school answer,' Gabriel said.

'Double fuck you. What's in it for me?'

'They'll turn the book you write into a movie. You'll get on late-night television and show off your pleasant personality.' He paused. 'Should I take it to the *Post* –'

'I need something to convince a skeptical editor.'

Gabriel heard silence on the other end of the line, and in the silence he heard what he expected – the telltale electronic signature of a wiretap. 'I have a document that dots the 'i's and crosses the 't's. A dead man's parting gift. Names you'll recognize. Evil will combust when you shine light on it.'

There was a pause. 'It better be that good.'

'6.00 p.m. tonight. Take an umbrella.'

'Which station?'

'Connecticut Avenue.'

'It hasn't opened yet.'

'You can duck under the barrier. I did it yesterday. It's near you. No one will be out in the storm except you and me.'

*And the men listening to the conversation.* 'Names' would get the attention of the men Gabriel wanted. A lie, to be believable, only had to offer the possibility of truth.

# 25

## RIGGS BANK
## PENNSYLVANIA AVENUE

CLAIRE CHOSE A TELLER window served by a woman with a pleasant face, thinking that speaking to a woman would give her confidence. She stepped up to the brass grill. She wore a large floppy hat and dark glasses that she'd bought in the pharmacy, hoping for a good disguise, but now they felt awkward.

'How can I help you?' The woman smiled politely.

Claire removed her glasses. 'Good morning.' *Be natural.* 'Terrible weather.' She smiled. 'I need to initiate a wire transfer.' She pushed a completed bank transfer form under the grill. 'I thought you might close early with the hurricane coming.'

'I wish,' the teller said. Her long fingernails were painted a bold carnelian red, and Claire found herself staring.

'Excuse me,' the teller said. 'You want to transfer funds from an account here to an account at BCCI. Is that correct, ma'am?'

'Yes.' She clutched her bag. 'That's right.'

'How much are you transferring?'

Claire pointed through the grill at the amount written on the form. 'Ten million dollars.'

The teller looked up. Claire didn't allow herself to react to the teller's surprise.

'I'll need to see identification.'

'This is the identification.' Claire passed a note under the grill with the answer to the security question. 'Mr Withers handles the account. He can confirm this answer.'

'And your name?'

'It's a code-three numbered account. You don't need a name.'

'I need to know who is requesting the transfer. An amount this large has special requirements.'

Claire paused. Had she overlooked a step, or missed an instruction? Had her husband forgotten to give her a critical piece of information? Alarms rang in her head. 'You don't need my name,' she said. 'The security question' – she pointed again through the grill – 'is the unique identification for a code-three account. That is all you need to initiate a transfer on this particular account. Is it clear? Account number 13-2020719-Q.'

The teller's smile slackened. She didn't appreciate being corrected. 'Let me ask?'

Claire looked away from the teller, who retreated into the back, and glanced across the cathedral atrium toward the heavy bronze doors that opened onto Pennsylvania Avenue. She had left Sara outside the bank with the instruction to wait thirty minutes, and if Claire didn't return in that time, Sara was to call her aunt, who'd come and collect her. She'd given Sara the phone number and change, pointed toward the nearby phone booth, and then she'd hugged her. 'You'll be fine,' she'd said. 'I'll be out soon.'

But now waiting, Claire worried. *How long will this take?* Echoing quiet was broken by a guard's footsteps on the marble floor and the loud whispers of a couple in the waiting area. Claire was aware of everything at once – her wait, the huge chandelier hanging on a long chain from the atrium ceiling, a balcony below a frieze of leaded windows, and the testy impatience of a customer at the adjacent teller window.

'Ma'am?'

225

Claire was being summoned by the teller, who stood at the end of the bank of windows and motioned Claire to entered a locked gate.

'Follow me, ma'am.'

Claire hesitated. Her first thought was that thirty minutes was too little time to accomplish the transfer, and Sara would be gone. Her second thought was that she was going to be arrested.

'I don't have much time,' she said, passing through the gate.

'Mr Withers needs to speak with you.'

Claire was shown into a glass-walled office with a view of the working tellers, but the enclosure, even as transparent as it was, gave the confined space an intimate and confidential feeling. Assistant Vice President Withers sat behind a dark Victorian desk. He was short with a pale face creased by wire-rim glasses and a fastidious smile, which invited Claire to sit in a chair opposite the desk.

'I don't have much time,' she said, sitting forward on the edge of the chair. 'This transaction doesn't require a name. It's a numbered account, as you can see, and the authorization code is all you need. We don't give names,' she said. 'You can appreciate that matters of national security require complete confidentiality.' Claire was polite but irritated. She was aware that she had perspired through her blouse.

Withers leaned forward, comparing an account file card to the wire transfer form. 'The account, please?'

'13-2020719-Q.' *Nine digits and a letter.* She repeated it more slowly, watching him match against the card.

'This is a restricted account. Our tellers don't have access to it. In the past customers making a transfer asked for me.'

'That's what I did.'

Withers turned to the teller, who stood rebuked. 'There

are a few formalities I need to go through before we process a transfer of this size. Do you mind?'

'Please.'

'What is the account name?'

'There is no account name. It's a numbered account.'

'The amount of the last transfer?'

'Two million two hundred thousand dollars.'

'From?'

'Arab National Bank.'

'The authorized signatory?'

Gabriel hadn't given her one. 'There is none. It's a numbered account.'

'This says the money is going to BCCI. Is that right?'

'Yes. Numbered account. Paris branch. 799DH128FT1.' *Eleven digits and letters.*

'I'll be just a moment.'

Claire saw him take a walking cane from behind his desk and step out. Her eyes moved to the huge wall clock high in the cavernous space. The six-foot second hand jerked forward on the Roman numerals, slicing off a bit of the future. How long would she wait? Again she looked at the exit and stared at the guard by the bronze doors.

'Hello, ma'am.'

Claire saw a new man standing in the doorway. He was Withers's physical opposite, older, thinner, sterner. He patted the air to insist she remain seated, and then he took the seat beside her, putting on a patronizing show of avuncular concern and offering an ingratiating smile.

'I'm sorry, ma'am, I don't have your name.'

'Ma'am will do.' She returned his gaze with prickly coldness. 'This isn't a social call. I am here on Agency business.'

'Yes, yes. Let's get to that. I am Mr Leacock, branch manager. This is a very large sum of money. I'm sure you can appreciate that we have our internal controls.'

'Is there a problem?'

'No, no. Everything is in order, but you're new to us. The account is usually accessed by someone else. That person is the only one we know, so I'd like to ask why you're here and not her?'

'That person is a man. Mr Gabriel was called to the White House. He delegated this matter to me. Is there a problem?'

'No. It's a formality.'

Claire's eyes narrowed. 'Let's get past the formalities, shall we? What do you want to know?'

'Can Mr Gabriel come in tomorrow?'

'Will you be open tomorrow? Will you come into the office in the hurricane?'

Leacock contemplated the answer but said nothing.

'This transaction is urgent,' she said. 'We established this account to serve the Agency's needs. We brought our business here knowing you were a cooperative bank and your chairman understands our need for confidentiality.' She looked at Leacock. 'Time is urgent, gentlemen.'

She looked from one banker to the next, and when neither spoke, she stood to leave. At the door, she turned. 'Transfers come from Adnan Khashoggi without question. We expected them to go out without question.' She was through the door, when she heard Leacock ask her to stop. She had her eyes on the guard, who had turned to the commotion.

'Ma'am, please. Have a seat.'

Claire's heart raced, and she was desperate to reach her daughter. She turned on her heels and confronted the two men. She glanced at the clock. Twenty minutes had passed. 'What?'

'It will take a minute,' Leacock said. 'There's coffee. I'll be right back.'

Claire didn't sit. She stood firmly in one spot and then glanced at the clock, and she stared at Withers with an indignant expression. Her mind's eye saw Sara on the street, witness to her mother being escorted out of the bank in handcuffs. She turned suddenly and stopped. Leacock blocked the door.

'The wire is complete,' he said, and handed her a slip with the transaction confirmation number. 'Thank you for your patience.'

Claire took it without reading it. She walked numbly across the vast atrium hall, eyes focused on the bronze doors, trying desperately not to let her eagerness quicken her stride and betray the fraud.

She found Sara beside the bank's massive stone columns, where she had been told to wait. Sara's face paled with joyous relief when she saw Claire, and she rushed forward and embraced. 'What took so long?'

*

Claire stood inside a telephone booth a few blocks away and dialed the number Gabriel had written down. She listened to the ringing, and on the sixth ring she glanced at her wristwatch. The time was right. Her eyes drifted across the street as government workers left their offices early to escape the hurricane. *So many normal people*, she thought. She dialed again and recognized her husband's voice.

'It's done. I'll never do this again.'

'What happened?'

'Nothing. It's done. Now I know why you guys die of heart attacks.'

*

229

Eastern Airlines flight 67 from National Airport to San Juan pushed back from its gate at 4:05 p.m., an on-time departure. It was one of the last flights out of Washington that afternoon.

Claire sat in a window seat near the rear of the Boeing 737 and gazed out at the approaching storm. A wrathful sky birthed nearby lightning, and thunder rattled the plane. Passengers nervously looked about or cinched seat belts tighter. Landing lights of arriving aircraft emerged from the low cloud cover that darkened the day and illuminated rain sweeping across the tarmac. The precision required for landing an aircraft had always fascinated her. It gave her a feeling of excitement to be on the verge of a journey – the leaving, the arrival, the open-ended adventure of going someplace different. There was none of that now.

The pilot's calm voice on the intercom did little to reassure passengers frightened by the violent weather. The aircraft nudged forward, gathering speed, as it positioned itself for take-off. Dim runway lights lined the tarmac. Claire felt the engines' powerful thrust push the plane forward.

She looked out the window. She was abandoning a comfortable life, a good career, friends, their home, and taking up an uncertain future. This wasn't the life she had planned for or counted on.

She smiled at Sara, patting her daughter's hand.

'What are you thinking?' Sara asked.

'I'm thinking about my grandmother. She left Ireland as a young girl and never returned. She could have gone back, but she never did.'

'But we're coming back, aren't we?'

'Of course.' She looked out the window, unsure if they ever would.

# 26

## DUPONT CIRCLE

HURRICANE ELOISE FOLLOWED A steady westward path across the Atlantic, becoming a tropical storm and, subsequently, a hurricane north of Puerto Rico. The eye of the hurricane moved over Cuba, then to the Gulf, and advanced on an evacuated Pensacola. Wind gusts of 140 miles per hour sheared telephone poles, stripped roofs from houses, upended cars, and overwhelmed emergency response teams. It made its way north overland, losing some energy, but moisture pulled from the Gulf was released in a slow-moving deluge that arrived at Washington, D.C., that night.

*

Gabriel stared. His eyes were fixed but unfocused, gazing blindly into the swirling storm beyond the windshield. The wind howled with the lunacy of banshees, and the maddening sound made it hard for him to think. He turned on the wipers, and for intermittent moments the landscape took on shape and dimension. The street was empty and rain lashed the nearby Metro station.

It was time. Gabriel checked his 9mm Hi-Power. He had kept up his marksmanship with weekend visits to a gun range in Virginia, and he knew from his time in Vietnam that it operated well in foul weather. The satin nickel pistol was heavy in his hand, and he didn't allow himself to consider what it would mean to point the gun at a friend. He released the catch to confirm the bullets were inserted properly, and he chambered a round. He tucked the pistol under his belt.

Pitiless rain pelted him when he stepped out of the car. He hop-stepped across the deserted street and entered the shelter of the Metro's well-lit glass canopy. A waist-high construction barrier denied access to the gleaming new subway station that was set to open in a week's time. All around the hurricane raged. Trees in Dupont Circle groaned against the wind, and a metal garbage can bounced down the street in a riot of sound. Fierce gusts drove sheeting rain sideways under the canopy, and temperatures had fallen. He was wet and cold, and he rubbed his hands together for warmth, but he could do nothing about rain that swept in sideways.

Gabriel had seen one solitary man approach the station from Connecticut Avenue, but when he looked again the man was gone. Instinct told him that he had been spotted, but that was his plan, to place himself where he could be easily seen – alone and well-lit.

The plan was dangerously simple. All it required was that he identify his adversaries before they inflicted harm. It was madness, he told himself – madness to deliberately do the wrong thing, but he was matched against dangerous men, and he'd never known a trap to succeed without the madness of putting oneself at risk.

Gabriel suspected there were two men, possibly three. He didn't know all their names, but he knew who to suspect, which led him to this conclusion. He had reviewed the omissions, redactions, and gaps in the documents to see where the missing information pointed within his understanding of the old

Agency's lax rules. And he had Weisenthal's claim: *Three men.* He was confident about Treacher. Who were the other two?

Now, like an audience seated in a darkened theater, he waited for actors to enter center stage. Their presence out in the storm would be indictment and verdict enough, and Gabriel would use his 9mm pistol to administer the punishment. He had come to terms with the terrible thing that he would do.

Gabriel's eyes moved slowly across the storefronts and then toward Dupont Circle and the dark tree line. A storm drain had backed up, and water spouted into the street. Flooding was everywhere, and water cascaded down the Metro station's escalator. It was past the hour of rendezvous and coming to the time Ostroff said he would arrive. *How much longer? Have they been scared off by the storm?* His hand reflexively touched the clear plastic bag under his raincoat that held the bait – an empty envelope.

Gabriel hadn't found a way to warn off Ostroff. Any call to Ostroff risked alerting the men he sought, so he'd moved forward knowing he was putting Ostroff in danger. And then there he was across the street. Early. Eager for his scoop. *Idiot.* Ostroff stood in the shelter of a shop's awning with his baseball cap and an umbrella, the ribs popped backward, making it useless. The two men were separated by thirty yards of storm, one yelling at the other, each trying to make himself heard. Gabriel waved for Ostroff to stay where he was, and in that moment Gabriel saw the *Times* reporter frantically wave back.

Gabriel gauged the direction of Ostroff's hand to calculate the location of the danger. Gabriel read caution on Ostroff's face, yelling words that were swallowed by the howling wind. He turned where Ostroff had pointed, and he saw the solitary man again. He was in full rain gear, moving from the cover of one parked car to the next, hunched over, approaching the

Metro station. The man held a pistol, and his hood shadowed his face.

Gabriel saw Ostroff start to cross the avenue, walking into harm's way. He aimed his pistol and fired one warning round at Ostroff that shattered the plate glass window behind him. Stunned, Ostroff stayed rooted in the open, and Gabriel emptied his pistol at targets all around the startled man, striking a lamppost, the pavement, and the store's brick façade. Ostroff retreated in the face of the danger, and Gabriel loaded another clip, firing twice more, high into the dark where Ostroff had disappeared. Gabriel looked again, to confirm Ostroff had retreated, and thought it was just as well. Ostroff had played his part, and now he was gone.

Gabriel had reduced his profile, dropping to his knees, and he again looked where Ostroff had pointed. A second man emerged from behind the marble fountain in the center of Dupont Circle. He moved across the plaza, running bent over to gain the cover of the tree line, advancing against the rain, forging forward. The skirt of his mackintosh snapped in the wind.

Gabriel glanced from one man to the next, frustrated that he couldn't identify them. He pressed close to the station's bulwark and peered beyond the meager shelter. The hoods and the darkness denied him a view of their faces, but their guns were drawn, and seeing Gabriel, they saw each other. Gabriel watched them coordinate their assault and felt the danger he was in, but that was his plan. He moved toward the yawning mouth of the station's escalator.

Beneath Washington, the first sections of the city's grandiose urban transportation project were being completed after years of construction inconvenience. Massive steel boring machines had cut through the hard schist and gneiss of a remnant mountain under Connecticut Avenue and the particularly hard bedrock had required pilot holes that were filled with dynamite and exploded, leaving mounds of shattered rock and volatile fumes that were evacuated through air tunnels onto the street, sickening residents. The big, incomplete engineering project left portions of downtown planked in cut-and-cover quarrying. Washington was fatigued by the endless project. And now, the first stations were opening as work on others continued, and deep escalators led into a new underworld.

Gabriel took the steel treads of the unmoving escalator two at a time, entering the wide concrete arch that angled into the earth. He descended into subterranean darkness knowing that when his business was done, he would cross the station and escape through the exit at the other end. He looked over his shoulder, and in the keyhole of light at the top, he saw two hatted silhouettes in raincoats follow him down.

Gabriel reached the bottom of the cavernous station and jumped the turnstile. It was a quiet place, removed from the hurricane's fury. Dim lights illuminated the regular geometry of the vaulted ceiling, but the platform was dark and obscure. The lingering smell of volatile chemicals from freshly painted iridescent caution stripes hung in the air and the vague forms of kiosks were still wrapped in protective plastic. Tracks on either side were filled with rushing currents that crested at the platform's edge. Water poured into the station from the tunnel with a violent babbling sound, frothy and swirling in eddies and waves. Branches torn from trees were carried along in the strong current and then disappeared in the tunnel at the other end of the station.

Gabriel stood in the dark station that was now a tributary of Rock Creek, then ran toward a rolling work lamp that loomed over the last area of construction in the center of the platform. At the other end he saw the second escalator that would enable his escape, and then Gabriel saw a third man. He had emerged from behind a kiosk, so Gabriel saw only a dark shape, but when Gabriel's pursuers yelled his name, the third man stepped back behind the kiosk.

Again his name was called. The two pursuers had jumped the turnstile, and they now blocked Gabriel's retreat. Gabriel looked where he'd planned to escape, and then he looked back where he'd entered the station – danger in both directions. They knew he was there, but he hadn't been seen. Faint ceiling lights created vague shadows that frustrated alert eyes, and everywhere confusing shapes lurked in the darkness.

Gabriel's hand worked quickly to find the switch on the thousand-watt lamp that he'd positioned during an earlier trip to the station. A metal-halide bulb sat in a large silver cone.

'Jack.'

Gabriel stood perfectly still. Dark human forms advanced on him, coming in range of the work lamp, and he removed the Hi-Power from his belt. He gauged the danger and looked where the third man blocked his escape route, but he was gone. Gabriel glanced left and right at the dark, muddy water pouring past on either side, looking for alternatives. The current surged over branches lodged under the platform, producing an uncouth sound in the vaulted space. His eagerness to survive tempered his plan; his mind was divided by an urge for retribution and the jeopardy when he acted. His mind played a trick on his judgment, seeing what he wanted to see. He was tempted by the idea that he could finish his work and swim his escape.

'I wouldn't do that, Jack. You'd be pulled under.'

The man who spoke was thirty feet away, a dark figure of average height, bulky in rain gear, a pistol in one hand and a flashlight in the other. Gabriel thought he knew the voice. When the beam found Gabriel, he quickly stepped back into the dark, and his hand went for the arc lamp's switch. Brilliant light filled the vaulted space and illuminated two men standing center stage, stunned and blinded, deer in headlights.

'So, it's you.'

'Are you disappointed? Shut that thing off.'

Gabriel's anger stirred as he observed the two men bathed in light. 'Put your arms down. I want to see your faces.'

Treacher lowered his forearm, squinting. 'Surprised?' He held a Colt pistol at his side.

Gabriel smiled confidently because they were now equally matched. 'There are no surprises.'

'Still the arrogant Jack Gabriel. Always thinking you're the better man.' Treacher shielded his eyes with his hand.

A gunshot rang out. The lamp sparked and then exploded, casting the station into darkness. Slowly the pitch black resolved to murkiness as the men's eyes adjusted. In the darkness, Gabriel had moved a short distance, and now he was a few steps from Treacher, pistol at his side. Gabriel watched Treacher remove his hood and knock rain water from his baseball cap. His face was ghoulish in the shadow of his flashlight's beam. Gabriel considered his old acquaintance, and everything began to fall into place – Treacher's abrupt departure from the CIA, then his rise through the apparatus of government, always moving quickly upward, a man pushing himself to succeed. Gabriel was not shocked to see Treacher standing before him, but later he realized how angry he had been to discover it was Treacher.

'I thought we'd sort this out,' Treacher said.

'Just the two of us?'

'Him, too. Three of us. You've met Michael Casey, I understand. Office of Security. One of the old guard.'

Gabriel looked past Treacher, and the apparition behind became a man. When Casey lowered his flashlight, he took on a human form and his face was grim.

*Three of us?* Gabriel thought of the other man who'd

come and gone. He glanced back at the far exit.

'Go ahead,' Casey said. 'You're a confident guy. Make a run for it. You might make it.' Casey pulled back the barrel of his service pistol, recharging the chamber with a bullet.

Gabriel smiled, declining the invitation, which he found too eagerly offered. They had the advantage, and he felt peril in the man's ready posture.

'It was you.'

'Me?' Treacher said.

'Nick Arndt. Phillip Treacher. You killed Wilson. You and him.'

There was a long silence, and the three men were small and motionless in the grotto. Gabriel had his eyes on the other two. He moved a step closer, keeping an eye on each. 'You're hoarding your words,' Gabriel said. 'Speak. Tell me why I'm wrong. Tell me the pathologist's report is wrong.'

Gabriel took another step forward. 'Let me hear the ways you've justified his murder to yourself. The Soviet threat. Fear of what he knew. How those times were different. Your name sullied by scandal. Go ahead. Make your case.' Gabriel's caustic voice rose to a mocking pitch. 'I want to know.'

'That's close enough, Jack,' Treacher replied. 'Yes, I was there. By chance. I stepped into the breach. They pulled me in at the last minute. My luck to be the low man on holiday duty that night. Missed my first Thanksgiving with Tammy. She still brings it up when she's angry. Damned by fate, you could say, as I have heard you say many times. Like you, here in this place.' Treacher's eyes cast about the station. 'Taking on this cold case.'

'Weisenthal?' Gabriel asked.

'What's to tell? Wanted to be a prophet.'

Gabriel glanced behind Treacher to Casey. 'What was his prophecy?'

Treacher grunted his answer. 'Beware Communism. But that era has passed. The Soviets are a depleted economy, a humiliated Army, a bankrupt ideology. They'll collapse. Weisenthal needed a new conviction, which he found by rejecting everything he once believed.'

'*Jesus fuck.*'

'Me?' Treacher laughed. 'Too much in your mind, Jack. It's all in the past. Leave it there.'

'What happened to Weisenthal?'

'The death he got is the death he deserved. A chameleon who found a good disguise in the shadings of our times.'

Gabriel heard in Treacher's voice the velvet arguments of a man hoping to close a sale. Gabriel again looked at Casey, whose eyes were coals on a granite face.

'I want what you're giving the *Times*,' Treacher said. 'Hand it over, then fly off. Live the rest of your life on a beach somewhere.'

Gabriel removed the manila envelope from its plastic cover and showed that it was empty. 'It's in the mail. On its way.' His lie came out easily. His index finger slipped onto his pistol's trigger. 'I have what I came for. My death, should it happen in this place, will complete the story and seal your fate.'

Silence lengthened among the men as the dimensions of Gabriel's treachery sank in.

'It's winging its way to an eager audience,' Gabriel said. 'On its way. Gone.'

Gabriel saw Treacher glance back at Casey, who stood a dozen yards behind. Treacher was turned. It was just for a moment, but that was enough. Old anger warmed Gabriel's heart, and contempt coursed through his blood. His reserve, which had always made him cautious and contained his desire to punish Treacher's sense of entitlement, vanished. Gabriel hit Treacher in the jaw with his pistol's handle, knocking him to one knee. Gabriel's blow, coming while Treacher's eyes were turned, caused Treacher to drop his Colt, which skidded twenty feet along the platform.

The two old acquaintances looked at each other. Treacher rubbed his jaw. Blood flowed from his split lip, and Treacher looked up from his crimson palm. He smiled. 'Well done.'

Gabriel pointed his Hi-Power at Treacher's temple, inches away. His eyes flicked to Casey, who'd gone perfectly still as he calculated the changed circumstance.

Then Gabriel looked at Treacher's humbled face. He saw the deep exhaustion of a guilty man whose crime was catching up with him.

Treacher raised his bloody hand, eyes wide in a vague plea. 'I deserve what you want to do. Pull the trigger. Shoot me,' he said. 'Spare me the suffering. Hyenas in this town will feast. We both know how it ends. Renounced. Picked over. Careers don't recover. Fallen men never rise – jealousy, envy, retribution attack the wounded beast.'

Gabriel's urge to avenge weakened. He felt oddly sympathetic to this kneeling man.

'Here we are,' Treacher said. 'Victor and vanquished. The only time I've lost to you. Don't pity me. Don't hate me either. Kill me.'

Gabriel stood above the dishonored man. His rage was calmed by the man's plea to take his life rather than endure opprobrium. The words were swaying Gabriel little by little, and as he listened, he felt a corrupting kindness weaken his resolve to punish the man. This wasn't about Good and Evil. Those Romantic abstractions didn't apply to Washington's civilized corruption, which rewarded selfish and convenient choices, however base and disreputable.

'Who was responsible in the Agency?' Gabriel asked. 'You authorized it?'

'Not me.'

'Somebody else higher up? You have no idea who, I suppose. Or do you?'

Treacher's bleeding mouth opened to speak. His eyes widened, but his voice was silenced by something that caught his attention.

'Who ran the operation inside the Agency?' Gabriel demanded.

Treacher pointed past Gabriel. Gabriel pivoted and saw James Coffin standing twenty feet away in dim light, having stepped away from the kiosk. He had recovered Treacher's Colt and now held it in two hands, arms extended, feet spread.

'Drop the weapon.'

Gabriel placed his gun on the platform and watched Coffin, whose marksman's eye sighted along the barrel. Gabriel saw the muzzle flash, and the gun's blast reverberated inside the vaulted space, a deafening explosion of sound. Gabriel had blinked, and the explosion erased a moment of time. He touched his chest, certain he would find blood and a mortal wound, but there was no blood and no pain, nor did he see a wound on Treacher. He looked back and saw Casey was on his back on the platform, motionless. His gun had fallen from his hand and lay useless at his side.

'He was going to shoot you,' Coffin said to Gabriel.

Gabriel stared at the fallen man lit by his dropped flashlight. Crimson leaked from a small round entry wound on Casey's forehead, and a slowly enlarging pool of blood came from the exit wound on the back of his head. Casey's eyes were open and unfocused in the chill of death.

And then a second gunshot hallowed out the station's ringing quiet.

Gabriel looked down at Treacher. He'd been shot in the ear at close range, execution style. Coffin was at Gabriel's side, wiping his finger prints from the Colt, which he placed on the platform beside Treacher.

'You look like you've seen a ghost, Jack. Don't forget to breathe. This is what you wanted.'

Gabriel stared at Coffin and took a moment to comprehend the incomprehensible. His mind tried to pattern an answer from the unexpected shock, feeling disoriented and suddenly struck by the suddenness of his circumstance. He looked down at Treacher, his old adversary but also a sort of friend. He didn't feel anger or outrage, only pity and kindness evoked by the harmless dead.

'It's a simple story,' Coffin said, pointing at the two bodies. 'Murder and suicide. Old demons rose up between two conspirators who no longer trusted each other. Something from deep in their past that isn't known and is now unknowable. The story is unbelievable given who they are, but it will convince everyone because in substance it is true.'

Coffin was matter-of-fact, but his conviction was real, his reasoning was real, and the two dead men on the platform were real. All that was false was his smile.

\*

Coffin and Gabriel stood silently over the two corpses. The entombing silence of the space was broken by gurgling floodwaters. It was only Coffin's echoing footsteps that got Gabriel to shift his eyes from Treacher and take his mind off their sorry history.

Coffin was seated on a bench in the center of the platform, and he patted the seat, inviting Gabriel to join him. Coffin drew on his filtered cigarette and released a lungful of smoke in a steady stream. He raised the cigarette, observing the glowing tip in his long fingers.

'I followed you here,' he said.

Gabriel turned to Coffin.

'I expected something like this from you,' Coffin added. 'I didn't know what you had on your mind when I left you at the Botanical Gardens, but I knew you were on to something. You've been a dog with a bone about this Wilson thing. You have your answer now.'

'*An* answer, yes. *The* answer?'

Coffin laughed.

'Tell me that what lays here on the concrete is the truth,' Gabriel pressed.

Coffin drew again on his cigarette and patiently released smoke from his mouth, forming rings in the air. He considered his answer. 'We had no gulag to send Wilson to. What were we to do with him? He was unstable and in possession of a terrible state secret. We treasure our civil liberties, but in Wilson's case the Soviet gulag system would have given us a better choice. But we didn't have that choice.'

Again Coffin studied the lengthening ash of the tip. He looked at Gabriel. 'Speak up, Jack. Your tongue is a stringless instrument.'

'Weisenthal?'

'Conscience makes wise men mad.'

'Casey?'

'His wickedness contaminated his office.'

'Treacher?'

'Bad luck to pull holiday duty.'

'Me?'

'You?' Coffin paused a moment before offering his judgment. 'Good heart. Great talent. Self-righteous prick.' He looked off. 'Our Agency is an unweeded garden that needs tending. Care must be taken. We can't raise the Agency against itself. The whole enterprise would fall. We need to take care of our own, quietly.'

'Weisenthal and now them,' Gabriel said. 'You've purchased time, that's all.'

Gabriel was aware that his Hi-Power was on the concrete a few yards away. He didn't know if Coffin had brought his own pistol. 'You think all this will go unknown,' Gabriel said. 'I know it. Or maybe I'll be the means for you to tie up loose ends. Is there a window nearby?'

Coffin looked at Gabriel. 'You are sawing the air, Jack. Nothing has to happen. We can know the truth and not share it. Wilson was a security risk, and we couldn't be undone by one unstable man full of scruples.'

Gabriel contemplated Coffin's remark. When Gabriel spoke, his voice was thick with sarcasm. 'You are a noble man, James. You acted improperly, but for a proper reason. Yes, that is the sign of a noble man. You saw danger in Wilson's confused mind. You feared he'd blow the whistle on our use of terrible weapons, so you sacrificed your scruples to defend freedom, incriminated yourself for a good cause, gave up peace of mind so that we might keep ours. You are a selfless patriot, James. A noble man.'

Coffin had thrown his cigarette to the platform and ground it with his heel. 'Too much in your head, Jack.' He pulled a pistol from his raincoat and put the steel muzzle hard against Gabriel's chest. His eyes were dull and weary.

'Stand up. Move to the edge of the platform.'

Gabriel was on his feet. He coveted the Hi-Power that was far out of reach. 'You killed Weisenthal, too,' he said. 'And Kelly.' He had suspected that in the Botanical Gardens. Only the murderer would confidently place Kelly among those implicated in Wilson's death. Coffin's silence was Gabriel's answer, just as it had been an answer to Gabriel's claim that it had all begun in Berlin. He saw in Coffin the executioner's stamina for killing.

Gabriel was at the platform's edge, and he looked down into the swirling water. He was conscious of powerful currents bearing him ceaselessly into the past. This was his time to die. He felt the noose on his neck, and he stared down from the hangman's platform into the void below the water's surface.

Gabriel's eyes caught the motion. Coffin had lifted his pistol, and in so doing his sleeve pulled back. Gabriel saw the pistol's blue-black barrel, but his eyes settled on the man's bespoke wristwatch in the traditional English style, graced with a tonneau crystal. Gabriel raised his wrist to reveal his own watch's graceful bezel with tonneau shape and dual time-zone face. 'I gave a similar watch to Wilson. He saved my life, and then you took his.'

Gabriel's savage vengeance flared in a fury. Grief and anger burned hot in his chest. The sight of the elegant timepiece swept away all reserve that was confederate to his surrender. Memory stung. His fist erupted from his side, knocking Coffin's arm away so the bullet, when it came, harmlessly ricocheted from the platform. Gabriel's left fist followed with indignant force that caught the unbalanced Coffin, and the startled man tipped into the sucking current.

Coffin gave a cry but said nothing, pulled by the rushing water. His arms thrashed wildly, but the weight of his wet clothes dragged him under and, still thrashing, he disappeared into the dark tunnel.

## ST. LUCIA STRAITS

'WE ARE WELL,' GABRIEL had written the director, without disclosing their whereabouts. He saved the director from choosing duty over friendship, knowing how that choice would come out. He'd given a redacted account of what happened in the Metro station to prepare the director for the heightened scrutiny the Agency would receive after the violent deaths of three men linked to the CIA. Gabriel had also written that he wouldn't add to the widening scandal by making public the circumstances of Wilson's death. As far as Gabriel was concerned, his work was finished. He needed to put the past to bed. The killing was over, and his spirit was stilled by the sweeping skies and tranquil horizons aboard their sixty-three-foot ketch.

\*

Gabriel had the director's response in his hands. It was a personal letter that had found its way to Gabriel via the reverse of the circuitous route Gabriel's note had taken – Claire's sister to a post office box in Miami where a retired Cuban who owed Gabriel a favor reposted the letter to a second post office box in Martinique.

'Thank you for returning the carbons of your report,' the director's letter began. 'You didn't explain how they got out of Headquarters, but I'll assume it was an oversight. I am glad to have them. I was hasty when I shredded the original, and I'm glad to get the carbons so we can recreate your memo and make it a part of our history. One day the story will be told. Let the next director make that choice.

'You might hold me responsible for what happened, and I am partly to blame, but not in the way you imagine. I forced you out not because I'd lost confidence in you. I had complete confidence in you. I suspected Coffin, but he was untouchable – a fox in his hole who had to be flushed. You were the best man for this, and you wanted to leave anyway. I counted on your pique to keep you on the case from the outside, and I was right about that. We got to know each other in the Central Highlands, and I used that knowledge against you. This note is an apology of sorts. I was glad to get your letter because it gave me an opportunity to reflect.

'I suspected Coffin, but I had nothing to go on except that he was among a handful of senior men in the Agency in '53. The only way forward was to have him think you would expose him. Mueller was uncomfortable being the stocking-masked snitch pointing you in directions that vexed Coffin, but in the end he agreed to go along. Pushing you out the door made it look like I'd lost interest. I wanted Coffin to play his hand, and he did. What a piece of work: noble in reason, honorable in intent, infinite in cruelty. The best of us are rich in contradictions, and that makes us interesting, but James was at the extreme of contradictions and that made him deeply, mysteriously fascinating. He was a staunch Cold Warrior – the coldest warrior.

'Knowing the truth is a very lonely thing, and I appreciate that you've chosen to stay silent. People wouldn't understand the story. They would doubt it completely or accept it glibly, saying,

'Well of course the CIA kills people.' But even they wouldn't believe that we would kill one of our own.

'At your urging, I attended Wilson's interment. His remains were placed in a new casket and returned to his grave. I stood in the back, but Antony Wilson recognized me. When the brief ceremony was finished, he approached. He was bitter, and he said no one should have to dig up his father. I had him and his sister to lunch at the Agency, and I gave them the documents that you discovered in the archive. He was grateful to have evidence that confirmed some of what he already suspected. I didn't tell him that his father was murdered. I know that's what he believes, and I didn't dissuade him of his belief, but I didn't confirm it.

'It was a great burden to stay silent and not give him the satisfaction of knowing what we know. Keeping the truth from the family is necessary even if it's a wretched thing. Harm to us outweighs whatever closure knowledge would bring him. 'Closure' – such a terrible word. It suggests that reconciliation accompanies knowledge when in fact, as you wrote, one answer begets another question, question following question, and in the end the things that were in men's minds remain forever mysterious, like life itself.

'I am rambling and writing more than I intended. I too am troubled by the Wilson incident, but I have to keep personal feelings away from the job of running the Agency. It's a lonely office. We err on the side of secrecy – sometimes too eagerly. Wilson's murder is one of those bad secrets that should be declassified, but it's wrapped inside a good secret, and therefore, regrettably, it must remain secret. I feel for Antony, but I can't run this Agency on feelings.

'I went from Wilson's interment to Treacher's funeral in the National Cathedral. I should have skipped it, but I wanted to see how much fuss was made. A big, solemn, standing-room-only *event. Not a dry eye, but, I suspect, not much grief. He got what he wanted – a big send-off. The president delivered a kind eulogy.*

'*No one mentioned how he died. Forensics confirmed both men were shot with Treacher's pistol, and there aren't many incontrovertible conclusions you can reach. Coffin was found drowned in Rock Creek a mile from Dupont Circle. We had to announce his death, but we've kept the circumstances quiet. The unnatural death of the CIA's head of Counterintelligence would excite the fevered imaginations of the press. We'll make a further statement when we have more to say, but now there is nothing, except the coincidence that three senior government men died the night Hurricane Eloise hit Washington. Your note was vague on your role that night. Is there anything I should know?*'

Gabriel looked at the director's question, and he realized the letter's candid tone was a clever seduction. How like him, Gabriel thought, pleasantly dissembling to elicit information. Gabriel continued to read.

'*The FBI is investigating diligently. You have made their list of fugitives, and the allegations against you grow daily. Hard to imagine one man being able to do everything you're now accused of. Your sudden disappearance has become the basis for implicating you in several crimes, including the fraud at Riggs Bank. Your wife's face was matched to photos taken by the bank's security camera. Best you stay away for now. I would help you clear your name, but my circumstances have become complicated. My testimony to the Senate committee is under investigation, and I have had to hire an attorney to defend against a charge of perjury.*'

\*

Gabriel returned the letter to its envelope. He placed it under a weighted dive belt and turned his attention to the ketch. He was at the helm, steering the boat south under a sky singed orange by a dying sun that peaked over cumulus clouds. The sun had tanned his face, and wind lifted his hair. He watched swells grow as they entered the open water on their crossing to St. Lucia. Telltales high on the sheeted mast snapped in the breeze.

As an amateur sailor he knew that the line between a sunny day and a violent storm was a minor shift in upper atmosphere wind direction, or a small temperature difference between colliding air masses. He had seen high tufted clouds on the sail out of Fort-de-France, but he had dismissed the messengers announcing the arrival of a cold front. To the west he saw a tropical storm birthing. Broad cloud galleons clipped like anvils darkened the sky.

Gabriel's eyes came away from the distant lightning strikes and answered Sara's question. 'We're okay. We'll make landfall before it hits.' They were now joined by a tabby kitten that harmlessly pawed at the gulls gliding overhead, honking like French horns. One occasionally broke off only to rejoin the rear of the formation. Father and daughter watched the new member of the family, and they smiled together, finding amusement in the kitten's antics. Sara took a string to join the kitten in play. Gabriel looked for a sign that she was doing well, but when he saw nothing to confirm his hope, he turned back to the weather. He kissed her forehead. 'Go get your mother?'

Sara stood, and the kitten hopped off her lap.

'Don't forget these.' Gabriel tossed snorkel, face mask, and fins. 'Stow everything on deck. Take your algebra book. Tell your mother we'll eat here to keep an eye on the storm.'

Once a week they made the twenty-six-mile trip across the St. Lucia Strait to Martinique to withdraw funds from their bank account at Credit Suisse. They ate lunch on the beach, bought an American newspaper at the tourist hotel, and then returned to St. Lucia with whatever mail Claire's sister had forwarded. Washington seemed remote now.

Claire sat beside him. She'd wrapped her hair in a scarf and wore a bikini from their morning dive. Claire looked at her husband gazing at the storm. They had entered the open channel, and both his hands held the wheel against the powerful swells. Claire placed the serving tray with its dishes on the table and sipped a glass of wine, offering him a taste. She looked toward the western sky. 'Are we safe?'

'The storm won't hit until after we reach Castries.'

'Are we safe from Washington?'

Gabriel turned away from the approaching storm. 'We're safe for now.'

She nodded at the letter under the dive belt. 'What did he say?'

'He claims he used me. He fired me to get to Coffin.'

'You believe him?'

He frowned. 'Self-deception is the occupational hazard of a job that rewards lies.'

Claire laughed. Her voice deepened with disdain. 'Men strut their time in power and then are heard from no more. He'll be gone.' She looked at Gabriel. 'Did he tell Antony?'

Gabriel shook his head.

Claire was aghast and indignant. She glared. 'It's time. It's over.'

Was it over? Gabriel knew what had happened, but knowing the facts didn't settle the matter in his mind, and it wouldn't settle the matter for Antony. Knowledge was a bitter root. Here was the question that had dogged Gabriel since he had discovered that his erstwhile friend's doubt rang alarm bells and that he'd paid the price. Why hadn't he quit? Spoken up? Gotten out? There were no answers. Just the man. The knowing soul. But he didn't know enough to save himself. Just the man who enjoyed his dry martini, a poem's hug, and a weekend with his children, who didn't want the complications of a security clearance, who found himself in a dark labyrinth not of his making. Wilson was dead, yes, but how he died lived on, the tragedy endured, the cover-up continued. All that was over were the lives of three prominent men.

Large swells broke over the ketch's bow, sending cooling sea spray over the deck and onto them. He tasted salt in the air and felt Claire's eyes on him.

'If he didn't tell Antony,' she said, 'then you must.'

# ACKNOWLEDGMENTS

*The Coldest Warrior* is based on the case of Frank Olson, who died sometime around 2:30 a.m. on November 28, 1953, when he 'fell or jumped' from his room on the thirteenth floor of the Statler Hotel in New York City. The New York Medical Examiner's report contained that ambiguous description of how Olson came to land on the sidewalk early that morning, and it was that description that shaped how Olson's death would be viewed over three decades. Olson, forty-three at the time of his death, was a highly skilled Army scientist who worked at Fort Detrick, Maryland, a top secret U.S. Army facility that researched and tested biological warfare agents. He had been accompanied to New York by Robert Lashbrook, a CIA employee, who worked in the Agency's Chemical Branch. Olson's flag-draped coffin was lowered into its vault in Linden Hills Cemetery on December 1, 1953, three days later. His body had been embalmed in New York and transported to Frederick in a sealed casket. My aunt Alice, Frank's widow, was told that disfiguring injuries suffered in his fall made it ill advised to hold his funeral service with an open casket – the first of many, many lies that she was told over thirty years.

I am deeply indebted to Frank's two sons, particularly Eric, his eldest, for providing a wealth of information that he collected over a lifetime in his search for the truth about his father's death. Most importantly, I witnessed the torment of a family from whom the CIA had withheld the terrible circumstances of Olson's death.

Several books and magazine articles were indispensable sources of information about the Frank Olson case. They are: David Kairys, *Philadelphia Freedom: Memoir of a Civil Rights Lawyer* (University of Michigan Press, 2008); James Starrs with Katherine Ramsland, *A Voice from the Dead: A Forensic Investigator's Pursuit of the Truth in the Grave* (Putnam, 2005); Stephen Endicott and Edward Hagerman, *The United States and Biological Warfare* (Indiana University Press, 1998); Jonathan Vankin and John Whalen, *The 80 Greatest Conspiracies of All Time* (Citadel Press, 2004); William Colby, *Honorable Men: My Life in the CIA* (Hutchinson, 1978); H. P. Albarelli Jr., *A Terrible Mistake* (Trine Day LLC, 2009); Michael Ignatieff, 'What Did the CIA Do to His Father?,' *The New York Times Magazine*, April 1, 2001; and Ted Gup, 'The Coldest Warrior,' *The Washington Post Magazine*, December 16, 2001. The Frank Olson Project website provided numerous original source materials, as did transcripts of hearings held by the U.S. Senate Select Committee on Intelligence in 1977.

Several characters in the novel quote or paraphrase other works. They are William Shakespeare: 'It is a wise man who knows his own child' and 'His tongue is now a stringless instrument'; Paul Celan: 'Only one thing remained reachable, close and secure amid all losses: language'; Harold Pinter: 'Sometimes you feel you have the truth of a moment in your hand, then it slips through your fingers and is lost.'

My agent Will Roberts's enthusiasm for the book was critical in helping it find its place in the world, and Ion Mills, my UK editor, served as an indispensable champion and advocate. Pegasus Book's Katie McGuire embraced the story with enthusiasm and expertly polished the text. I am grateful to the book's early readers, who provided insights and suggestions that improved the text in large and small ways: Rae Edelson, Bruce Dow, Andrew Feinstein, Marc Levin, Emily Bestler, my brother Joe Vidich, and my fellow writers in the Neumann Leathers Writers Group: Mauro Altamura, Amy Kiger-Williams, Aimee Rinehart, Dawn Ryan, and Brett Duquette. Brendan Cahill, Elizabeth Kostova, Milena Deleva, Lauren Cerand, Joseph Kanon, Michael Harvey, Helen Phillips, Susan Isaacs, Kevin Larimer, and Elliot Figman and his colleagues at *Poets & Writers* have been gracious with their support and encouragement. And thanks to my sons, Arturo and Joe, who have helped me understand the few things that matter and the many things that don't. And to my wife, Linda, partner, teacher, muse, and collaborator once again. She encouraged me to write the book and helped shape it.